I opened my e   in
my own bed. Farra   a
storm of dark green
darkness. His thumb   ....me his
fingers had slid deepe   ...ot gripping or
pulling, just resting, like   ....onged there.

"What are you doing?" I whispered.

I wasn't sure I wanted to know the answer. Whatever he was doing felt good. Too good. I didn't want him to stop and that scared me. I didn't like giving someone else control over my happiness.

Little zings of sensation continued to radiate from where he touched me.

"Your magic calls to me." Part of his stony expression dropped, and I could see astonishment and maybe a little fear. "You've started the change."

"No." Apprehension crept into my awareness, pushing aside some of the warm fuzzy feelings.

"The magic is in you." It would have sounded hokey if he hadn't been so sincere. I'd have to remember that line the next time I was writing.

"No, it's not." Great, Theo, argue with a fae who was probably an expert on magic. Real productive.

His smile was hesitant and, for some reason, helped to calm my rising panic. "The magic is there. It senses my magic and responds. Do you not feel it too?"

I nodded, not quite ready to give his theory verbal affirmation.

Praise for Everlyn C Thompson

"Theodora is not your typical female main character, and it's so refreshing! She's plain, overweight, and has an obsession for chocolate cake. There's an inner beauty that comes out of her. She's so spunky and charming. She wields quips like a buccaneer wields a sword. Through all of her trials her humor has been her emotional shield, so when she's totally serious, that's when you know her heart is broken. It's quite poignant. Such an original take on the fae and on vampires. I find the story delightful. Jam-packed with self-deprecating humor and laugh-out-loud quips and snarkiness."

~ Author Mark Payne

Grave-Reaping Hermit

by

Everlyn C Thompson

Grave Reaper Series

Grave-Reaping Hermit

COPYRIGHT © 2022 by Everlyn C Thompson

Cover Art by *Kristian Norris*

The Wild Rose Press, Inc.
PO Box 708
Adams Basin, NY 14410-0708
Visit us at www.thewildrosepress.com

Publishing History
First Edition, 2023
Trade Paperback ISBN 978-1-5092-4808-7
Digital ISBN 978-1-5092-4809-4

Grave Reaper Series
Published in the United States of America

Dedication

For all the narcoleptics and the vampires that love them.

Chapter One

Cobwebs coated my hair in sticky clumps, and the aroma of dead skunk was slowly crawling up my nose.

This was not how I'd envisioned spending my Friday morning. Or any morning, really.

On the bright side, I'd found the source of the funky smell that had been taunting me for the last two weeks.

I reached behind me for the shovel that I'd dragged into the small crawlspace beneath my cabin, and with a little twisting and a lot of grunting, I managed to get the stupid thing pointed at the skunk and slid it under the pile of black and white fur. The corpse came free from the ground with a squishy sucking sound.

The shovel scraped against the hardpacked dirt as I slowly inched back out the way I'd come, dragging my grotesque prize with me. I tried not to look too hard at the dark drag marks the shovel left in its wake. Something skittered past my peripheral, and I shuddered. I had no idea why all the local creepy-crawlies had decided to take up residence beneath my particular cabin, but this seemed to be their favorite place to hang out.

By the time I crawled through the narrow opening next to my back porch steps, my knees were scraped, my head had a few new bumps, and I was grinning like an idiot. I couldn't deny the perverse satisfaction that came from accomplishing something for myself. Even if I'd been forced to brave the spider-infested shaft to do it.

I stretched out the kinks in my neck from being crammed into such a small space and then knelt to examine the poor animal that had met his demise on my property. It was definitely a skunk. The white stripe running down his back was a dead giveaway, confirming what my nose had already deduced.

Mother Nature had gifted us with a second summer this year, so I'd been hoping the warmer weather might have dried out the body and mummified it. But apparently, that's not how death worked. So much for Mother Nature's clean-up crew.

I'd never seen a dead body before—animal or otherwise—so the squishy bloated sack of skin and bones was a bit of a shocker. Its right ear was missing, and the eyes remained open in death, a milky gray that stared unseeing at the sky above. The large laceration down the length of its back was probably what had killed the poor thing.

When something on the shovel moved, I stumbled back a few steps with images of furry woodland creatures going *The Living Dead* route filling my head. The skunk didn't immediately jump up and go for my throat, so I leaned in until I realized there were maggots wriggling in the matted fur. *Gross.*

I clapped a hand over my mouth and tried not to lose my breakfast.

After a few deep breaths, I hefted the shovel and carried my stinky treasure across the yard and into the woods. Once I'd found a flat patch of dirt between two large pine trees, I dug a hole where Mr. Skunk could take his eternal sleep. Honestly, it wasn't such a bad way to go—surrounded by the peace of the forest, rather than lodged in a coyote's digestive tract.

My hands were blistered by the time I'd returned all the dirt to the hole, and something still smelled awful.

This time I couldn't blame it on the skunk.

****

I quickly stripped and tossed my filthy shirt and pants into the bathroom hamper. I'd have to do a load of laundry tonight before I went out, otherwise the whole damn place would smell like a dead animal by morning.

The shower started without a fuss, the old pipes creaking behind the wall as the water temperature climbed to a decent level. I jumped in before it was more than lukewarm; the water heater was older than I was, and it was only a matter of time until it crapped out completely. But until that day came, I'd be grateful that I managed to wrangle one more shower out of the old hunk of junk. Replacing it wouldn't be cheap. Or easy. I'm not the handiest of homeowners. I'm more of a learn-as-I-go-and-hope-I-don't-burn-the-house-down-in-the-process kind of girl.

On any other day, I wouldn't have given the mountain of yeti hair on my legs a second thought. But today was the one day out of the *entire* month that I had plans.

Against my better judgement, I'd been wrangled into another girls' night out with my friend Katie. I'd only agreed since a) she was my best friend (my only friend, actually) and b) she insisted that it was for my own good. I can't say she didn't have a valid point.

While I hadn't exactly enjoyed my first two trips to Tamarac's rundown watering hole, it had been good to get out of the cabin for a few hours.

So, because Katie was counting on me to drag my butt into town that night, I did my best to clean up the small tracks of blood that ran down the backs of my legs. The towel felt like sandpaper, thanks to the damn dryer that broke last week. You can use all the fabric softener you want, but you'll still end up with scratchy towels if they've been hung outside to dry. The only silver lining was that I finally found out why the box of bandages came with all those tiny little strips that I'd previously thought were useless.

A glance at the alarm clock on my weathered nightstand confirmed that I had another five hours until I had to leave. Plenty of time to do some work on my laptop.

Admittedly, it felt good to be productive. All the years of hitting roadblocks and never finding answers had gotten to me.

And honestly, anything was better than sitting and thinking about my upcoming social outing.

This was my chance to find a little happiness, I thought to myself.

And I was going to try. Really.

Although, sometimes, it's better to keep your goals small so they're more attainable. So, for then, I was just hoping to feel normal. Happy could wait.

****

What girl doesn't like to find a single red rose waiting on her doorstep?

Actually, this girl doesn't.

Yeah, you could say I'm a bit of an anomaly.

I have trouble getting on board with the whole flowers-equal-romance concept, because it makes me think of the slightly outdated practice of cavemen dragging home dead animals to present to their cavewomen. Also, who wants to watch something vibrant and full of life slowly wither away, knowing it has been cut from its roots and suffocated in plastic just for the purpose of earning affection?

So, when I stepped outside and discovered the rose, I didn't feel thrilled; I crossed my arms and scowled at the unexpected gift. Who in their right mind would send me a flower? Nobody knew I lived here, aside from the lawyer who handled the paperwork when I bought the place, and I'd been damn sure to impress upon him my desire to keep the sale private.

Glancing at the gravel road that dead-ended directly in front of my cabin, I briefly considered the possibility that someone had left it at the wrong door. It was pretty unlikely. My property was built directly at the end of the turnaround, and each of the five driveways were marked with a thick wooden post and a large white number nailed to the top. Even in the dark, the numbers were easy to read, despite the lack of any streetlights. A deliveryman would have had to drive past the other four cabins to reach mine.

The midday sun had left the velvety petals slightly wilted; they must have been sitting out here for the better part of the morning. I crouched down and spotted a small white card tucked underneath.

You Are My Sunshine...

The note was on plain white cardstock; no company name or logo. There wasn't even a delivery slip. I frowned at the handwritten letters, confused and more than a little creeped out. I didn't like that someone had been on my porch without my knowledge or permission.

When I didn't spot any rose-wielding deliverymen lurking in the bushes, I let myself out and locked the door behind me.

****

In today's society, class goes a long way. But it's not something that you can fake. You've either got it, or you don't.

The Boot Scoot, one of Tamarac's finer establishments, didn't have a single ounce of class.

The scent of stale beer mingled with cheap perfume hit me before I'd even pulled into the parking lot. The Boot Scoot's older building was the only one not yet abandoned or boarded up on the block. The neon cowboy boot glowed happily in the window, letting me know that they were indeed still in business; they hadn't been shut down due to an untimely health code inspection. Not that I'd had my fingers crossed for that to happen.

After parking in the overgrown lot beside the weathered western bar, I shimmied down my skirt that had ridden up to indecent heights during the twenty-minute drive into town, and I stuffed my keys, ID, phone, and a few twenties in my pocket. I left the old truck unlocked; I didn't want to have to replace a smashed window if someone broke in just to steal half a bottle of water and a cupholder full of quarters. I wasn't worried about the old beast getting stolen, because what car thief in his right mind would want a late-80s half-ton with over 300,000 kilometers on it?

Trying not to stumble while walking on the parking

lot's uneven ground, I shivered as goose bumps ran up and down my arms. The hairs on the back of my neck stood up, and I got a disturbing feeling that someone was watching me. I slowed my pace, darting glances at every shadow big enough to hide a threat.

Why hadn't I brought my bear-spray? *So stupid, Theo!* I needed to carry a purse. Not that I was afraid of bears. This was a small town, but that didn't mean it was free from crime.

To my left, something in one of the pools of darkness caught my eye. I did a double take and realized that a man was lurking between the dumpster and the building. My heart kicked into high gear, and my tongue was suddenly dryer than burnt toast. I doubted that I would have enough moisture left in my mouth to scream for help if I needed to.

Why the hell is he just standing there?

As I stood indecisively between the safety of the Boot Scoot and my truck, my eyes had adjusted to the dark enough to see the faint outline of his face surrounded by dark hair and dark clothes. Who the hell creeps around in the shadows dressed all emo, in black? *Nobody up to anything good, that's for sure.*

Jamming my hand into my pocket, I yanked out the small key ring. The old truck key wasn't particularly sharp, but it was better than nothing. Risking a glance down to make sure I had the right key, I gripped it between my knuckles. If the guy made a move toward me, I wasn't going to go down without a fight. I'd poke his damn eyes out if I could. And then I'd kick him in the junk if I got the chance.

My lungs seized up when I suddenly realized that he was no longer standing in the shadows. I quickly surveyed the entire lot, and I still didn't see him. He'd somehow disappeared in the small amount of time it had taken me to check my keys.

If things had gotten physical, I have no doubt I would have gotten my butt handed to me; I'd never been in a fight before. And what crook in his right mind would show up without a gun or at least a knife?

But the guy had disappeared without demanding my wallet, or worse, dragging me into the alley with him. Who knows, maybe he was a local cat-burglar casing the bar for a future break-in. Or maybe he was just a patron who didn't want to wait in line for the men's room. I could stand here all night imagining what he had been doing, but Katie would be waiting for me. So I took a deep breath and dragged myself toward the front of the bar.

I already spent too much time fantasizing about mysterious dark strangers when I was writing—tonight I was going to enjoy some time in the land of the living.

****

The bar wasn't as packed as I'd assumed it would be on a Friday evening. It was still summer though, so some of the potential clientele could have opted for the cheaper option of building a bonfire and bringing their own drinks. Not that I was complaining. The twenty-or-so people who turned to watch me walk through the front doors made me want to crawl under the nearest table. Quickly, until I was no longer the object of their attention. While it wasn't a huge crowd, it was still early by any normal working-person standards. The place would continue to fill up as the night went on, but anything over a party of two was too crowded for my liking.

"Theo!" At the sound of my friend's voice, I turned with no small amount of relief.

My closest—well, my only—friend in Tamarac, Katie Sunderland, waved enthusiastically from the other side of the room, her blonde curls bouncing up and down. She continued to call my name even after I'd sent her a small wave and worked my way toward her.

I bumped into a few people as I crossed the room, or, rather, a few people bumped into me, even though the place wasn't crowded. All of them were men, so I figured it was intentional and a part of the awkward mating rituals that I hadn't participated in since my teens. Part of me was shocked and a little flattered that I'd been included. Seriously, these guys must have some pretty low standards. Or they were just flat out desperate.

Don't get me wrong, I'm not hideous or anything like that. It was just obvious that I was out of my league as I subtly observed the other women in the room. They were all taller than I was, even though I'd had the foresight to wear my boots with two-inch heels. That was the best I could manage; anything that could get me over the five-and-a-half-feet mark would probably lead to me breaking an ankle.

Before leaving home, I had scrambled through the cupboard under my bathroom sink and dug out my old make-up bag. I hadn't used it in years but managed to apply a bit of eyeliner without poking my eye out, and I even added a touch of mascara. The tube had dried to a thick crunchy paste, but a few drops of hot water had it loosened up enough that it didn't clump on the wand. Probably not the most hygienic thing I'd ever done. I treated expiry dates as more of a guideline. Hopefully there hadn't been any bacteria or fungus making a nice home for itself in the expired tube that would lead to me going blind.

I'd been feeling pretty good about my hair and makeup when I'd left home, but then at the Boot Scoot I realized anything less than a quarter inch of foundation applied with a trowel wasn't going to cut it. The shades of eyeshadow that I spotted on the other women ranged from electric blue to amber red. Their lipstick was bold and so thick I could see cracks in it when they smiled. Suddenly, my watermelon-scented lip gloss seemed childish in comparison. I wished I hadn't even made the attempt at improving my appearance; it would have been better if I'd just shown up au natural.

Big hair, teased as high as it would go, must have been a small-town Saskatchewan thing. I had to remind myself not to stare as I passed a woman with her blonde hair piled on top of her head, surrounded by a cloud of hairspray that made me cough. My own plain brown hair hung down my back. I'd lost my blow-dryer and straightener during the move, so I hadn't done anything aside from washing it that day.

"I'm so glad you came!" Katie's genuine smile was a welcome distraction from my self-doubting inner-monologuing. She embraced me in one of those weird hugs where we both bent at the waist and leaned in so only our shoulders were touching. I've always wondered if some women hugged like that just so they would have a reason to stick their butts out.

"I got you a drink," she said.

I took a seat next to her and accepted the glass of wine she slid across the scarred table toward me.

"Thanks," I responded. "I thought you didn't like wine."

She shrugged daintily. "I don't. I thought it would look more elegant than a bottle of beer."

I hid an unladylike snort in my wineglass; Katie could be chugging bleach straight from the jug and she'd still be the most refined, put-together person I'd ever met. With her hair perfectly moussed into loose curls, every fingernail lacquered ruby red, and her long willowy limbs, she was the walking definition of sophistication and grace.

"So, how's work going?" I asked.

"Good. Things are slowing down now that the fall orders are almost finished." Katie was the owner of Country Customs, Tamarac's only bridal boutique. It was unlike any of the big-box wedding-dress stores that I'd ever been in. The gowns and formal wear were all rustic and simple, very country chic. Brides-to-be came from all over Western Canada for Katie's signature selection.

"How's the book coming?" Katie looked at me over the edge of her wineglass and wiggled her perfectly shaped eyebrows. The girl was a sucker for romance novels and was always looking for juicy snippets from whatever I was working on.

"Still not finished," I said, hoping to evade another sex-scene discussion.

"Please tell me the duke finds Priscilla when she sneaks out into the garden!" Katie's bright green eyes took on a dreamy look as she stared off somewhere past my shoulder. I wanted to bang my head on the table. I had already lost her to the steamy interludes playing through her mind, featuring my latest characters. "Does he—"

"No!" I cut her off, before she demanded explicit details. I had no desire to discuss an imaginary man's anatomy, and what he was potentially going to do with said anatomy, in such a public place. Self-consciously, I glanced around to see if anyone was listening. I was grateful that we hadn't caught any attention, aside from the usual glances from every single male in the place.

I wouldn't say I was ashamed of the fact that I wrote novels that included some descriptive sex scenes; but I also wouldn't have gone out of my way to advertise it. I'd always used a pen name to keep my erotic imagination under wraps. Katie was the only local who knew what I did for a living, and I preferred to keep it that way.

Twelve years ago, I'd successfully published my first novel. By the time my third book hit the shelves, I had earned the right to precede my name with "New York Times Best-Selling Author." What had started out as a hobby had turned into a career; it was something I had been extremely proud of. My next three books, a trilogy set in the sixteenth century, quadrupled my sales in under six months. Apparently, I had managed to tap into a small but passionate historical romance fan-base.

Racking my brain for a way to steer the conversation away from fictional trysts, I scanned the room hoping I'd see—Yep, right on time. Two guys leaned against the bar, both looking in our direction. They were both attractive, with sandy brown hair and light blue eyes. One was a little taller than the other, but their facial features were similar enough for me to assume that they were brothers.

"Two hotties at the bar." My casual remark worked

like a charm, directing Katie's attention away from fictional men to the real ones across the room. She subtly adjusted her bright red, strapless bustier, displaying her cleavage to its maximum potential. Flipping her curls artfully over her shoulder, she glanced coyly toward the men at the bar. One of them raised his beer and nodded a greeting with a small smile.

I took a long drink of my wine. This was always how a night with Katie went. She'd mingle, she'd flirt, she'd drink, and she'd dance. And I'd get dragged along for the whole damn ride.

Well, not actually the *whole* ride, thank God. Just up until she left with whichever lucky guy caught her eye, and then I'd climb in my truck and return to my empty cabin.

"Hi, there, ladies," the men said as they sauntered up to our table.

Katie flashed them a dazzling smile. I tried to muster up a genuine smile, but it probably came out as more of a toothy grimace.

Katie nudged one of the unoccupied chairs away from the table with the toe of her strappy stiletto. "Join us for a drink?"

The men took their seats across the table from us and introduced themselves as Tim and Joey. I'd originally thought they were young, late twenties or so, but now that they were closer, I could see they were likely closer to my own age, thirty-two.

"I'm Katie, and this is my friend Theodora."

"Theo. It's just Theo," I told them, while sending Katie a glare. She knew that I never used my full name.

Tim, the one who'd raised his drink to us earlier,

was dressed in a green plaid shirt with its sleeves rolled up to his elbows, revealing tanned, muscular forearms. He'd left his top two buttons undone, revealing a hint of chest hair without any tan lines. Tamarac was full of hard-working people, so my guess was that he worked outdoors, probably doing something physical if he spent much time in the sun without a shirt. I hadn't seen many sunbathers since I'd moved here.

"Hi, Theo." Joey's cadence was slightly softer than his brother's when he spoke.

I smiled back, trying to look friendly. My social awkwardness had nothing to do with these guys, so I tried to appear eager to be part of a real conversation with other adults.

"So, do you come here often?" Joey asked.

I couldn't help myself; I laughed at his terrible pick-up line.

"Sorry, that was pretty lame," he admitted, running a hand through his short hair.

"I've heard worse," I said, not wanting him to feel bad. It wasn't a total lie either; I *had* heard worse, but I'd take a cheesy line any day over a guy that couldn't be bothered with conversation because he was too busy staring at my boobs. And Joey had already earned a few bonus points since I hadn't caught his eyes dropping below my face.

"And, no, I don't come here often." I wasn't about to tell him I was new in town; just because he had a nice smile didn't mean that he was entitled to all my personal info.

The waitress toddled over, wearing heels that would give any normal woman loonie-sized blisters by the end of the night. Brushing her long brown hair over

14

her shoulder, she bent to drop off another round of beer for the boys and wine for us. The hot pink push-up bra, now right at my eyelevel, trembled under the sudden pressure. I hoped it was strong enough to do its job while she showed off her impressive bosom; I sure didn't want another woman's D-cups landing in my lap. I waved her away when she tried to replace my empty glass with a full one. "No, thanks, I'm driving."

"Aww, come on, Theo! You've got time to dance it off," Katie protested.

It was still pretty early, so I probably would be fine in a few hours. Hopefully Katie and her new friend Tim were planning on sticking around that long before they took the party back to his place. Or the ladies' room. Or the park by the elementary school. I'd never actually asked where she took her hook-ups.

"Okay." I ignored the waitress's smirk; she could think I was being a pushover if she wanted to. I was going to drink because I *wanted* to drink, not because other people wanted me to.

"So, what do you boys do for fun?" Katie asked. I was sure she knew about (and had tried) every possible fun thing to do in a town this small, from stargazing to skinny-dipping, but it was all part of her flirty routine to ask.

Tim took the bait with an aw-shucks grin. "Well, Joey and I work at Bill's." He must have caught my blank look and elaborated. "Bill's Buffalo Farm, north of town."

I nodded knowingly, even though I had no idea what he was talking about. Did people really farm buffalo? I didn't remember ever seeing buffalo steaks at the grocery store, but it's not like I'd been looking.

Tamarac was mostly surrounded by crown land occupied by boreal forest, although now that I was thinking about it, some of the roads were bordered by old barbwire fencing. Would I have even noticed if I passed a herd of buffalo? Probably not. The only trips that I made into town were supply runs, not for sight-seeing.

I kept up my fake smile without really listening, while Tim prattled on about buffalo. Apparently, work was his idea of fun. I jumped when Joey reached across the table and touched my hand. "Hey, do you want to dance?"

I studied his face, looking for any sign that he was messing with me. He stared back, patiently waiting for me to decide. His expression was honest enough, and I even caught a hint of vulnerability in his eyes.

Did I want to dance? Hell, yes. I loved to dance, and it had been forever since I'd felt a man's arms around me. And if I said no, he'd just find someone else who would, and then I'd be stuck as the third wheel while Katie used her feminine wiles on Tim.

"Sure." The floor wobbled a bit when I stood, and Joey offered me his arm to hold. It was steady beneath my fingers, and I made it all the way to the dance floor without falling on my ass.

There were only a handful of other couples dancing, most of them doing an awkward side-to-side shuffle with their arms wrapped around each other. Their dancing brought back memories of junior high school dances. I was expecting Joey to do the same, so I was surprised when he guided my left hand onto his shoulder and took my right hand in his. It didn't take long for us to find a steady rhythm as he guided me slowly through the other couples.

"You're really good at this," I told him, tilting my head back to see his face.

"Thanks." His grin was boyish, and I found myself smiling back.

The song ended and something with a faster tempo came on. Other couples were using the music as an excuse to get closer to their partner, but instead of hurtling us across the dancefloor or wildly spinning me around, Joey kept an easy pace, and I mentally awarded him more bonus points.

It didn't take long for the current song to end and for a few more to roll by. Joey kept up a steady stream of small talk, while he guided me effortlessly through the growing press of bodies, using only his hand on the small of my back to steer me where he wanted me to go.

"Do you want to get something to drink?" he asked.

"Sure," I answered lamely. I'd gladly have stayed on the dancefloor all wrapped up in his strong arms for another twenty songs, but I didn't want to openly admit it. Technically, I was still married, so wanting another man's attention was wrong.

This was wrong.

Guilt pooled in my belly and crawled up my throat, tasting like bile. My husband was missing; he could be in danger or wounded somewhere and I was living it up on the dancefloor, lusting after another man. I was no better than any other unfaithful spouse.

Lacing his fingers through mine, Joey tugged me toward the table where Katie was examining Tim's tonsils with her tongue. They stopped to come up for air when I flopped into my chair.

"How was the dancing?" Katie managed to make the question sound innocent and dirty at the same time.

"Fine," I told her, letting all the irritation I was feeling toward myself leak into the word.

Joey sat down beside me, and I accepted the glass he offered. Screw sober driving, I was having another drink. Or five.

Chapter Two

I can't say I knew what it was like to wake up in bed with a stranger.

I'd never done it, so up until then, I'd always imagined it would be somewhat of a romantic scene. You know, with our clothing littered across the floor leading to our entwined bodies, tangled in rumpled sheets. There'd be some sort of awkward "good morning" conversation that would quickly morph into us making slow passionate love while looking into each other's eyes, followed by breakfast and hastily made plans to see each other the following night.

Just to set the record straight, it doesn't happen like that to girls like me.

"The *fuck*?" I cracked one heavy eyelid and peered around.

My living room was dark and smelled like cheap wine and good coffee. The pounding in my head increased when I tried to sit up, and the whole room tilted. Strong hands grabbed my shoulders and helped guide me into a sitting position.

"Here, this will help," a man's deep voice advised me, and a mug pressed into my hands. It was still warm, and a tentative sip revealed it was coffee. Deliciously sweet but not too strong, just the way I liked it. I took another gulp, hoping a large dose of caffeine would silence the marching band that had taken up residence in my head.

"Go slow. I'm *not* carrying you into the bathroom if you throw up again."

Well, that explained why the inside of my mouth tasted like a public toilet that hadn't been cleaned in six months. Ugh, I would have literally killed my own grandmother for a toothbrush and some mouthwash right then.

Prying my eyelids open felt like acquiring a new superpower, and my head felt sixty pounds heavier than it should. The outline of a broad set of shoulders came into focus directly in front of me, and I yelped in surprise. The mug of hot coffee slipped from my fingers, but his hand shot out to catch it before it landed in my lap.

"Careful!" The sharp word was barked from a voice far deeper than Joey's, and the realization slapped sobriety into me faster than the coffee ever could have. I barely felt the hot liquid scalding its way down my chest and into my bra.

"What the hell?" I stared in absolute disbelief at the stranger sitting next to me on the couch. Even in the semi-darkness, I could tell I'd never met this man before. He was a freaking *giant*.

Red hair, the kind that came from genetics and couldn't be replicated in a salon, stood up in messy tufts on his head. A strong jaw and slightly crooked, angular nose tipped him from handsome into dangerously-beautiful-but-able-to-kick-your-ass-if-you-mention-it territory. He was wearing a black leather coat that hugged shoulders twice as wide as mine. He made me think if he'd had a big bushy beard and plaid shirt, he'd look like a lumberjack.

"Calm down, woman; I'm not here to hurt you. Theodora—"

"Theo. It's just Theo," I automatically corrected him.

"Okay, *Theo*, I'm Oscar Alderidge. I'm investigating the disappearance of your husband." He enunciated my name like he was annoyed, but I couldn't tell if it was because I interrupted him or because he just didn't like my nickname.

"You're looking for Will?" The fog in my brain was dissipating, and I took another gulp from my mug. So he wasn't a serial killer who had broken into my place for a little torture and murder play session. Hopefully.

"Yes, I believe he's in the area. Has he been in contact with you?"

Will was here? That wasn't possible. He didn't even know where I lived anymore. Nobody did.

After five long years of searching, I'd used up every penny to my name and been forced to throw in the towel on my search. I still had quarterly royalties coming in, but I knew it wouldn't be enough to keep up with the costs of the house we owned in Saskatoon. So, after selling our beautiful two-story home in the suburbs, I'd bought this run-down cabin in the woods. "No, I haven't seen him in over six years." I kept my words bland, not wanting to parade my grief around in front of a stranger.

"Any calls? Letters? Emails?" he asked.

"No. My cell reception is crappy out here; I usually don't even have my phone on." I was rambling now and forced my mouth shut. I finished my coffee and got up to refill my mug.

Oscar followed me into the small kitchen and looked around as if he suspected that Will might jump out of one of the cupboards at any moment. I was stupidly relieved that I had washed and put away all my dishes last night. And that it no longer smelled like a dead skunk. Oscar was the first house guest I'd had over since I moved. "House guest" being a pretty loose term for the man taking up half my kitchen.

While he studied my outdated cabinets and vintage appliances, I studied him. His plain black slacks didn't tell me much; he could use them for anything from ballroom dancing to breaking into a museum *Ocean's Eleven*-style. His pale gray shirt with dark gray pinstriping was subtle, and he'd left the top few buttons undone to reveal a hint of chest hair that confirmed he was a natural redhead. He didn't really look like an Oscar; the name seemed just a little too hoity-toity to go with his casual appearance. He looked more like an Ozzy.

"Why do you think Will might be here?" The question slipped out before I could stop it. The desperate hope filling my voice made me turn and stare out the window into the dark backyard. I didn't want to feel hope. It always led to disappointment. I wasn't going to get back on that depressing ride again.

"There have been a few sightings in Tamarac and some of the smaller communities east of here."

"Sightings? By whom? Who here even knows who Will is? In Saskatoon, he was a nobody, and the police stopped looking years ago." I shot the words out bitterly.

When the police had grown tired of my weekly visits, they basically gave up on finding him. The detective in charge had said, "We'll continue following up on any new leads; he's bound to show up sooner or later." But his face and careless shrug seemed to say, "What am I supposed to do? He doesn't want to be found."

"I've got some local connections."

Right, 'cause that wasn't vague at all.

"Who did you say you work for?"

"I didn't."

When he didn't elaborate, I crossed my arms and stared at him. God, did the guy never blink? The way he was looking at me was just freaky. His eyes were gray; the same color as hard granite. It would be easy for a girl to get lost in them.

Not wanting to admit defeat by looking away, I mustered every bit of snarkiness that I had and told him, "Get the hell out of my house."

"Theo—" He raised his hands placatingly, but I'd already heard enough. My head was pounding with the first hangover I'd had in years, and I wanted to be alone so I could fall into bed and sleep for the next three days.

"Just go." I walked to the front door and held it open. After a few tense moments in which I wasn't sure he'd listen, he followed me but paused in the threshold of the doorway.

"Here's my card." He slid a small white card into my hand. "Call if he reaches out to you."

I nodded as he stepped outside into the cooler night air.

"And Theo?" He turned, and my heartrate spiked at the intensity in his gaze. "There have been five murders and even more unexplained disappearances in the area; there's a good chance Will's involved. If he shows up, don't let him in. Just call me; I'll be able to get here faster than anyone else." He looked like he was debating saying more, but eventually, he turned and walked across my decrepit old porch and into the shadows.

I shut the door and hoped my elderly neighbor, Mrs. Swazle, hadn't caught sight of my visitor. She'd probably have an aneurism if she thought I was having gentleman callers at night—or lumberjack callers.

What time was it anyway?

I turned out my pockets, but I couldn't find my cell phone. My truck keys were missing, too.

I tossed the couch cushions, finding nothing but cracker crumbs. The bedroom turned up zilch, and I was seriously entertaining the possibility that Ozzy was an identity thief. Well, too bad for him that my phone didn't have much personal info on it. I did all my emailing and online banking from my laptop, so he was shit-outta-luck. And, yes, my laptop was still sitting where I'd left it on the kitchen table before I went out last night. Thank goodness.

So, worst-case scenario would be that Ozzy, or whoever found my phone, got access to the half-dozen contacts I had. Plus, the keys to my truck and cabin. I had a spare set of both around here somewhere, but I really didn't like the idea of someone having the ability to waltz right into my home without my permission. This was my safe space. This cabin was *mine*.

Peeling off my shirt and skirt, I tossed them in the laundry basket. The clock on the microwave told me it was four in the morning, so I brushed my teeth and scrubbed the remnants of mascara off my face.

Before I climbed into bed, I went back into the

living room, pulled aside the thick curtains, and glanced outside. The road was dark, but the sky was lightening with the first hints of coming daylight. And neatly backed into my gravel driveway, was my truck.

I was ready to run out the door to see if it was really my truck, when I realized I was still in my underwear. Out of consideration for the neighbors—because *nobody* needed to see my big thighs—I went back to the bedroom and climbed under the blankets.

Something in my chest eased a little when I realized the old beast was safely parked outside. I'd intentionally bought a big, piece of crap truck, because it was just one other thing to which I didn't want to get attached. It might just disappear at some point. Better to not get emotionally involved. But, dammit, I was relieved. Stupid me.

Had I driven it home myself? That would have been beyond idiotic, even for me. I'd been planning on sleeping off all the wine in the parking lot last night before driving home. The last thing I remembered was spinning around the dance floor with Joey. That was around midnight, but everything between then and waking up on my couch was just a big blank spot in my memory.

And who was Oscar Alderidge? Had I brought him home with me, or had he been waiting for me when I got here? And was he really law enforcement? Or did he have another reason to be looking for Will? He'd never said who he worked for. Maybe he was a private investigator.

Was he even looking for Will? Maybe that was just a cover story, and he was after something else. But after what? It's not as though I'm super rich or own a diamond mine or have mafia connections.

God, I was still feeling tipsy from all the booze, and my stupid imagination was hard to rein in on a regular day. Today, it was nearly impossible. There were literally *millions* of possible explanations for what was going on, and my brain wanted to explore every single one of them.

Fantasies continued to run rampant in my dreams when I fell into a welcome sleep.

****

The absolute best part of living alone was being able to have chocolate cake for breakfast. Gooey, moist, fudgy cake with thick sticky icing was exactly what a hangover called for. And since, technically, I didn't get up until after noon, it was more of a lunch or afternoon snack.

Will hadn't cared for sweets (Crazy, right? Who doesn't love sweets!?), so I'd focused my culinary skills on improving our supper options. Now that I was cooking for one, I'd adopted more of a screw-it-I-want-cake-so-I'm-making-cake attitude in the kitchen.

Freshly showered and dressed in comfy sweatpants and a tank top, I took my plate and laptop into the backyard. I'd already been over every inch of my truck, and there was no sign of my cell or keys. I'd have to buy another phone next time I was in town.

A slight breeze made the yellowing leaves in the trees dance and rustle against one another. I loved the soft music they made. Pretty soon, the leaves would start falling, and then I'd lose some of the privacy they provided. Right now, my entire property was cocooned by foliage so thick I couldn't even see Mrs. Swazle's white bungalow from where I sat.

The small patio table and two mismatched chairs had come with the place. I had positioned myself with my back to the cabin so I was facing the woods. The wall of trees wasn't the most picturesque of views, but it always eased some of the tension in my head and chest. It was peaceful in a way that a photo or painting could never be.

A small path continued past my property for about a quarter of a mile until it reached Tamarac Lake. You wouldn't be able to find it on Google Maps; you could only reach it from the five cabins on my street. I'd never actually seen anyone else using it.

I opened my laptop and lost myself in the complicated twists that kept the duke and Priscilla from their happily ever after. Long after my butt began to ache and my legs became numb from sitting for too long, I stood and stretched. The sun was a lot farther along in its journey than when I'd started writing.

My stomach growled, reminding me that chocolate cake alone couldn't sustain my size twelve figure. The remaining half of the cake in the fridge called to me, but I figured I should have at least one healthy meal today. My tastebuds disagreed, but my guilt won out.

I grabbed my flint knife from beneath the table where I'd superglued its holder. Yeah, I was too lazy to walk back to the cabin every time I wanted to start a fire but didn't want it sitting out in the open where it could get stolen. Keeping it under the table kept it out of sight and protected from the elements.

The firepit, another gift from the previous owners, was a real work of art. The old bricks were neatly stacked as high as my chest on one side, with three sets of metal rods extending out at varying heights. The remaining three sides were only a foot high with small gaps to allow air flow. They were the perfect height to rest my feet on during cold nights when I had the fire blazing. The mortar holding everything together was cracking in a few places and would need to be replaced in a few years.

It took me a few minutes to get a flame started on the small curls of willow bark, but soon I had a decent fire going. Using a flint instead of something easy, such as matches, might seem somewhat pointless, but I'd learned a valuable lesson when Will had disappeared. Counting on anyone or anything was stupid. I was the only one I could depend on. So, even if there was a world-wide zombie apocalypse, and if all the match factories shut down, and I couldn't run out to a convenience store for a lighter, I'd still be able to make a fire. I'd survive.

After returning my laptop to the kitchen table, I dug a nice thick steak out of the fridge. Peeling off the brown paper, I wished that I'd thought to marinate it overnight. Oh well, dinner prep was the last thing on my mind last night.

It didn't take long to make a small salad, and once I'd topped it with feta and croutons, I headed back outside. The sun was just setting, coloring the clouds a vivid orange that made me smile. *This* was why I'd bought the cabin. The absolute solitude and serenity. I was finally getting close to making peace with where life had taken me. This wasn't what I had planned, but I was settling in. The dream of a big family and a house in the suburbs was long gone, even before Will had disappeared. I was already thirty-two, and I just didn't have it in me to try again.

I grabbed the old wire rack from next to the firepit and slid it onto the middle set of metal rods so it was resting about twenty inches above the ground. Just the right height to hold my steak above the flames, but still close enough to sear the meat.

Movement in the tree line caught my attention, and I froze. The long shadows that blanketed the forest blended together, making it hard to pick out any individual shapes. Mrs. Swazle had warned me that there were black bears in the area. I hadn't really taken her seriously until now.

A juicy drop of blood fell from the steak as it dangled on the end of my fork. Great. Not only had I caught the attention of a hungry wild animal, but I'd done it while smelling like raw meat.

I flopped the steak onto the waiting rack and took a few steps back. Weren't wild animals afraid of fire? Hopefully it would be enough to keep any predators at bay. My backup plan was to run for the cabin, rib eye be damned. It probably tasted better than I did, and it would slow the bear down.

Remembering something I'd read as a kid, I started singing in a whispered voice. A branch snapped next to the path, and I belted it out so loud my voice shook. There definitely weren't any karaoke bars in my future. And if my singing didn't manage to scare off the bear, my only foreseeable future was becoming bear food. This was not how I wanted to go out. Would poor Katie wonder what had happened to me?

A low whine came from the dark, cutting through my panic. I stopped singing and realized that if something was going to attack me, it would have come charging out of the woods by now. Listening, I waited but didn't hear anything beyond the crackling of the fire and the hiss of the meat as it burnt. Stabbing my fork into the steak, I gave it a quick flip.

Then I heard it again—definitely a whine.

I was no expert, but I didn't think bears whined.

"Hello?" I called. Maybe it was Mrs. Swazle. If she'd fallen and hurt herself, she might not be able to call for help. My heart was still going a little too fast and made it hard to hear, but I crept closer to the path.

Two golden eyes stared out of the darkness at me. I shrieked and backed away.

Holy shit!

Should I turn and run? I was a *city girl*; why didn't they teach city girls what to do in situations involving wild animals? If I survived this, I was going to write a very strongly worded letter to the public-school board.

My heel smacked into a root, and I landed hard on my backside.

Another soft whine, and I ceased backpedaling across the yard as a dark shape slunk out of the trees. My throat squeezed painfully, and I didn't even try to scream as the animal silently crept closer.

Once it stepped out of the shadows, I realized it was a dog.

I'd nearly given myself a heart attack over a stray dog.

A big black dog, maybe a rottweiler. The dog whined again, blinking big yellow eyes at me before lowering himself to his belly and army-crawling the rest of the way to where I sat on my bruised butt.

I didn't know much about animals, but it didn't look like he was going to attack me. His body language was submissive, not aggressive.

"Hi," I whispered, not sure what else to say. The grass was cold, so I lifted myself to my feet, backing up when the dog inched closer. "What are you doing here?"

I didn't really expect any answer, but his gaze darted over my shoulder to where my dinner was burning.

"Ah. You came to steal my supper."

He continued to stare longingly at me, and I forced myself to turn back to the fire and rescue what was left of my meal. Sharing with him would be a bad idea; it would only encourage him to come back the next time his belly was empty.

"Go home," I told him, without bothering to look back. I didn't want to see his big sad doggy eyes. I'd worked hard to cut off all ties since I'd gotten here; I didn't want the responsibility of someone depending on me. I'd built some damn tall walls around myself. Katie had wormed her way into my life, but I sure as hell wasn't letting anyone else in. Not even the stupid dog.

The steak was dried out and rock hard. I shook my head in disgust and yelled, "It's all your fault that I'll be eating salad for supper!"

Plunking myself down into a lawn chair, I scarfed down my salad like an angry rabbit. The dog, who hadn't left when I'd yelled at him, crept closer until he was huddled next to the woodpile.

Why was the big dummy still hanging around?

He sat with me while I watched the sun go down and the fire died out; the only light in the yard coming from my kitchen window. Goose bumps broke out on my arms as the temperature dropped, and I went inside to put on a hoodie and to find the remaining chocolate cake in my fridge.

Chapter Three

I had set my alarm for seven in the morning, planning to take a swim in the lake before breakfast. I wasn't athletic; being short with big curves had always made me shy away from sports. But the cake wasn't going to burn itself off my hips, and swimming was the one athletic pursuit with which I was comfortable. So I sucked up my embarrassment, braided my hair, and put on my bathing suit under a warm hoodie. Coffee would have to wait; swimming with a full tummy always made me feel sick.

I stepped off the back porch into the sunshine and pretended not to notice that the plate of steak I'd left outside last night was now empty.

Stupid dog. I hope it gave him heartburn.

Following the narrow path through the trees, I kept my eyes open for bears. I even sang out loud, hoping it would be enough to scare off any wild animals or people that I came across. The same damn song from last night was stuck in my head, and I tried to send some apologetic vibes to any small critters who were forced to endure my off-key humming.

The lake was crystal clear and smooth as glass. There wasn't much of a beach, just a section of small worn rocks that slopped into soft sand next to the edge of the water. As usual, there wasn't another soul around. It was perfect.

I left my hoodie resting on a boulder, and I waded into the cold water.

I would like to say I'm one of those girls that just rips the bandage off all at once, but I'm not. Instead, I took it inch by freezing inch until the water was lapping at the bottom of my breasts.

Damn, it's colder than a witch's tit!

This was always the moment of no return. I could still back out; it was never hard to think of an excuse. But, being the stubborn person I am, I closed my eyes and dove straight under, not coming up for air until my lungs were burning and I was deep enough that my toes couldn't touch the bottom.

After some unladylike gasping, I forced my body to move. The rhythm of a slow breaststroke eased some of the stiffness in my muscles, and soon I didn't even notice the frigid water. Late summer in northern Saskatchewan usually meant that the temperature wouldn't climb into the double digits until noon.

Once I'd burned enough calories, I headed for shore. I didn't like to go too far out; my athletic ability was underwhelming, so the prospect of being stranded in the middle of the lake was real. And while I'd never actually seen a boat on the lake this early in the morning, I didn't want to chance getting run over.

That would be a pretty crappy way to start the day.

A shiver crawled down my spine that had nothing to do with the weather. The chilling feeling of being watched filled me, and my stomach clenched in protest. Slowing my pace until I was treading water about fifteen yards from the shore, I scanned the trees but nothing seemed out of place.

I'm not sure how long I had stayed there, waiting

for something to jump out of the shadows at me, but eventually my arms were burning and I was forced to leave the safety of the water. Was I just being paranoid? The stupid dog from last night must have spooked me more than I thought.

I lumbered out of the lake like a big whale with legs. When I arrived at the boulder where I'd left my sweatshirt and shoes, they were gone.

What the hell?

Looking around, I didn't see them anywhere. I *know* I had left them right here. The same place as last time and the time before that. Maybe they'd smelled like smoke from my fire last night and the damned dog had run off with them.

Goose bumps ghosted across my skin, and I suddenly wanted to be home. I was too exposed out there in the open. Screw my hoodie and shoes; I planned to just find them later.

The urge to run was overwhelming, but my bare feet on the forest floor forced me to keep my pace to a stumbling jog. As I said, I'm not very athletic. I was huffing and puffing like the big bad wolf after only a minute or two. And running in a wet swimsuit wasn't exactly helping. The sound of my wet braid, slapping against the bare skin between my shoulder blades, was barely audible over my breathing.

Someone stepped out of the trees onto the path in front of me, and I let out a tiny shriek of surprise and came to an abrupt halt. Warning bells clanged in my head. Something wasn't right about the man. He was tall, taller than any man I'd ever seen before. And that was saying something, since the last man I'd seen was Ozzy, and he was well over six feet tall. Instead of a bodybuilder's physique, this guy was skinny in a sickly skeletal sort of way. He reminded me of a velociraptor, the way his shoulders were hunched over. A chiropractor would have a field day with this guy's posture.

A black hood covered his head, hiding his face in shadows, even though he was only ten feet away. He must have had gloves on, because his hands were long and ended in sharp pointy fingers that couldn't possibly be real. Not unless he was Freddy Krueger's cousin.

He didn't just look wrong, he *felt* wrong. My skin wanted to crawl off my body, like I'd swallowed a dozen rats that were trying to chew their way out of my stomach.

Oh shit, oh shit, oh shit—

My dread built, and it had nothing to do with the fact that I was standing nearly naked in front of someone. No, this had nothing to do with being self-conscious about the size of my hips; this type of fear was born from an ancient part of me that I'd inherited from my ancestors; it was entirely about survival. It was the same instinct that screamed *Predator!* when you found yourself cornered by a wild animal.

The man jumped, his legs bending in a way that human knees shouldn't have been able to, and then he was leaping toward me so fast that I only had time to throw my hands up to protect my face before he was on me. His fingers dug into my arm like claws, tearing and slicing as I toppled backward. My breath rushed out of my lungs, and then he was sitting on my chest, making it impossible for me to pull in more air.

I wanted to close my eyes, afraid that I'd see my death in his face if I looked too closely, but if this was really my last few seconds left on Earth, I didn't want anyone saying I went down without a fight. I kicked at the forest floor and tried to shout, "Get the fuck off!" but it came out more like, "Ge...fu...fff," and my attempt at fierceness was ruined by my breathlessness.

He leaned down, bringing the black hole where his face should have been close enough that I could feel his hot, moist breath on my cheek. It smelled as though he'd been eating rancid tacos that somebody else had already thrown up.

A rushing sound filled my ears, and I desperately tried to buck him off. My first move would have been to knee him in the groin, but my legs were trapped uselessly under his weight. Little black spots clouded my vision, and my arms were giving in to the weight pushing down on me. Blood ran down my arms and dripped onto my face, warm against my chilled skin. Why the hell hadn't I thought to bring a towel with me? My hands and feet had already gone numb. Although, judging by the amount of blood coming from my ruined arms, I was lucky not to be feeling anything in my extremities.

Then, just when my trembling arms collapsed, something shiny slid across my sight, followed by a wave of bright red. The body that had me pinned to the ground toppled sideways and rolled a few feet away. I blinked rapidly, trying to see what was happening. Swiping at my face, my hand came away red and sticky.

What the hell?

My lungs finally unseized, and I sucked in oxygen as though I'd just gotten back from a week-long vacation on the moon. I struggled to sit up, but I couldn't find the coordination needed to do anything but flop around like a fish.

Someone knelt beside me, and for a horrible moment, I thought that the attack was starting all over again. Then, my brain caught on to the fact that a second man had joined the party. The first man's body lay unmoving a few feet away.

The person next to me tugged back the hood of his dark green cloak and, to my immense relief, revealed a face that was human. Well, human-ish. He was far too beautiful to be considered just human; he was closer to a Greek god than any average man.

His long blond hair was swept straight back, giving an unobstructed view of his perfect porcelain skin. Damn, as soon as I caught my breath; I was going to ask him what moisturizer he used, because I was already getting a few wrinkles of my own.

Green eyes that managed to be dark, yet vibrant, impartially swept over every inch of me, and I tried not to blush. Directly above his full lips, a sharp elegant nose split a perfectly symmetrical face. In one smooth motion, he removed his cloak and draped it over my body.

Who the hell wore a full-length cloak these days? I guess it was none of my business; I was just grateful his questionable fashion choices meant I was now covered from my chin to toes in soft velvety fabric. I tried to tell him that I didn't want to get blood all over his beautiful clothes (cosplay costumes probably weren't cheap), but my lips didn't seem to be working. Which seemed kind of weird, since I know I'd been screaming only a few seconds ago.

Actually, nothing seemed to be working anymore.

Even my involuntary shivering had stopped.

The man, who I'd started referring to as Legolas in my head (since he reminded me of Tolkien's elf) lifted me into his arms and strode purposefully through the trees. I couldn't tell if we were heading toward the lake or my cabin, and I didn't particularly care. His chest was hard against my softer body, and he kept my head tucked between his shoulder and neck so it didn't flop around. I wanted to tell him I could walk by myself; carrying around a hundred and sixty pounds of anything would likely put his back out.

"Hush," he told me when I tried to slur out some words of protest on his behalf.

Fine, he could go ahead and torture himself if he wanted to. Just saying, even with the strong arms I could feel holding me, he was going to be hurting tomorrow. I'm not a small girl.

I gave up on warning him, and I tried to enjoy the weird sensation of floating while still being cradled against a rock-hard body. I was probably going to end up with bruises from how tightly I was pressed against him. Not that I was complaining.

****

I must have fallen asleep, because when I opened my eyes, I was once again lying on my ugly striped burgundy couch with a strange man next to me.

I really had to figure out how this was happening; two days in a row was a little concerning.

Pain exploded up my arms as my body warmed up enough to regain some feeling, and I choked on a moan.

Son of a bitch!

My back bowed off the couch as shivers simultaneously wracked my entire body.

Legolas spared me a glance before he continued to tape gauze across my left arm. My right arm was already engulfed in white bandages. Holy shit, it *hurt*, and I tried to squirm out of his grip.

"Hush," he said.

"It hurts." I tried not to whine.

"It will heal." Easy for him to say. Good thing he had a great bedside manner to go along with his giant lack of compassion.

"I'll probably need stitches." There had been so much blood; how could I *not* need stitches? Without a phone to call Katie for a ride, I'd have to drive myself. Dragging myself off the couch and out to my truck was about as likely as me fitting into a size six bikini. I wondered if Legolas would drive me into town to the walk-in clinic…Maybe if I asked really nicely.

"What *was* that thing?" I ignored the tremble in my voice. Knowing the truth, even if it was terrifying, was always preferable to ignorance.

"What thing?" he asked casually, his fingers tightening on the bandages, gauze, and tape as he stuffed them back into the first-aid kit. His fingers were long and graceful, like the fingers of a pianist.

"The thing in the woods! The monster that attacked me!" I looked from my injured arms to his face and back to my arms. I had *not* been imagining things. Something had definitely happened, and I wanted to know what the hell it was.

He shrugged, and my eyes were drawn to the simple white shirt he wore. If one of the characters in my books were wearing it, I'd have called it a homespun tunic. But here in the modern world, it was easier to describe as a gender-neutral blouse. Probably silk, or something equally expensive. I doubted that even a drycleaner could get all of my blood out of its pale fabric.

"Seriously? You're going to stick your head in the sand and pretend that didn't just happen?" I demanded.

He looked at me blankly, and I wished I wasn't so light-headed so I could smack some understanding into him.

"Ignoring things doesn't make them go away," I explained, sounding like I was addressing a roomful of toddlers. "And the bad thing is still out there." Oh, God, what if it went after poor Mrs. Swazle next door?

"You needn't worry. I killed him."

"Wait, what? You killed it?"

"Yes." He stood and returned my first-aid kit to the bathroom before rummaging through my fridge.

"Why?"

"He would have killed you." He set a glass of water and my last piece of chocolate cake on the coffee table and helped me to sit up. "You need to replenish the blood you lost."

It didn't take much convincing to get my hands to cooperate, and I drank the entire glass of water.

"So it was a he?" I speared a forkful of cake and shoved it in my mouth. After my swim and near-naked run through the woods, I'd worked up quite an appetite.

"Yes, Lebolus was a male."

I shivered and tried not to think about the thing in the woods; something that scary shouldn't have a gender. Tornados and earthquakes didn't have genders, and they were no less dangerous.

"Lebolus was not native to these woods. I suspect he was suffering from some type of...mental illness."

He chose his words carefully, as though he was unfamiliar with them. "The responsibility of capturing him and returning him…ah, home was mine." The slight crinkle between his eyebrows made me think that he was making this explanation up as he talked. He might not be lying, but he definitely wasn't giving me the whole story.

The cake must've given my blood sugar a boost, because I was feeling more like myself and less like a helpless bimbo in a B-list psycho/thriller movie. It wasn't lost on me that I was still wearing nothing but a wet bathing suit, wrapped in a cloak, with a strange man in my house. Just because he saved me from that thing in the woods didn't mean I trusted him. Some predators liked to play with their prey before killing it.

"Who are you?"

"Farranen." He inclined his head without breaking eye contact.

"Theo," I told him, once I realized he was waiting for me to respond with my own name.

"That is a man's name." He didn't sound like he was judging, more like he was curious.

"Theodora." I don't know what made me tell him; I hadn't used that name since I was a kid.

"I'll get you some more water, Theodora." I watched him walk away. The view was pretty spectacular; his pants looked like leather and fit him like a glove.

Maybe I've become overly suspicious in my old age, but something about this whole situation wasn't sitting right with me. "*How* did you kill him?" I asked. It's not like he had a giant hunting rifle slung over his shoulder. Maybe he'd left it outside on my back steps.

"I cut off his head." He handed me a full glass, and I nearly dropped it.

"You *cut off* his *head*?"

"Yes."

I looked at the empty plate on the coffee table and wondered if I had enough eggs to make another cake. Somehow, I doubted there was enough cake in the world to make this conversation sound normal. I was totally going to regret asking, but I asked anyway. "*How* did you cut off his head?" Unless Farranen had his own retractable claws like Lebolus did, he must be hiding one heck of a hunting knife up his sleeve.

He stared at me with indecision bouncing back and forth in his eyes. Just when I figured he wasn't going to answer me at all, he stood and said, "I should not be telling you this. It is forbidden to involve your kind in my world; but since Lebolus has already revealed himself, the damage has already been done."

Well, that sounded ominous. Kind of like the big speech a serial killer gave before cutting off someone's body parts.

Farranen reached over his left shoulder with his right hand like he was grabbing something, and then, suddenly, there was a sword in his hand. A freaking *sword!*

"Holy *crap!*" I jumped to my feet, only staggering slightly at the sudden dizziness that rolled through me.

Moving slowly, he lowered the sword, pointing the tip at the floor. At least two and a half feet long, the shiny silver blade reflected the morning sunlight that streamed through the window. There were vines, or something floral, etched at the base, continuing up the hilt and under his hand. It looked far more real than anything you'd carry as part of a cosplay costume.

"Theodora—" The way he lowered his voice, like he was talking to a scared child, made me angry. I was *not* a scared child.

"Where the hell did that come from?" I gave him my strongest glare, hoping it hid the fear in my eyes.

"It is glamoured, a gift from my queen, spelled so that I might carry it into this world to fulfil my duties as a guardian of the gate." He stated it so matter-of-factly, that I truly believed *he* believed it.

What the hell was I supposed to say to that? Pretend like I bought his crazy story? Spend the next ten minutes of my life arguing with him that the sword in his hand couldn't possibly be real? It sure as hell *looked* real.

"I should get dressed." And maybe a psych evaluation.

"Of course." He swung the sword over his shoulder, and it disappeared just as fast as it had appeared. Lowering his hands gracefully until they hung at his sides in a nonthreatening manner, he must have sensed my desire to scrutinize his outrageous claims, and he held perfectly still while I studied every inch of him.

"Turn around." I twirled my finger in the air for emphasis, and he obligingly did a slow turn. It was physically impossible to tuck a full-length sword down his shirt or under his ponytail.

"It is still here; the scabbard is glamoured to conceal it."

"Oh." Right, because that was going to be my next guess. "I'm just going to find something warmer to wear…" I backed toward my bedroom, leaving damp footprints in my wake. Once I was safely across the threshold, I shut the door and locked it. Not that the flimsy antique doorknob would stop anyone for more than half a second, but at least I'd have some warning.

After the bear-that-was-really-a-dog incident last night, I'd realized how vulnerable I was out here by myself, so I'd taken some precautions. It had taken some digging, but I'd found the old shotgun that Will had inherited when his grandfather had passed away. It took a lot of trying, but I'd succeeded in getting it loaded without shooting my foot off. I still wasn't sure if it would work, but I had slept better knowing it was tucked between my mattress and headboard.

I scrambled around the bed like a three-legged hippo and gingerly freed the shotgun from the hidey-hole that I'd made for it. The wooden part was smooth in my hands, and it felt like safety.

I briefly considered climbing out the window instead of dealing with the man in my living room.

No. This is my home. I am a strong, independent woman and can take care of myself.

The bandages on my arms would beg to differ, but now was not the time to think about that.

With my cold, stiff fingers wrapped around the shotgun, I pulled open the bedroom door and looked straight into Farranen's dark green eyes. Aside from the slight raising of his left eyebrow, he didn't look surprised to be facing down a short woman with a large gun. He didn't even mention that my shivering was making the barrel of the gun jump from side to side.

"Get the hell out of my house." I'd used the exact same words yesterday. I should put them on a T-shirt or wreath for my door so I could save myself the trouble of repeating them again.

Farranen dipped his head and turned for the door. "As you wish."

I didn't lower the gun until I heard his footsteps on the back porch, and then I tiptoed to the kitchen window just in time to see him disappear into the woods. The view was still spectacular, but this time it filled me with a huge sense of relief.

Chapter Four

Monsters with featureless faces chased me through my dreams, and I woke feeling unrested.

The burning in my arms had subsided to a deep ache, and a chill that had settled into my bones was gone, thanks to every blanket that I owned piled on top of my bed while I'd slept. The two pairs of socks with fuzzy slippers might have been overkill, but at least I was finally feeling warm again.

I must have slept the entire day away, because my cabin was completely dark. I lay there for a few minutes, letting the silence wrap itself around me, until I was a part of it. Then, at my bladder's insistence, I shuffled to the bathroom and took care of business.

Once my teeth were minty-fresh, I wandered into the kitchen and poked around in the freezer. *Hmm, beef stroganoff or chicken alfredo?*

Something behind me made a scratching noise, and I nearly jumped out of my skin as the silence was broken. Every hair on the back of my neck stood straight up. The sound came again; somebody was on my back porch. I really, really didn't want to turn around and look, but keeping my head buried in the freezer all night wasn't an option.

Scritch...Scritch...

Why had I left the shotgun in my bedroom? Did I have time to run back and get it before whoever, or whatever was outside broke in to eat me? Anything that came through the door would have me backed into the kitchen without any place to run or hide. Yeah, some of the lower cupboards were pretty big, but not big enough to hide anything with my size of hips.

I ran for the bedroom. Tossing aside unmade bedding, I lunged for the shotgun like a drowning woman would scramble for a life preserver. My nerves calmed considerably once I had the heavy butt pressed against my shoulder. I was damn sick of people showing up unannounced.

I stalked toward the back door in my slippers. They didn't make me look very threatening, but I figured the gun would more than make up for it.

Scritch...

Opening the door would be a stupid move. If I did that, it would have been like handing whoever was there some dinner napkins for when they were done ripping my face off. But the shotgun was heavy, and I didn't want to stand here waiting for them to break in. Who knows how long that would take?

I could just shoot the damn door and hope it hit whoever was outside, too. But then I'd have to replace the door, and the idea of being without one overnight made me queasy.

I tried to think like the duke—what would he do if somebody was lurking outside his manor home?

I backed quickly across the living room and peered out the window. When nothing moved, I returned to the front door, quietly turned the deadbolts, and cracked it open. Without any street lights, I had to rely on the moon's ambient light to see in the near darkness.

The yard was silent; my truck was still backed into

its usual spot on the gravel pad next to the front porch. Keeping one ear on the scratching sound still coming from the back of the cabin, I inched outside and down the stairs. My slippered feet barely made a whisper of sound on the old stairs. Huh. Usually, I sounded like an entire family of tap-dancing elephants on the creaky wooden planks, but my fuzzy pink footwear seemed to be helping. That was damn handy and made me think the nine-dollar purchase had been worth it.

The leaves on the ground were freshly fallen and didn't crunch under my feet as I rounded the north side of my cabin. I didn't want to chance Mrs. Swazle glancing out her window; if she saw me, she might scream, and then I'd jump, and that would be dangerous with a loaded gun in my arms.

I kept to the tree line, and once I was past the side of the cabin, I could see something big and dark on the back porch. *Oh God, please don't let it be Lebolus, having come to avenge the loss of his head!*

A small whine preceded the scratching, and I squinted, trying to make out what was on my porch. The thing turned, and I instantly recognized the big golden eyes. "Dog?" I asked, disbelief making my voice sound higher than it should have been.

He stopped mauling my door and gave a slight tail-wag before he lay down with his head on his giant paws.

"What do you think you're doing? Look at my door!" I climbed the steps and examined the scratches in the brown paint. They weren't all from him, and I was more pissed that he'd scared the crap out of me, than at the minor damage. "Bad dog!" I would have wagged a finger in his direction, but the shotgun required all the waning strength of both my injured arms. I turned and marched back around the house, since I hadn't thought to bring the keys for the back door with me.

Stupid dog.

I didn't want to admit it, but I was still scared. My imagination was working overtime, seeing monsters in every shadow. Even the half-moon seemed to be leering down at me.

By the time I got back inside, my arms were cramping up from carrying the gun, so I dumped it on the coffee table. The damn thing must have weighed twenty pounds.

The dog whined from the open doorway, and I slapped a hand over my mouth to stifle the small shriek that had escaped. "Don't *do* that! You scared me!" I hissed at him.

He lowered his head, and I felt like a jerk for yelling at a dog.

Once my heart stopped trying to pound its way out of my chest, I asked him, "Are you hungry?"

Judging from his doggy expression, he clearly thought I was an idiot for even asking. I held up a hand when he took a tentative step inside. "No, you don't. Go wait outside, and I'll see what I can find for supper."

He whined but stepped back until he was at the edge of the porch and lay down at the top of the stairs. I felt marginally safer knowing he was outside. Of course, I had no doubt that anyone with a fresh T-bone could bribe their way past him.

I locked the deadbolts for good measure. I was halfway across the living room when I got that same feeling in my gut again that said I wasn't alone. Goose bumps rose on my arms and back, followed by a cold sweat. Everything looked exactly as I'd left it, but I knew something was off. My spidey-senses were tingling something fierce.

Maybe being out here alone for so long had messed with my tolerance for other people; maybe I was still reeling from having two different people in my personal space uninvited. Four, if you counted Dog and Lebolus.

Figuring I'd rather face an intruder armed, I grabbed for the shotgun on the coffee table. Its weight was still unfamiliar in my hands, and I fumbled, trying to make sure I didn't accidentally grab the trigger. The creaking of my old wooden floor was the only warning I got before someone grabbed me from behind. I screamed, and the shotgun went off, creating a sudden flash of light and deafening me with a sound like thunder caught indoors.

The man—I assumed it was a man, since he felt like a brick wall against my back—lifted me until my pink slippers dangled off the floor. His arms locked around me in a giant bear hug, effectively pinning my arms and the gun against my chest. I lashed out with my heels, but he didn't even acknowledge the blows to his shins. If I survived this, I was going to start wearing steel-toed boots to bed.

I screamed as long and loud as I could, even though I knew the only other person who lived on the street was Mrs. Swazle, and by now she'd probably taken out her hearing-aid and gone to bed. When my lungs ran out of air, I gulped in more. I wasn't going to let this guy walk away without at least one perforated eardrum.

"Theo!" My attacker grunted and muttered something I couldn't hear because I was screaming again. He gave me a little shake, like a dog with a toy, and my teeth clicked together. "*Theo! Cut it out—*"

I knew that voice. I paused mid-shriek, and the silence was nearly as loud as the shotgun blast had been.

"Jesus Christ, woman. I'll put you down if you promise not to shoot me with that thing." The way he rolled his r's, right along with the way he infused his words with indignant irritation, was familiar.

"Ozzy?" I asked, trying not to sound as confused as I felt.

He set me down but kept a firm grip on the shotgun while I scrambled to put a few steps between us. He could keep it; the damn thing hadn't done me any good when I needed it.

The light from the kitchen cast funny shadows across his eyebrows as he scowled down at me. "Don't call me that." Right, like he had any right to be offended by a nickname when he'd just manhandled me like a rag doll.

"What are you doing here?" I tried to sound accusing, but I was still shaking from the adrenaline rush he'd caused. I fisted my hands in the fabric of my sweatpants so he wouldn't see me quivering, but that made the cuts on my arms burn so I forced myself to let go.

"I came to check on you."

"You broke into my place *to check on me?*" I put just the right amount of disbelief into my words so I sounded just as aloof as he did.

"I didn't break in. Your door was wide open;

you're lucky I wasn't here to abduct you, or rob you blind!"

I arched a brow, letting him know the jury was still out on that one.

"Well, I'm fine. Thanks for stopping by. And for the physical assault. And for nearly giving me a heart attack. That was nice and all. I'll show you to the door." I turned to the door and stopped when I saw the moonlight pooling on my hardwood. Which was totally wrong, since it wasn't coming from the window.

"What the hell?" A brand-new hole in the wall, directly between the front door and living room window glared down at me. It was about a dozen feet up, right at the apex of the pointed ceiling. "My wall!" The stupid shotgun had blasted right through the drywall, insulation, and siding.

He cracked the shotgun in half, and the remaining shot fell out. "Oh, .224s. You know, these could take a man's head off. Best not to keep it loaded."

I gave him my best scathing look, even though I knew my face was burning with embarrassment. He was right; I shouldn't have been waving around a loaded shotgun without learning how to use it properly first.

"What the hell am I supposed to do now? I don't have any plywood to patch it. Every damn squirrel out there will be moved in by morning!"

"Maybe you should have thought of that before you shot a hole in your wall," he suggested casually.

"I don't have time for this. You can leave." There might be an old tarp in the shed that I could nail over the hole to cover it until I could go into town for supplies. My rickety aluminum ladder was sketchy, but it should be able to reach that high. I just hoped it didn't have a weight limit.

"First, you need to explain to me why I found a trail of blood leading from your back door into the woods." All his casual pretense was gone, replaced with an aggression that had me backing up a few steps.

"The blood—it was mine," I stammered.

"Yes, I know it was yours. *Why* is it out there"—he pointed toward my backyard—"instead of in *there*?" His finger jabbed at my chest, and I slapped it away.

"I had an accident, but I'm fine now."

"An accident?" he scoffed. "What kind of accident?"

"None of your business." I'd had enough of him treating me like a misbehaving child. I didn't have to answer to him.

"Theo, there are things going on here that you don't understand." He raked a hand through his hair, and I realized why it was always standing up. "I saw all the blood and assumed he'd gotten to you."

"Who are you talking about?"

"Will."

"Will?" Part of me wanted to laugh, while part of me wanted to cry. "What are you talking about?"

"Will tried to follow you home from the bar."

Will was here? My heart squeezed painfully before crawling into my throat. "He was here? My Will?" I blinked back tears of joy, and I hoped they'd stay hidden until I was alone. I slumped onto the couch before my knees gave out.

"He was at the Boot Scoot last night."

I still couldn't remember anything from the night before. Had I seen Will? Oh God, I was the crappiest wife ever.

"I don't know how much you remember, but I drove you home. I suspected he would try to contact you. The agent tailing him lost him between here and the bar, so I don't think he actually knows where you're living now."

"I should go back. To the bar, I mean. So he can find me." I was babbling but didn't care. I had so many questions; if I could just see Will, he'd straighten this whole mess out.

"No. I can't let you do that."

"What?" I looked at him in disbelief.

"Will isn't here to rekindle your dead marriage, Theo." I flinched as if he'd slapped me. "He's hunting you." He held up a hand to hold off the questions that I'd already opened my mouth to ask. "I don't know what he wants from you. Theo, listen to me; he's not the same man you knew six years ago. He kidnapped a woman last night. He's a monster."

The blood drained from my face, and I was glad I was already sitting. What the hell was going on? Will was a monster? Like the monster who had attacked me this morning?

No, that wasn't possible. Will wasn't a monster. He was a gentleman. Maybe a little boring, but definitely not a monster.

"What woman?" I asked, my voice little more than a whisper.

"A waitress at the bar last night. He must have realized I was in the truck with you, or maybe he knew he was being followed. Either way, he circled back and grabbed her from the parking lot after the bar closed."

"How do you know it was him?" It could have

been anyone.

"She looked just like you. Same height, same build, long brown hair."

"Lots of women have long brown hair," I protested.

"D cup, hazel eyes—"

"Mine are just brown." And I was a double D, but I wasn't going to tell him that.

He flicked the light switch on the wall, and I blinked in the sudden brightness. "What the hell?"

The couch dipped next to me, and then Ozzy grabbed my jaw in his huge hand and tilted my face toward his. "Nope, they're hazel."

Asshole.

I shrugged out of his grip and tried to remember what we'd originally been talking about.

"So, you think Will kidnapped a waitress and then turned into a monster?"

"No, he turned into a monster six years ago. There are at least two dozen missing women we've been able to link back to him."

"You think he's a *serial killer?*" Holy shit, this was insane. Will had been repulsed by the thought of hunting or fishing; he couldn't possibly stomach murder. He'd barf all over his victims before he got to the actual killing part.

A bead of sweat trickled down my back, and I pulled my hoodie off. My cabin felt warmer than usual; to think I was worried about the hole in the wall letting out all the heat. Guess I'd been wrong.

"What the fuck happened to you?"

I looked down at my arms; the cuts still hurt, but I'd nearly forgotten about them with all the talk about my husband and murdered women. Blood had soaked into the white bandages thanks to the giant bear hug Ozzy had put me in.

"Yeah, about that—" Before I could decide how much to tell him, he was dragging me by my wrist into the bathroom. He shoved me onto the toilet and dug in the cabinet under the sink. "Hey! Is that anyway to treat an injured woman?"

"It is when she's too stupid to take care of herself," he huffed.

Once he had opened the first-aid kit, he donned a pair of latex gloves and peeled my bandages off.

"Ouch! You don't have to rip off all the arm hair and skin with it!" A backhoe would have been gentler than Ozzy. And wouldn't have scowled so much, either.

"Better to get it over with quickly."

"Your bedside manner sucks." That earned me a smirk which quickly disappeared when Ozzy saw my arm. Four deep gashes cut across my forearm, with a smaller one on the softer inside skin closer to my wrist.

"What the fuck, Theo?"

"You should see the other guy," I joked lamely. When he glowered at me, I just shrugged. What was I supposed to do, feel guilty for getting attacked? "Seriously, the left one isn't nearly as bad."

He made a noise in the back of his throat that sounded like a growl as he ripped off the second piece of gauze. After putting a towel across my lap, he dumped a bottle of peroxide on my injuries.

Then there was a lot of screaming. And probably some profanity. I can't say for sure, since I was too busy doing the screaming to really pay attention. I think he grinned when I called him a monkey-butt-faced son-of-a-bitch.

"You're lucky the muscles and tendons aren't damaged."

"Yep, that's me—damned lucky."

He was surprisingly efficient as he used new gauze pads to soak up the blood that kept leaking from the wounds. Once the oozing seemed to have stopped, he pulled out his cell and snapped a pic of the gashes.

"Did Will do this?" He looked up at me from where he knelt on the bathroom floor, his expression deadly serious.

"What? No!" Hadn't he been listening when I told him I hadn't seen my husband for the last six years?

"These are defensive wounds. Tell me what happened." He said it softly, before returning his attention to opening non-stick gauze packages.

I figured, what the hell, he would either believe me or not. I wasn't sure if *I* actually believed me.

"I was walking home from the lake this morning, and this guy, this *thing*, jumped out at me. His fingers were like claws." I shuddered at the memory. "Then, someone else showed up and cut off his head. End of story."

Ozzy's fingers stalled, and he looked at me like he was questioning my sanity. I couldn't even say he was the only one here who thought I might be crazy.

"Cut off his head?" he repeated, like maybe he hadn't heard me correctly.

"Yep." I dragged a finger across my neck and mimed having my head cut off. "With a sword."

"Describe it." He used his teeth to rip off a piece of medical tape from the roll, but he was watching me out of the corner of his eye.

"The sword or the monster?"

"The thing that attacked you."

"Oh. Tall, maybe six and a half or seven feet. Everyone looks tall to me; it's hard to say for sure. Skinny, like he hadn't eaten in months. Dressed in all black, and the hood hid his face, but it was all shadowy where his face should have been. He smelled like a mouse that had died in someone's old gym shoes." I let out a nervous laugh; I sounded like a kid describing the boogeyman after a bad dream. "He looked like the Grim Reaper." I blinked back tears at the fear that tried to overwhelm me. Damn it, I was stronger than this. "His name was Lebolus."

"You talked to him?" The calm intensity in his face made me want to shrink away, but I had nowhere to go.

"No, I was too busy being mauled to carry on much of a conversation." I don't think he appreciated my sarcasm, but I continued talking anyway. "Farranen told me. Right before I put the shotgun in his face and told him to get out."

"Who—"

"The guy with the sword."

With my arms freshly bandaged, Ozzy put away the supplies and tossed his gloves in the garbage. Before I could stand and leave the bathroom that was making me claustrophobic, he pulled out a flashlight and shone it directly in my face.

"Hey!" The new tape pulled at my arms when I threw them up to block eyes. "What the hell?"

"Just checking to see if you have a concussion." The light clicked off, but my vision was shot; all I could see were a bunch of white spots. Ozzy's hands slid into my hair, making me jump. This seemed like a pretty inappropriate time and place for a scalp massage.

"I don't feel any bumps. Do you remember hitting your head?" he asked.

"No, my head is fine." My poor butt was still bruised, but he didn't need to know that.

"Your injuries look a lot like a bear attack. A blow to your head would explain the man with the sword."

I bristled at the implication that I didn't know what I was talking about.

"Theo, only your blood was found at the scene. If someone, or something, had been decapitated, there would have been blood. And what happened to the body?"

"I don't know! Why don't you ask Farranen?" I pushed past him, banging my shoulder on the doorjamb on my way out. Just perfect; like I needed another bruise. "And how do you know it was my blood, huh?" Wouldn't I have noticed an entire crime scene investigation team traipsing through my backyard?

"It's my job to know."

I scowled. That was such a cliché cop-out answer.

I marched across my living room, only banging my shin twice, and threw open the front door. My pink fuzzy slippers detracted from my badassery, but only a tiny bit.

"Get the hell out of my house." I gestured with my chin to the waiting door.

"Theo…" He ran his hand through his hair, and when I didn't say anything, he sighed and stepped outside onto the empty porch. He paused for a second, and it almost looked like he was sniffing the air. Yeah, 'cause that wouldn't be creepy. Then he was just gone.

Dog was MIA, so it looked like I was on my own.

Just the way I liked it.

****

After a frozen TV dinner and not nearly enough sleep, I climbed into my truck the next morning and headed into town.

Mid-September was unusually warm this year, but there was no way in hell I was going for a swim this morning. After Ozzy's surprise visit last night, I was questioning whether I'd really seen something supernatural in the woods, or if maybe I'd imagined the whole thing. It was actually more likely that Farranen and Lebolus were figments of my own imagination. If so, I would have to consider ditching historical romance writing once I was done with the duke and Priscilla. With a male protagonist as hot as Farranen, I'd have no trouble breaking into the paranormal romance genre.

My mind was already compiling a character bio for the heroine. Maybe she'd be short with too many curves and plain brown hair.

Yeah, maybe not. Who would want to read about someone boring like that?

My fridge and pantry were getting pretty bare, so I stopped at the Shop 'n' Save to pick up groceries. Normally, I would have stopped by Country Customs, but I didn't want to have to explain my injured arms to Katie.

After a quick run through a drive-through for lunch, I was back on the highway headed home. I nearly choked on a fry when I had to suddenly slam on my brakes to avoid hitting a deer in the middle of the road. Two of my plastic bags of food slid to the floor as I wrenched the wheel hard to the left. Thank goodness nobody was in the oncoming lane.

Once my vehicle came to a stop, with only minor fishtailing but huge skid marks in my wake, I pried my fingers off the wheel one by one.

Holy. Shit.

A glance in the rear-view mirror showed the buck still standing in the middle of the road, oblivious to the brush with death he'd just had.

I moved to take my foot off the brakes, but something in the mirror caught my eye. The deer was looking toward my truck with an odd amount of concentration, but that wasn't what had my attention. The sun was high in the morning sky, highlighting the deer in stark relief against the blacktop, and it made the deer look like it was glowing.

Weird.

I gave a shaky exhale and surprised myself with a giddy laugh. I really should have bought a lottery ticket before I left town. Two sort of break-ins (one with a magical sword), one monster attack, a shotgun hole in my living room, a near head-on collision with some radiant wildlife, and I was still breathing. Yay for me.

I looked down at the mess of fries scattered on the floormat and frowned. After all I'd been though in the last two days, I should deserve *something* good.

Maybe I'd make a cake when I got home.

Chapter Five

Once again, I found unexpected company waiting for me when I got home. At least this time, he'd had the manners to wait outside.

Dog greeted me with a hesitant tail wag and mournful eyes, as if he wasn't sure he was welcome.

"You have some nerve showing your face here," I told him.

His tail drooped guiltily. Rightfully so, since he'd left me high and dry when Ozzy had pulled his cat-burglar act last night. Dog whined in agreement.

"Why am I talking to a dog?" I asked. His golden eyes were sympathetic, like he knew my pitiful social life revolved around conversations with a K9. "Arrgh!" My frustration caused him to belly-crawl back a few inches, no doubt thinking I was mad at him.

"I'm sorry," I told him. "I just feel like an idiot for thinking you were watching out for me." And for talking to a dog. "You gotta do you, and I'll just do me." It would be better that way; nobody to let you down but yourself.

"Are you hungry?" His big, pointy ears perked up. "Stupid question, right? I bought some chicken thighs for supper." To be honest, it was nice to have someone who appreciated my culinary skills; although, I doubted Dog had very discerning taste buds.

After I filled the fridge with my grocery store haul,

I threw ingredients for a strawberry shortcake together in a pan and popped it in the oven. It didn't take long to whip up some frosting, and I carried my laptop outside to wait for the oven timer to go off.

Dog was lying in the shade with his scruffy black fur blending into the deeper shadows, so that only his yellow eyes were noticeable. It would have been creepy, apart from the fact that I'd temporarily paid for his loyalty with the cold fries from my truck. I'd be safe while his belly was full.

The rest of the afternoon was spent in a peaceful silence, with Priscilla and the duke's unlikely love flowing from my fingertips, while Dog snored softly under a large pine tree.

I stopped for a midafternoon cake-break before plunging back into my work. What can I say? I needed to replenish my body after the recent blood loss, right?

Movement on the other side of the yard made me freeze with my fork halfway to my mouth. Something small darted between the trees before emerging from the shadows. A skinny white cat strolled through my backyard without disturbing a single fallen leaf. It froze when it caught sight of me, and I briefly wondered if Dog would chase it.

A quick glance to my right showed that Dog couldn't have cared less. He didn't give the cat any sign of acknowledgement; he just continued to stare longingly at my forkful of shortcake.

The cat contemplated me with pale blue eyes and then abruptly turned and continued to wander through my yard as though it owned the place. Jeez, first Dog, and now the cat. I wondered if I should be taking my garbage out more often; something must be attracting them to my property. Since they both looked as if they hadn't had a decent meal in a while, I assumed that they didn't have nice warm homes to go back to at night.

The cat ducked back into the shadows of the trees, and for a brief second it looked like it was glowing. I blinked, positive that I'd been staring at my laptop screen for too long. Of course all that bright white fur was going to stand out against the darkness of the surrounding forest.

I stood and stretched my stiff muscles. You know you're getting old when the mere act of sitting makes your body hurt. It was almost six o'clock, and the sun was already close to setting.

I used my flint knife to start a fire, and once it was burning steadily, I went inside to grab the chicken thighs. I drizzled them in olive oil, basil, parsley, garlic, and paprika and laid them in a large cast-iron pan. Making some cheesy garlic toast and a salad was an easy way to complete the meal, and soon I had everything lined up on the outside patio table.

With the meat sizzling in the pan over the fire, I shut down my laptop and carried it inside. I pulled on a clean hoodie to ward off the evening chill and went back out to check on supper.

The chicken was crispy and golden, so I removed the pan from the flames and tossed the toast on the highest wire rack. The cat was gone, and Dog had crept closer until he was camped out under the table. His big eyes followed every move I made.

"Would you just relax? It's not done yet."

His small chuff told me he was fine with undercooked toast.

Stupid dog.

Feeding stray animals wasn't a good idea. I'd never get rid of him now.

Once the cheese was melted into a gooey mess and the toast was perfectly crunchy, I divided it and the chicken onto two plates. I topped mine up with salad before setting Dog's on the ground. I only made it halfway through my salad before Dog had licked his plate clean.

"Did you even chew it?" I asked.

I watched the sky while I ate, waiting to see the first stars twinkle into sight. The fire had died down to a few glowing coals, and I'd forgotten to leave the back porch light on, so the yard was too dark to see across.

Dog sat up abruptly, his eyes no longer attempting to guilt me into sharing what was on my plate. He scanned the woods next to my cabin, and the fur on his back stood straight up. A low growl rolled out of his chest, and I shot to my feet.

"What is it?" I asked. Sitting outside in the dark suddenly didn't seem like the best plan.

Dog apparently agreed, because he tucked tail and ran for the trees at the back of my yard. Stupid dog! He ditched me after I'd fed him *twice* today. Stinkin' traitor.

So that left me with two options: follow him into the spooky woods (where I'd been attacked yesterday) or run for my cabin. I was a creative thinker, dammit! Why couldn't I come up with a third option? My brain always seemed to shut down under pressure. Given enough time, I could come up with thirty more options, but I needed to get my butt moving *now*. Funny how, standing out here in the yard alone, after dark, had never bothered me until two nights ago.

Surrounded by four solid walls with my shotgun in my bedroom seemed like the safest place to be. I ran for my cabin, not bothering to bring my half-eaten meal. Dog could have it, if he was brave enough to return for it.

I didn't bother with stealth, my sneakers pounded up the old wooden stairs like Lebolus's twin brother was on my heels, with his heart set on a gruesome revenge that involved disembowelment followed by decapitation. And maybe some torture thrown in for shits and giggles.

It did occur to me that Mrs. Swazle's place was on the other side of the trees I'd passed, so maybe she was out doing some evening raking and caught Dog's attention. Or maybe Dog had seen the white cat. He did seem like a pretty jumpy dog; anything could have spooked him.

I'd nearly talked myself into believing that I'd been jumping at shadows when someone stepped out of the shadows at the edge of the porch. I shrieked and grabbed for the doorknob.

"Theo." The deep baritone voice was familiar, but it still sent a chill down my spine.

"Ozzy?" Good Lord, did the man want to give me a heart attack? I clutched at my chest like I could calm my heartbeat through the fabric of my hoodie.

"Don't call me that." He stepped closer; he was still wearing the same black leather coat from last night. "We need to talk."

Talking was good; much better than him killing me.

"Do you want to come inside—" I started to invite him inside, thinking it was fortunate I'd made cake so I could try out my rusty hostess skills, but he cut me off before I could finish.

"I'm taking you into custody." One second, he was on the other side of the porch, and the next he was right next to me. Before my brain could try to process how fast he'd moved, he had grabbed my hands and cinched both my wrists together in front of me with a zip tie.

"What the hell are you *doing*?" I tried to sound outraged, but inside I was panicking. With my hands trapped in front of me, I felt helpless, and feeling helpless was something I'd worked very hard to avoid in the last few years.

"Get away from me!" I shouted. I tried to back away, but I already had my back pressed up against the cabin, so I had nowhere to go.

"Theo, this is for your own good." His giant hand pulled me by my elbow toward the stairs. "Damn it, woman, stop fighting me!"

I snarled some ugly words at him, but he just continued to drag my big butt across the weathered porch. Every female instinct I had was screaming that I needed to get away from him, that women who were tied up and dragged off into the night usually ended up with their faces on the side of a milk carton.

"Would you just calm down and listen to me?" The irritated tone in his voice made me think that he wasn't after a little heart-to-heart. When we reached the top of the stairs, he moved behind me so he could propel me forward down the steps.

The ladder that I'd used to repair the shotgun hole was still propped against the railing, waiting to be returned to the shed. And right next to it was my hammer.

Did I have the balls to do this?

Six years ago, I would have said heck no. Make some noise and hope the neighbors would call the police. Wait for rescue. Have faith that help would come.

But that was before. Now, there were no neighbors to hear my cries, nobody to save my hide but me.

I mentally hiked up my big girl panties and lunged for the hammer. It was heavy, and I lost my balance as I spun and swung upward with both hands. Whatever Ozzy had been saying was cut off with a sickening *thud* as the hammer connected with his head.

I was pretty sure I'd read somewhere that the softest part of the human skull is the temple—and I nailed his like it had a big red bull's-eye on it.

Momentum from the blow flung us apart. Ozzy was knocked backward, releasing his death grip on my elbow. I floundered at the top of the stairs for a few seconds before gravity won, and I toppled backward with a shriek.

The staircase of five steps was not too far a fall, but with my hands still zip-tied in front of me, it was like falling off a cliff in slow motion. The stairs rushed past in a blur, and my entire body tensed in anticipation of hitting the cold hard ground. I had a moment to be grateful that, if I was going to fall, at least I was landing on my backside where I had some extra padding to cushion the fall.

My butt never made it as far as the ground. Strong arms seized me from behind, and I landed against a hard chest that knocked the air out of me with an *oomph!*

I blinked in the near darkness and realized

Farranen had caught me. He spun us around so that he was between me and the cabin, then gently turned me in his arms so that we were face-to-face. His expression was just as serious as the last time I'd seen him; the slight wrinkle in his forehead was a mix of thoughtful and concerned.

"Are you all right?"

My first thought was, *He IS real! I knew it!*

"Theodora?"

I realized he was still talking, probably waiting for a coherent response from me. Not that I had one. I mean, other than some chafing from the zip ties, I was okay. But the whole abduction thing was really, really *not* okay. Thoughts flitted back and forth in my head, but my mouth decided to go with "Farranen? You're real."

Smooth, Theo. Real smooth.

His mouth quirked a small half smile, and I found myself smiling back. With lips like that, he really should smile more often.

"Yes, I am real. Did you doubt it?"

I opened my mouth to confirm that I had indeed thought he was a product of my overactive imagination, but the man bleeding all over my porch interrupted with "Jesus *Christ*, woman! That fucking *hurt*!"

Keeping one hand on my arm, Farranen turned to face Ozzy. And then, as if the situation wasn't surreal enough, Farranen reached over his shoulder and pulled out his sword. Yep, the freaking sword again. Which was also real. Obviously. And sort of cool, if you stopped to think about it.

"Theodora, who is your guest?" Farranen's words were civil, but his tone wasn't.

"Uh, this is Oscar Alderidge. Ozzy, this is Farranen." It was easy to fall back on social niceties when I had no idea what else to say. I wanted to add, "And his sword," but that seemed redundant. It would have been hard for Ozzy to miss, since it was pointed at his face and all.

So, so awkward.

I fidgeted from foot to foot, uncomfortable with Ozzy's bleeding and Farranen's sword.

"Ozzy just stopped by for a little abduction attempt. Nothing I couldn't handle." With my handy hammer. And some sarcasm.

"Explain." The word was cold; I could practically hear frost crystalizing on it as the temperature around us dropped in response.

"It wasn't an abduction; I was taking her into custody." The moon was just making its appearance for the night, and it was bright enough outside to see the trickle of blood running down Ozzy's forehead from his hairline.

"On whose authority?" Farranen demanded.

"The agency's." Ozzy stepped right up to the edge of the stairs and crossed his arms across his thick chest, as if he wasn't concerned at all about the sword tip inches from his face.

"On what grounds?" Farranen persisted.

"Those injuries on her arms are fae." Ozzy's eyes darted to me, and I thought I caught an apologetic look, but it was gone just as quick.

What the hell was he talking about?

"And?" Farranen threw the single syllable out like a challenge.

"If she turns—"

"That hasn't happened in centuries."

"—she'll be a danger to everyone."

The two men glared at each other, and I wondered if, maybe, I should take off into the woods like Dog had. They probably wouldn't have even noticed.

Instead, I opened my big mouth and asked, "What are you *talking* about?"

Chapter Six

That moment, a gust of wind chose to blow through my yard, tossing leaves everywhere as though we were trapped in a giant snow globe with yellow glitter. Ewww. I shivered, and my movement caused the zip ties to cut deeper into my skin. Before anyone could answer my question, I pointed at my dark cabin. "Can we do this inside? I'm freezing."

"Of course." Farranen gestured with his sword. "Move it, leech."

Ozzy scowled but let himself through the back door and didn't stop until he'd parked himself on the living room sofa.

I trailed behind the men, flipping on the lights as I went. "Is that really necessary?" I pointed at the sword.

Farranen slid it back into its hiding spot without a word.

"May I?" Farranen pulled my hands into his and carefully used a small dagger to cut through the plastic ties. Where had *that* come from? It disappeared just as fast as it had appeared, much like his sword had.

"Thank you." My words seemed inadequate, but he nodded in acknowledgement with a stiff smile.

Staying as far from Ozzy as possible while still being in the same room, I tried not to cringe at the damage that the hammer had done to his head. I couldn't tell if the injured side was swollen or indented from the impact, but it definitely didn't match the other half of his head. It was hard to say with the way his hair was standing up. Blood was smeared across his forehead, where he occasionally stopped to wipe it with his sleeve, so it wouldn't drip into his eye.

My mind shuffled through all the questions I wanted answered, so I started with "Am I under arrest?"

"No." Ozzy sounded surprised by my question.

"You said you were taking me into custody."

"Yes. For your protection."

"Why? What did I do?"

He sighed and ran a hand through his hair, grimacing when his fingers brushed against his open wound. "It's more of a quarantine. It's to keep you away from the human population until we know—"

"The *human* population?" I interrupted. "As opposed to what? The buffalo population?"

"Theo, those wounds on your arms—they were from a fae. It's not likely, but there's a chance you could be…infected."

"Infected? With what? And what's a fae?"

Farranen answered, even though I'd directed my question to Ozzy. "The fae folk." I must have looked confused, because he elaborated, "The fair folk? The hidden people? Wee folk? The people of the hill?"

"Fairies," Ozzy said flatly.

"Like the Tooth Fairy?" I didn't think the idea of someone sneaking into small children's bedrooms while they slept was funny, but Ozzy let out a man-sized guffaw.

"Yeah, just like the Tooth Fairy," he said.

"The thing in the woods didn't look like a fairy." I looked down at my arms, felt the cuts burning beneath my bandages and the fabric of my hoodie. "Do I need to get a rabies shot?"

People who were bitten by wild animals with rabies could die. I slumped into one of my dining room chairs and put my head on the table. This might be more serious than I'd thought.

The chair next to me scraped across the hardwood, making me jump. Farranen sat down, but he kept Ozzy in his line of sight.

"There's no shot or medical intervention that will help now that you've been exposed." I must have looked a little panicky, because he continued, "The chance of you being affected is incredibly remote. It hasn't happened in hundreds of years."

Okay, well, I guessed that was good news. I mean, Ebola had a death rate of like 80 percent, right? So this could have been worse.

"So what am I supposed to do? Should I go to the hospital?"

"Theo, let me take you in. Our facility is set up for quarantine. There are doctors who specialize in situations like this." Ozzy sounded so sincere; I thought that maybe I should go with him. The only thing stopping me was the fact that he'd tried to truss me up like a calf. Who knew what other liberties he'd take with my freedom?

"You'll put her in a cage, and then what? What will you do if she turns?" The anger in Farranen's voice was sharper than the dagger he'd used to cut me free.

"Why do you keep saying it like that?"

"He means if you turn fae," Ozzy sneered.

Wait—what? If I turned into a fairy? A missing piece of the puzzle clicked into place, and my gaze shot to the man sitting next to me.

"Lebolus was a *fairy*?"

"He was from the Dark Court; but, yes, he was fae."

I tried to reconcile the monster that had attacked me with the mental image that I had of tiny-winged creatures, dancing among wildflowers. The two opposites refused to mesh in my head.

"You think I'm going to turn into a *fairy*?" I felt crazy just saying the words. "And you"—I pointed to Ozzy—"want to lock me up in case I do?"

"If that's how you want to look at it. There's also the matter of Will to discuss."

"Who's Will?" Farranen asked.

Oh man, how to answer that one? Maybe I should put a pot of coffee on; we might be here a while.

"What does this have to do with Will?" My head was hurting, so I rested it on the table over my arms.

"He's been hunting her," Ozzy said. "I was sent to bring her into protective custody, but the mission changed when I saw the claw marks. An ankou, if I'm not mistaken?"

Farranen made some sort of affirmative sound.

"Well, that's…interesting." Ozzy sounded so carefully neutral, that I popped my head back up.

"What's interesting?" Yeah, I know I sounded stupidly suspicious. I'm going to blame it on my rusty social skills.

"Nothing; I'd just been under the assumption that ankou weren't allowed on this side of the gate." He sent a pointed look to Farranen.

"They're not," Farranen bit out. "The blame for his presence falls solely on me, and I will take care of it."

Ozzy, looking every bit the hot-tempered redhead, jumped to his feet. "How? How will you take care of it? Because from where I'm standing, all I see is a ticking timebomb waiting to go off. Even if she doesn't turn, she knows about the fae. How long do you think she has until the queen finds out?"

In one fluid motion Farranen was on his feet, with his sword in hand. "I will not allow you to take her." His words were deadly calm, like the undertow at a tropical beach.

The two men stared at each other like they were searching for weaknesses, and the levels of testosterone I was picking up were making me sick to my stomach.

"This is PIMP jurisdiction," Ozzy growled.

"You're a *pimp?*" What the hell? Had I been caught up in some fairy-tale sex-trafficking ring?

"I'm an agent of the Paranormal Intelligence Maintaining Peace Agency." Ozzy's haughty tone grated on my already frayed nerves.

"Enough!" I shouted. "You." I pointed at Ozzy and then at the door. "Get out."

"Theo, it's not safe for you to be here by yourself." I wasn't sure if he was referring to me possibly turning into a monster, or my potentially homicidal stalker husband, but it didn't really matter. There was no way in hell I was going anywhere with him.

"Sorry, but you lost all credibility when you tried to kidnap me."

"I was taking you into protective custody!"

"Get out!"

I expected him to argue some more, but he just shook his hand through his hair and walked to the front door. Before he let himself out, he looked back at

Farranen and told him, "If anything happens to her—"

"*Nothing* will happen to her."

Ozzy acknowledged the words with a nod before disappearing into the night.

Farranen crossed the living room and flipped all three deadbolts. "That's new," he commented casually, while he studied the sheet of plywood nailed above the front door.

"Don't try to change the subject." I put on my bossiest face and kicked his chair away from the table in a universal gesture of "sit the fuck down." "Explain. *Everything.*"

"As you wish—"

"*Princess Bride* fan?" I interjected.

"What?" Genuine confusion marred his forehead.

"*The Princess Bride*; you know, Westley and Buttercup? Never mind." I waved away my distracted thoughts. "Continue. Please."

"Of course. I am Farranen, guardian of the gate." I remembered him saying something along those lines yesterday. "I was born of the fae realm."

"You're a fae?" I couldn't help it; I snorted.

"Yes, of the Light Court." I must have offended him, judging by the tightness around his eyes.

"Sorry, I'm just...surprised is all. This is a lot to take in."

His eyes softened a bit, and I could tell he was weighing his words before he spoke. "I understand this is hard for you." He flexed his hands where they rested on the table, and I sensed he was thinking of reaching out to me. I sat back in my chair; if he touched me, I didn't know that I'd be able to stop myself from accepting the comfort.

"As a guardian, it is my duty to protect the gate; it is the door between my world and yours. Members of the Light Court, with the queen's permission, are allowed to cross the gate for several reasons. Those of the Dark Court are not. I am tasked with hunting those who cross over unlawfully. I was in the midst of hunting Lebolus when he found you."

In one swift motion, he slid out of his chair, dropping to one knee in front of me. "Theodora—"

"Theo," I corrected automatically.

"I cannot possibly tell you how sorry I am for the troubles that have befallen you due to my carelessness. Please accept my deepest apologies." An emotion that I couldn't name crossed his face, darkening his eyes from forest green to nearly black.

"Sure...No problem." It wasn't like he'd personally attacked me; I wasn't going to hold him responsible for someone else's actions.

"It is customary for the fae to complete an apology with an offering. As I have no monetary gifts to bestow upon you, I would like to offer you an oath of protection."

"Um...thanks?"

"Theodora Edwards, I pledge myself into your service, as your guardian and protector, from this moment forward until you choose to release me; on my word, you have my oath."

I squirmed in my chair, unsure how to respond to his formal words. Something tingled along my skin like static electricity with fingers, and I tried to brush it away.

When Farranen made no move to stand, I slid out of my chair and inched around him to the kitchen. I was tired, and a cup of peppermint tea sounded like a good idea.

The simple motions of filling the kettle and turning on the burner helped calm my jagged nerves. When I turned around, Farranen was standing directly behind me, and I let out a girly shriek. He caught my arm before I fell back against the hot stovetop. Damn, the man moved as silently as a cat.

"I would like to 'explain everything,' as you requested."

My arm tingled where he held it, and my brain produced an unexpected image of him closing the scant inch of distance separating us. I wondered if he'd taste as good as he smelled. Pine and something spicy...Maybe cinnamon.

"Yes, please," I told him, not really sure if I was asking for his explanation or something more physical.

"Allow me to share some of my realm's history." He led me back to the table like he was escorting me to a ballroom dance floor. "Let me start by saying that the fae are a very private people. There are serious repercussions for revealing ourselves to the human world."

"Is that why Lebolus got..." I made a slicing motion across my throat.

"Partially, yes. He was suffering from psychogenic atrophy, something that the older fae are prone to developing when they have trouble coping with immortality. His behavior had become more erratic in the last few decades, and his unsanctioned arrival confirmed that he was no longer in control of his actions."

"Oh." I wanted to feel sorry for him, but that would

be no different from giving sympathy to an Alzheimer's patient who had developed a bad case of the stabbies and taken up serial killing for a hobby.

"Light fac, like myself, lost the ability to turn a human many centuries ago. However, it is possible that a few of the older dark fae have retained the magic within themselves. The magic is unreliable, as well as forbidden to try.

"Try to understand: the fae numbers have been slowly declining while the human population has increased exponentially. Our world was once strong, a kingdom without rival. Then, over time, our ability to conceive young ended. Without the ability to procreate, some of the fae took to kidnapping humans and turning them. They were called changelings, and for a short time, this process was enough to increase our numbers to a sustainable level."

I nodded to let him know I was following along.

"The changelings were a great gift; not only were many of our kind able to find their true mates, but the changelings were accepting of our seed. Many were able to bear young, furthering our population." His gaze was locked on my face, and I caught a glimpse of the passion I heard in his voice. "Unfortunately, your world grew wise to our existence, due to many unexplained disappearances. Soon, fae who came through to this side failed to return. The humans hunted us rigorously, and the queen was forced to close the gates."

He sounded as if he was reading from a history textbook, without an ounce of animosity in his voice.

"Not long after that, our realm's magic started to fade. We were no longer able to impregnate the changelings. Our numbers dwindled, in part from psychogenic atrophy, as well as fighting amongst ourselves. There has not been a healthy babe born unto the fae in half a millennium. The last human that survived the turning was before that."

"I'm sorry." I don't know if it was the right thing to say; it wasn't nearly enough to address the magnitude of grief I could hear rolling off his tongue.

I was familiar with the pain his people were going through. Infertility was no joke. I'd had years to accept that I couldn't have children.

The endometriosis I had suffered from as a teen was bad in a can't-leave-my-room-for-five-days-a-month-because-I-have-to-change-my-pad-every-hour kind of way. Once I had hit my twenties, I became so anemic that I'd had to go for half a dozen blood transfusions in less than a year, so I'd had a hysterectomy.

The kettle interrupted the silence that had settled over us, and I was grateful to be pulled away from my dark thoughts. Allowing myself to dwell on hypothetical babies that would never be mine was only asking for more heartache.

I made two cups of peppermint tea. While they steeped, I cut a piece of shortcake and waved it toward him from the kitchen. "You want some?"

"A kind offer, but I will refrain."

"Your loss," I told him with a smile. That just meant more for me.

While I'd been busy in the kitchen, Farranen had retreated to the comfort of my couch. He'd removed his cloak and draped it across the back of the armchair. It looked like the one he'd wrapped me in after the dark fae's attack. I wondered if he had a closet full of them or access to a really good dry cleaner. Either way, the dark green fabric looked as soft as moss, without a hint of my blood staining it.

"So, why does Ozzy have such a hate on for the fae?"

He accepted the mug I handed him.

"I mean, he wanted to lock me up on the tiniest chance that I might turn into one. That seems pretty extreme."

"The likeliness if you turning is small, but should you become a changeling that was begot by one of the dark fae, you would take on some of the characteristics of the one who sired you."

"Wait, I'd become like Lebolus?"

"Yes, depending on how strong his magic was, you could inherit any number of his ankou traits."

"Oh my God, I would look like the Grim Reaper? Like, with claws and a black hole where my face should be?" On the plus side, a little added height wouldn't have been a bad thing. But as much as I'd wanted to drop a few pounds, I didn't think the living-below-the-poverty-line-in-a-third-world-country-during-a-famine look would work for me. How the hell would I write? Those triple-jointed claws weren't conductive to typing on a laptop, or even holding a pencil.

My head was pounding, and the cake I'd just eaten wasn't sitting well in my stomach.

"Theodora?" I looked up and realized Farranen had slid closer to me on the couch; from the concerned look on his face, he must have been trying to get my attention for a while.

I opened my mouth to apologize for spacing out—
Oh God—I was going to be sick.

I rushed for the bathroom, barely making it in time to lose the piece of cake I'd just eaten, followed by my meager supper. Ugh, I was never going to be able to look at strawberry shortcake the same way again. Even after my stomach was empty, I heaved until tears streamed down my face and my abs felt like I'd gone ten rounds against an angry woman who could swing a two-by-four with deadly accuracy.

I knelt on the chipped linoleum next to the toilet and tried to catch my breath. Beads of sweat dotted my face and ran down my back and between my breasts. I must have caught one hell of a stomach bug for it to come on so fast.

My body was too exhausted to protest when Farranen knelt beside me and pressed a cold washcloth into my trembling hand. Doubting my ability to form any coherent words, I just nodded my thanks. Later, when I was feeling human again, I would probably be horrified that he'd witnessed me puking my guts out, but for now, my emotions were as hollow as my stomach.

"Let's get you into the shower." His steady voice broke me out of my trance-like state; my brain had been caught in a loop of figuring out if I had the energy to drag myself to bed, or if I should sleep here.

A shower was probably a good idea; I could smell myself and there was something caught in my hair that I didn't want to look too closely at. I didn't protest when Farranen lifted my sweatshirt over my head, but when he reached for the hem of my shirt, I batted his hand away.

"Out." I wasn't helpless. And I definitely wasn't stripping down in front of a stranger. He'd already gotten an eyeful of me in my bathing suit when I'd been injured; I had no intentions of repaying his kindness by flashing him my cellulite a second time.

"As you wish. I'll be right outside the door."

After the monumental task of cleaning myself, I climbed over the lip of the old cast-iron tub and found my flannel pjs with smiling kittens waiting for me next to the sink. I probably should have been concerned that someone had snuck into the bathroom while I'd been showering, but I was too tired to care.

With limbs as heavy as cement blocks, I donned the clothes commando since there were no panties. At least I knew Farranen hadn't been rummaging through my underwear drawer. I'm pretty sure some of my unmentionables were old enough to be considered vintage.

Some toothpaste and mouthwash took care of the funky taste in my mouth, and I was officially ready for bed.

Chapter Seven

Since I'd gone from living like a hermit to entertaining gentlemen callers (and dogs) at all hours of the day, I shouldn't have been surprised when I found Farranen waiting for me outside the bathroom.

He stood with his hands clasped behind his back, like he was casually waiting for the bus. Or maybe a limo; I doubted many fae took public transport.

His shirt was light brown with a gold button or brooch at the neck, and it flowed over the contours of his body like liquid. His pants were darker and looked like leather. Tonight, his pale blond hair was gathered into a loose ponytail; the crappy lighting in my cabin made it look nearly white.

"Theodora, we should talk."

I was glad he didn't ask me how I was feeling. The answer was probably pretty apparent since I'd just ralphed all over myself. "Tired. Come back tomorrow." Or never. That would be better.

He followed me into my bedroom, and waited in the doorway until I'd crawled under the perfectly tucked sheets. I did love a tightly tucked bed. It always made me feel like a piece of meat plastic-wrapped to a Styrofoam tray, but in a really comforting way.

I rolled away from him onto my side, hoping he'd take the hint and leave.

No such luck.

He flicked off the light and sat on the edge of the bed. I didn't even jump when he put his hand on my forehead. Yay for me.

"You're feverish."

"Thanks, Mom." Apparently, the fae didn't get sarcasm.

He pushed my damp hair away from my face and rested his fingers over the pulse in my neck. It was nice having his cool fingers against my hot skin. *Maybe he could stick around for a little while longer,* I thought.

I must have nodded off. The tiny little sugarplum fairies dancing through my thoughts were suddenly washed away by a wave of heat. It tingled, like electricity was skipping from my head to my toes, touching everywhere in between. And I meant *everywhere.*

I opened my eyes, slightly surprised I was still in my own bed. Farranen looked down at me, his eyes a storm of dark green that I could see even in the near-darkness. His thumb gently stroked my neck while his fingers had slid deeper into my hair, not gripping or pulling, just resting, like they belonged there.

"What are you doing?" I whispered.

I wasn't sure I wanted to know the answer. Whatever he was doing felt good. *Too* good. I didn't want him to stop and that scared me. I didn't like giving someone else control over my happiness.

Little zings of sensation continued to radiate from where he touched me.

"Your magic calls to me." Part of his stony expression dropped, and I could see astonishment and maybe a little fear. "You've started the change."

"No." Apprehension crept into my awareness,

pushing aside some of the warm fuzzy feelings.

"The magic is in you." It would have sounded hokey if he hadn't been so sincere. I'd have to remember that line the next time I was writing.

"No, it's not." Great, Theo, argue with a fae who was probably an expert on magic. Real productive.

His smile was hesitant and, for some reason, helped to calm my rising panic. "The magic is there. It senses my magic and responds. Do you not feel it too?"

I nodded, not quite ready to give his theory verbal affirmation.

"The change has begun." The awe in his words matched the way he ran his fingers over my skin. Like I was something to cherish.

The thought left me feeling uneasy. I was nothing to cherish. I was just someone to use and eventually leave behind.

"But there's no guarantee it'll work. My body will probably just fight it off, right?" That's what I'd understood from our previous discussion.

"Yes." His smile disappeared, and most of the expression left his face. I let out a relived breath; it was easier to deal with his cold impassiveness than the thought that he might actually care. "You will either overcome the magic or your body will submit to the change. It's also possible…"

"What?"

His discomfort was palpable. "It's also possible…that your body will be unable to handle the change, and you will fade."

"Fade?" My instincts knew what he was tiptoeing around, but I needed to hear him say it.

"Die." All that honesty was like a big bucket of ice

water and doused any of the touchy-feely emotions I'd been enjoying. It took all of my remaining strength to pull away from him. My head felt like it was filled with lead, and I closed my eyes.

I'd have to say, growing claws was one of the better options here. Staying human sounded pretty damn good, too. That's where I'd throw my vote; except, I didn't get a vote.

"I'm going to sleep. Lock the door on your way out." I wanted to put some force behind the words, but I didn't have the energy. I'm not even sure if I managed to keep the words from slurring together.

"I will stay; your magic will find solace with mine and be less volatile." As if to prove a point, he ran his hand down my back, and a subtle buzzing followed in its wake. It was like taking a pot of boiling water off the burner: the heat was still there but the roiling bubbles had stopped. It was soothing but made me resentful. I didn't want to be soothed. I didn't need to be comforted. I'd been through worse by myself, and I didn't trust myself not to rely on him.

"G-Go," I tried to tell him.

After a moment, the sound of his footsteps echoed across my room and into the living room. An unwelcome pang of disappointment crept into my awareness as I pictured him leaving through the back door.

It was better this way. I shivered and burrowed a little farther under the covers. I should have gotten up and went to the bathroom for a headache pill but it was *so* far. Too far, as far as my body was concerned.

I was surprised when the bed dipped and Farranen settled his weight next to me. I didn't say anything as he shifted around, then pressed the full length of his body against mine. He was still on top of the covers, but he tucked my head under his chin and wrapped an arm under my breasts. It was deliciously warm in a way that stopped my shivers, without increasing my fever.

The electric sparks pulsed through my veins everywhere we touched.

"Thank you," I whispered, feeling like warm champagne was pumping through me instead of blood. The pain in my head faded to bearable levels, and I let myself relax next to another person in a way I'd never thought possible.

It must have been the kitten pajamas. Everybody feels safe when they're wearing kitten pajamas.

****

When I woke up, I was alone.

Well, actually, I had the mother of all headaches, but I didn't think that counted as sentient company.

I rolled over and stared at the ceiling while taking inventory of my body. I didn't foresee a mad dash to the bathroom again, so I took my time sitting up, like a mummy slowly rising from its sarcophagus in a bad sixties' horror movie. My tummy grumbled, reminding me that it was empty, but I didn't want to risk giving it any more ammunition in case I wasn't done being sick.

I toed on my pink fuzzy slippers and shuffled out into the living room. There was no sign of Farranen; his cloak was gone from the back of the couch, and the dishes had been cleared from the coffee table. As far as house guests went, he wasn't half bad. Definitely top three.

I wandered from the living room to the kitchen and then back again. My body still felt too hot, and it was making me restless. Deciding it would be cooler outside, I turned on the front porch light and let myself out the door.

It was a clear night, without a single cloud blocking the moon. I could see my breath every time I exhaled, and frost covered my truck windshield in a thin layer. It would snow in another month or so. I should probably clean out the eavestroughs while I still had the ladder on the back porch. Of course, if the change ended up killing me, it wouldn't matter if I'd finished all the fall maintenance to my cabin.

I was still feeling weak, so I rested my elbows on the railing as I stared out into the darkness.

My cabin wasn't technically part of the hamlet of Tamarac; the five properties on my street were nearly a mile from our closest neighbors. The street was aptly named Broken Road, since it dead-ended next to my property and was surrounded by a rugged boreal forest. Aside from a small smattering of lakes and farmland, there wasn't much this far north in Saskatchewan. This seclusion was exactly what had appealed to me. I was done with all the bullshit that came with living in a big city. Too many people, too much traffic, too much noise.

Right here, surrounded by peace and quiet, I could truly relax.

And maybe someday, I could finally let go of some of the baggage that Will's disappearance had caused. But not today. And I was okay with that.

My eyes wandered down my driveway, over the willow and pine trees that lined it, to the part of the street I could see from my porch. Next to the road, something moved in the shadows. I froze, trying not to call attention to myself. Maybe it was Dog, coming to finish the meal we'd started earlier. I stared at the same spot so long my eyes watered, and I had to remind myself to blink.

It must have been nothing.

Feeling stupid for jumping at shadows, I stretched my arms out and tried to relieve some of the aches in my joints. They were stiff, like I'd been immobile for too long. The cuts on my arms didn't burn anymore, but the tape on the bandages protested the movement.

I shivered, goose bumps breaking out under my flannel pjs. My nice toasty bed was sounding like a good idea. I could probably catch a few more hours of sleep before morning.

The snap of a dry twig breaking jerked my head up. The sound had come from the edge of the driveway, and I held my breath as I scanned the tree line for movement. Something snagged my attention, and I realized that one of the shadows I'd dismissed as a tree was actually a man. I probably wouldn't have even noticed him, except for his slight movement, as if he'd merely shifted his weight from one foot to the other.

My initial panic grew as I realized the man didn't have Ozzy's wide shoulders or Farranen's pale hair. I really wasn't up for another visitor. Why did this keep happening?

At this time of night, I doubted it was a delivery guy or someone selling security systems. Also, the way he just lurked there was super sketchy; he obviously didn't want to be noticed.

My brain threw out a mental image of Lebolus as he'd attacked me, and I shook like my porch was suddenly caught in the grip of an earthquake. For all the clear sky around me, I couldn't seem to find a single breath of air.

With thoughts of the empty shotgun in my bedroom, I stumbled backward toward the door, banging my hip on the jamb in the process. My hands were shaking, and it took me a few tries to get all the deadbolts slammed home.

"Theodora?"

I screamed loud enough to frighten any of the local wildlife in a three-mile radius.

"Farranen!" Good Lord, where had he come from? "Don't *do* that!"

"I apologize, it wasn't my intent to startle you." His expression was sincere, and it's a good thing, since I probably would have slapped him if I'd seen a smirk.

"How did you get in here? I woke up, and you were gone." My words came out too fast, just like the air I was trying not to hyperventilate on.

"There was a disturbance at the gate. I left the back door unlocked; I didn't anticipate being gone for so long."

I knew it! I knew I'd seen someone or something in the yard.

"You should be resting."

I didn't protest when he took my arm; I was already shaking like a leaf, and the only thing holding me up was the door at my back. A little jolt of pleasure shot up my arm when he touched me, and I tried not to melt into a gooey puddle of neediness.

"In the yard—outside—I saw him." The words fell out of my mouth as my brain struggled to keep up.

"What? Who's outside?" The gentle curve of his arm that had been supporting me suddenly propelled me toward the couch, and I landed on my ass without any sort of grace. Before I could warn him not to, he opened the door and stepped outside.

Colder air streamed in from the doorway, cooling the beads of sweat on my skin. My adrenaline from earlier hadn't faded yet, but Farranen's sudden exit sent another shot of it into my blood, making me dizzy. Or maybe it was just the sudden lack of his body next to mine.

I struggled to my feet for a few seconds, but I ended up back on my butt on the ugly burgundy couch. Stupid balance.

Before I could think of any number of horrible situations that Farranen could be rushing headlong into, he soundlessly walked back in and shut the door. He swung his sword back over his shoulder, magically poofing it back where it came from. I was just glad to see he hadn't been outside empty-handed.

"There's nobody out there." He almost sounded apologetic, like he was sorry he hadn't been able to bring me someone's head on a spike.

"I saw them. By the driveway." Like presenting a decent argument would make the mystery man reappear.

"They're gone now." He helped me to my feet, and I wished that I had taken the time to put on some pants and a sweater. Because, yeah, it must be the kittens and fuzzy slippers making me feel so weak.

"Was it another fae? Like…" I didn't want to say his name, so I settled for saying, "…like before?"

"No one came through the gate."

We reached my room, and I practically collapsed face-first on the bed in my haste to reunite with my pillow and sheets.

"But you said someone was at the gate."

"I said there was a disturbance. The dark prince arrived, unaware that his visitation had been revoked." He removed his cloak and draped it over the foot of my bed as he spoke.

"Oh." That sounded like an interesting story. I'd have to ask about the mysterious-sounding dark prince when I wasn't so tired.

The springs in my mattress creaked and dipped as Farranen settled himself next to me. I mumbled a protest, but he silenced me with a finger to my lips. When I opened my eyes, he looked as shocked as I felt.

"What are you doing?" I asked in a hushed voice, not wanting to ruin the perfectly good silence that had settled over us. He leaned back against the headboard, and I thought maybe he wasn't going to answer me.

"I've never attended a human in the midst of the change; I have no firsthand knowledge of the transition. I fear by relying on rumors and supposition, I have put you in a precarious position, and any misstep on my part will prove fatal for you."

This wasn't his fault. I wasn't his responsibility to deal with.

"I'm fine. It was really nice of you to come check up on me, but you don't have to stay. I can take care of myself." I mean, the guy had stuck around, even after I'd barfed up pink cake. Not many men could say they'd do that for little old me. So, yeah, I was going to cut him some slack and set him free.

"You misunderstand my intentions," he said. "My presence isn't just to monitor your progress. The magic in your blood is new and vulnerable, and it can be unpredictable while it grows and settles. Contact with fae magic is necessary; it will help sustain you through the change. I can provide that for you, if you will allow me the honor."

He held out his hand, palm up. It was the same strong hand that had held a sword to decapitate another fae only days ago. I should have been afraid, but I wasn't. After a brief hesitation, I slid my hand into his and was rewarded by that delicious tingle that slid though my body into places that hadn't tingled in years.

His voice was slightly hoarse as he continued, "I've been told that, when a human was chosen, only the strongest of the fae were granted permission to attend them, to increase the likeliness of success."

The pounding in my head increased like an icepick was stabbing its way out through my forehead. I made an involuntary pathetic whimpering sound, and Farranen slid his fingers into my hair, like he already knew where I was hurting. He didn't offer any empty words or tell me I was going to be okay, and I was glad because we both knew he couldn't make that kind of guarantee.

The headache was making me nauseous, and I wanted to ask how long I'd be stuck in this weird limbo of maybe changing into a fae or maybe dying. Actually, I had a lot of questions about the whole process in general, but my ability to form coherent sentences was dwindling by the second.

"Fae magic can be shared through physical contact." His voice was carefully neutral. When I didn't say anything, he scooted closer and slid his arm under my head. "May I give you more contact?"

That sounded like a really old school way of asking

"Wait—let me explain." He sounded flustered.

I took a deep breath and tried to calm down enough to think. The first thing that I noticed was his hair, still neatly tied up in the leather string. It certainly didn't look like the tousled mess from my dream. And with no small amount of relief, I found my kitten pajamas, in the exact same place I'd left them—on my body. The shirt was all hiked up where Farranen's hands continued to grip me like he was afraid I'd run away if he didn't hold on tight enough, but all the buttons were present and doing their job. Thank God.

"I feared my magic wouldn't be enough. Changelings sometimes required two or three fae to see them through, so I thought to increase our physical connection. My clothing was a barrier between our magic, so I removed it." Coming from any other guy, it would have been a lame excuse, but coming from Farranen, it sounded apologetic and sincere.

"And you just assumed I wouldn't notice that you're *naked*?" I need to stop saying it that way; I sounded like a prude.

"Theodora, I would never presume to partake of your body without consent." I can't say why, but I believed him. "But once again, I find myself asking for your forgiveness."

The paranoid, suspicious part of my brain sat up and took notice. "For what?"

I knew we hadn't had sex; after years of forced celibacy, I would still be feeling every aerobic minute if we had done anything last night.

"The dream walking."

"The what?"

His thumbs massaged little circles into my skin as

he talked. "Dream walking is essentially dream sharing. Some fae can open their thoughts to those in the dream realm and pull them into a shared existence for a brief time. It is…*intimate,* and therefore requires consent. It can be extremely satisfying, or it can have the completely opposite effect; it is up to the fae who guides the journey to ensure the pleasure is mutual."

"So, that's why I was dreaming about…" Yeah, I couldn't make myself say the words out loud.

"Yes, I created the image and the magic in your blood allowed you to be pulled in." The corners of his mouth tilted up in a smile, and I could hear the pride in his voice. "Your magic grows stronger. It continues to reach for mine, even in the dreamscape."

"That's…good." I told him, not sure if I actually meant it. Did I really want fae magic growing in my body, changing me?

His face turned serious once more. "The change rendered you unconscious, and I could not wake you. Reaching you through dream walking was my only choice. I am sorry for the intrusion; I needed to get your attention."

He had certainly gotten my attention. Still had it in fact. There was no way I was going to be able to close my eyes at night without seeing the sharp cut of his muscles thrusting or hearing his ragged breathing when he'd increased the tempo—

His irises flared brighter, and I had a moment of panic as I wondered if fae could read minds. That being said, I was pretty sure that my thoughts were written all over my face, so he wouldn't actually have to bother with what was going on in my head to know how aroused I was.

"I want you to come with me."

I blinked at his bold words. Replayed them in my head. Probably blinked some more.

Uhh...Yes, please. I was rusty but willing to try.

Maybe I should shower first; I hadn't shaved my legs since I'd gone out with Katie. *I should probably brush my teeth too,* I thought.

"I need to return to the gate. There was an unsanctioned crossing while you slept." He rolled away from me and sat up. "That is why I woke you. If I tarry much longer, my absence will be noticed."

My brain took its sweet time understanding that he hadn't been talking about hanky-panky.

"I would like for you to come with me." Geez, did he have to keep saying it like that?

He stood up, and my ego suddenly didn't feel quite so bruised; he hadn't been as unaffected by the erotic images we'd co-starred in as I'd thought. And the icing on the cake was seeing all that aroused maleness straining against a pair of black boxer briefs with "Mr. Boxer" running along the waistband. The odd contrast of such modern underwear combined with the old-fashioned pants that he was pulling up was shocking.

I knew I was staring, but I didn't care. I just hoped I wasn't drooling.

"I do not anticipate being gone long."

"Can I just stay here?" My head was throbbing again now that I couldn't feel his magic seeping into me.

He frowned as he pulled on his boots. "I do not think it wise to leave you unattended."

"I'll just get in the way. What if the other guy has a sword? I'll be an unnecessary distraction."

Images of Lebolus danced across my awareness, and I pulled the covers up to my chin. I definitely didn't want to go outside with another crazy fae wandering through the woods, looking for an easy target.

Farranen, now fully dressed, knelt next to my side of the bed. "You will be safe with me; I give you my oath that your protection is my first responsibility."

"That's sweet, but I think I'll just take a nap while you're gone."

He touched my cheek, and I sighed as I soaked up his magic like a sponge.

"I am sorry, but it is too dangerous to risk leaving you alone."

"I'm good. I've got a shotgun." I didn't mention that I didn't have any experience to go with it.

"I have no doubt that you are capable of defending yourself. It is your transition that worries me." I cracked my eyes open to see if he looked as worried as he sounded. "Theodora, I need you to listen. You're in the midst of the change, I can feel it. Without the magic of Fairie to sustain you, you will fade. Do you understand? Here, in the mortal realm, there *is no* magic."

I opened my eyes again, not remembering when I'd decided to close them. "But I can feel your magic."

"Yes." He smiled. "And I will gladly continue to offer my magic, but we need to be in close proximity."

"Oh." I was catching on. I was like a ball and chain that he couldn't put down.

"Please; we must go. The longer we dally, the longer it will take to hunt whoever has entered your realm."

"Okay," I relented. "Grab me a hoodie from the

closet."

****

Can I just say that never in my wildest dreams had I thought I'd find myself walking through the woods, holding hands with an incredibly attractive man. Fae. Whatever.

The contrast between Farranen and me was conspicuous. His strength to my weakness; his beauty to my blandness; his elegant cloak and shirt to my kitten pjs and bright pink "Kindness Day 2012" sweatshirt. At least I'd put on a decent pair of runners instead of fuzzy slippers.

Shorter days meant that the nights were getting cooler, and small patches of fog had rolled off the lake to settle in the low spots between the trees. After following the path from my backyard toward the lake for about a hundred yards, we turned off onto a smaller footpath that I had always assumed was from the local deer. The path wound to the east, with small rises and dips that were heavy with aboveground roots and years of deadfall. After passing the third rotting log that was lying parallel to the path, I realized it had been dragged off to the side to keep the path unobstructed. Interesting, since Tamarac County wasn't known to draw a hiking crowd, and most of the quadding trails were on the other side of the lake. Someone must have been using the path regularly.

There wasn't enough room to walk side by side, so I followed behind Farranen and tried to pretend I wasn't ogling the wide set of his shoulders. After about ten minutes, we reached a clearing that was twice as big as my backyard. The tall scraggly pine and birch trees formed a perfectly round circle, but I didn't see any signs that they'd been cleared by hand. I doubted Farranen would drag a lawnmower down the narrow path once a week.

Standing in the center of the open space was the biggest, most beautiful tree I'd ever seen. Its branches gracefully arched out, creating an elaborate canopy of rich orange and yellow leaves that glowed like a living halo in the moonlight. It was easily three or four stories high, with one massive trunk that branched off into dozens of smaller ones and many thick roots that twisted around the bottom before slanting downward into the dirt. It looked like something the Headless Horseman would call home.

What? Just because I write romance, doesn't mean I didn't enjoy old school fiction.

"The akura created the gates to connect our worlds, back when our magic and numbers were plentiful. They took hawthorn trees that already existed in Fairie and created pockets of magic that allowed the trees to appear in this realm as well."

I ran my fingers over the rough bark and felt the faint buzz of its magic reach out to me. It was like Farranen, warm and comforting, but without any of the sexual undertones. I wondered what other magical things were growing in the woods behind my house that I didn't know about. I could write an entire book with all the ideas my imagination was throwing out.

"Originally, there were forty gates. Now there are six." Weariness carved shallow lines around his eyes.

"There are five more gates?" I asked.

"Yes, all scattered across this part of your world."

"What happened to the other ones?"

"Some were destroyed by the need for more

developed land in this world, and some were destroyed by fae."

"Why would the fae destroy them? They created them."

"Not all of the fae want a doorway between our realms. Some fear persecution, some wish to restrict movement to acquire more power; there are any number of reasons really."

I took a seat on one of the tree's roots that was shaped like a small bench.

"The queen eliminated some of them personally. She deemed them too close to the growing populace here. It was an unnecessary temptation for our people, once the act of creating changelings was forbidden."

Somewhere in the distance, a squirrel chittered, and its familiar sound made me smile. Saskatoon hadn't had much of a wildlife population, but even in the winter you could catch glimpses of their furry bodies scampering along the power lines.

"So, how does the whole gate thing work?" There wasn't anything that looked like an actual door, so I had to assume there was some sort of hocus pocus involved.

"Allow me to show you." Before I could ask any more questions, he stepped over the tangle of roots and pressed his hand on the main trunk of the tree. Between that second and the next, he was gone.

"Hey!" I jumped to my feet, more than a little freaked out. He'd literally disappeared into thin air. "Farranen?"

Taking cautious steps, I approached the spot he'd been standing in. There was nothing there but the same rough bark running in vertical strips up and down the tree. I poked at it, and even stuck my hand into a few of the thick crevices that had formed where the branches grew.

Nothing.

My breathing ratcheted up another notch. I went for a walk around the tree, peering into every nook and hollow.

Still nothing.

How the hell had someone six feet tall disappeared so completely?

As I made it back around the tree to where I'd started, Farranen was standing exactly where I'd last seen him, casually leaning on the tree with his arms crossed over his chest. The slightest hint of a smile teased his lips, and I got the impression he was enjoying my momentary panic.

"Where were you?" I demanded.

"Fairie."

I eyed him suspiciously. Somehow, I'd been expecting something a little more dramatic. A little more *Star Trek*-ish.

He straightened up and walked across the clearing to where the forest stretched out. "Come. I must find the fae who came through the gate."

Chapter Nine

You know what would make tromping through the woods a little less depressing?

Cake.

I'd have to remember to bring a big slice of cake the next time I was out hunting mythical creatures in the middle of nowhere. Black forest cake would be perfect, but at this point I was so hungry, any cake would do.

And a big-ass travel mug of coffee to go with it. I was exhausted, and some caffeine would have gone a long way to keep my feet from dragging.

"How did you know someone came through the gate without permission?" I asked, just to keep my mind off my grumbling belly.

"I am alerted anytime the gate opens. I return home once a day for updates on impending arrivals."

"Yeah, but *how* do you find out? Do you get an email? A telegraph? Is there even cell service in Fairie?" I fired questions at him as fast as I could think of them.

"Human technology does not work there. All guardians undergo a ceremony in which the queen gives them the ability to communicate with their gate." He knelt and peered at the ground. "This way."

I have no idea how he knew which way to go just by looking at fallen leaves and bare, thorny branches, but I followed without questioning his methods.

"What does it feel like when the gate opens?" I ducked under a narrow branch and tried to walk quietly. I still made more noise than a herd of wildebeests with arthritis tramping through the leaves.

"I believe it's called a 'gut feeling.' " He pointed at his stomach. "It's an internal awareness. One of the many benefits bestowed upon a guardian."

"Yeah? What other cool tricks can you do?" I was falling behind, my breath panting in and out as if we were at a much higher elevation. Farranen stopped and waited for me to catch up before holding out his hand. I gladly took it, and the relief was immediate. I should probably have felt guilty about using him as my own personal battery.

"The increase to my personal magic was a gift beyond compare. It allows me to temporarily lock the gate, something only the queen has the power to do. I have free rein to cross whenever I deem necessary. Glamouring requires none of the usual effort or concentration that is necessary for its constant maintenance in this realm." He spoke without any of the pride I would have expected, like he was reading from a cookbook.

"My status was raised significantly as my magic grew." He glanced down to where our hands were linked. "I must confess, until now I had taken my magic for granted. The frivolous privileges I've been afforded mattered not. But this…" He lifted our hands. "*This* is something I had not thought possible."

"Me stealing your magic?"

"No. What is freely offered cannot be stolen. I was referencing the change. Never had I thought, after all this time, that there would be another changeling. And to not only witness it firsthand, but attend you personally; well, I must say I am extremely grateful for every bit of magic I now have."

I knew he was hoping that I'd turn fae. I even understood why, but I was getting tired of him talking like it was a done deal. I mean, there was still the possibility that I could kick it at any time.

"You're counting your chickens before they're hatched," I told him and laughed when he raised an eyebrow. "I just mean, it's not a sure thing that I'll turn into...you know, a fae. This might end up being a big fat waste of your time. And magic."

"Theodora." He pulled me to a halt and stared down at me with solemn eyes. "Even if you remain human, the experience has been well worth the cost."

Easy for him to say, since he hadn't puked his guts out in front of a stranger.

"Magic is like blood; the more you expend, the more your body will make to replace it. And time holds little meaning for someone who has already lived centuries."

Holy crap, how old was he? I would have guessed early to midthirties, but apparently, I'd been way off. I opened my mouth to make a lame joke about holding hands with someone older than my grandparents, but the sudden snapping of a branch stopped me.

Another *crack* followed, and Farranen moved toward the noise. He freed his sword as he steadily turned in a slow circle, the blade sliding into existence the same way he hunted his prey: silent and deadly.

"Show yourself!" He stopped spinning and stalked toward a thick grouping of birch. Something moved in the dark space between the trees, and remembering the last fae I'd stumbled upon in the woods, I took a few steps back.

Words that I couldn't understand carried across the forest, their cadence light and musical like a child's. Farranen tilted his head, listening as the voice flowed around us.

"No, I will escort you back to Fairie. Any punishment levied against you will be determined by the dark prince." He lowered his sword from an attack position, pointing it downward. The casual way it hung from his hand was probably to put his opponent at ease. I wasn't fooled. From the taut lines in his back, to the way he balanced on the balls of his feet, I knew he was ready to strike at the slightest sign of trouble.

More of the magical song that I assumed came from another fae filled the air. It was really quite pretty.

"I understand, but I merely uphold the laws; I did not make them." He listened to a short burst of words, then replied, "Come out now, or I shall use force."

Someone small stepped from behind a fallen pine, and I held my breath, anticipating the moment when they'd leap for Farranen's throat. As the figure got closer, I realized it was a woman. Maybe just a girl. She was small, her arms and legs like knobby sticks as they poked out of clothing that looked like a crudely made nightshirt from the *Little House on the Prairie* era.

Her skin was light brown and rough, like the bark on a young poplar tree, complete with the occasional knot. Her nearly human face was pretty with a slight nose and big brown eyes. Her tangled hair was pulled back into a ponytail, its color and texture the same as straw. Her hands and feet were bare, and too big for her body. Each digit had an extra joint.

"Carameena of the Dark Court, surrender unto me, and I shall provide you safe passage back to Fairie." Farranen relaxed his battle stance and pulled a set of handcuffs from beneath the folds of his cloak.

The little fae, no more than five feet tall, asked something in a worried, tinkling voice.

"You have my word, as guardian of the gate."

Stepping cautiously toward Farranen, Carameena stopped when she caught sight of me. Her eyes grew even bigger in her face, and she shouted something shrill.

"You are correct; she is human. But you have nothing to fear."

She pointed an accusing finger in my direction, and her inflection indicated that whatever she said wasn't kind.

"What is she saying?" I bared my teeth and tried to look intimating. Judging by the look on her face, it was working. Probably because I had at least seventy pounds on her. And, you know, the kitten pjs were badass, too.

"She accuses me of fraternizing with humans. My voice is glamoured to sound human in this realm, but she still hears me speaking in our native tongue."

Farranen put his sword away and slowly approached the girl, all the while offering her small platitudes, telling her that it was okay, that he would protect her.

I can't say that I was impressed with the nonexistent daggers she tried to glare in my direction. If she hadn't looked so afraid of me, I probably would have wanted to punch her in the face. The handcuffs

Farranen used to secure her tiny wrists shrank as soon as they clicked shut. It looked like chunky costume jewelry, not something strong enough to hold a rampaging fae.

"Are you sure that will hold her?" I asked, even though I doubted she was too dangerous. Her spindly legs probably meant she'd be able to haul ass given the proper motivation. She didn't strike me as a fighter, especially after seeing her undramatic surrender.

"Positive. They're iron." He backed her up to a fallen log, then told her, "Sit."

She sank down without protest, her eyes remaining hard, while the rest of her body slumped in defeat. The nightgown pooled around her small body, hiding her too-big feet.

I moved closer, but he held up his hand to hold me off. That's when I caught the flash of a small blade, probably the same dagger I'd seen him use at my cabin on the zip ties. He kept it close to his side, concealed in the folds of his cloak, and I realized he still had his attention on the woods surrounding us, like he was scanning for threats.

If this were an old-school Wild West novel, I'd have whipped out a sawed-off shotgun and put my back to Farranen's, like a badass sidekick was supposed to. Unfortunately, this was real life, and due to my new acquaintance with all the things that went bump in the night (and day), I was pretty much useless. And where the hell was I supposed to stuff a shotgun? Down the leg of my flannel pjs?

If, by some miracle, I managed to survive the change, I was going to invest a good percentage of what I had in the bank at Tamarac's local gym. Maybe I could find someone in town who taught martial arts. Constantly relying on someone else while I was in life-threatening situations just did not sit right with me.

And who knows? Maybe I'd finally get down to a size 8. Then I'd definitely go the Black Widow route, with a sexy, skin-tight catsuit. Oooh! I could get Katie to design it for me.

The attack came from the same direction we'd found Carameena in. A man, tall and thin with coloring like Carameena, jumped from one of the lower branches in a large birch tree. With his arms and legs splayed, he looked like a giant, hairless flying squirrel as he aimed to land on Farranen's back.

"*Look out!*" I screamed.

Farranen turned just as the other fae crashed into him, taking the majority of the impact on his shoulder. They rolled across the dirt, their arms and legs tangled while Farranen's green cloak billowed out around them and blocked my view. Moonlight reflected off the blade of Farranen's dagger as he tried to angle it toward the other fae.

The newcomer to our little party had features similar enough to Carameena, that I assumed they were related. His worn pants and shirt made him look like a bundle of twigs wrapped in an old sack. He might not have been strong, but he was nimble and, so far, had managed to evade Farranen's blade.

The confined spaces of the forest didn't offer a lot of room for Farranen to maneuver. He reached for his sword a few times, but the smaller fae was still clinging to him like a spider monkey on crack. When their scuffle through the leaves changed direction, I backed up out of the way.

The heel of my sneaker caught on something, and I fell backward with my arms windmilling until I landed flat on my back, with the wind knocked out of my chest. Which was actually a good thing, since I probably would have shrieked otherwise, potentially distracting Farranen. It took a few seconds for my lungs to figure out how to breathe again, and even longer for the world to stop spinning while I reoxygenated myself.

Just as I lifted my head to see if the fight was over, Carameena landed on my chest. My newfound supply of O2 dried up, and I struggled to push her off. I expected her arms to be hard and scratchy like tree bark, but they were actually petal-soft.

She grated out words I couldn't understand, and then used the delicate chains on her handcuffs to choke me. My vision swam in and out of focus, and little spots flickered in my peripheral vision.

Oh, hell, no! I was not going out like this. I'd survived Lebolus' attack; I was not going to let this bitch take me down. She was half his weight and had none of the deadly claws to maul me with. The only thing she had going for her was the chain she was strangling me with.

It took all of two seconds to wrap my hands around her skinny waist and roll her under me.

Ha! I don't think I'd ever truly appreciated my plus-sized body until now. I was going to make an entire tray of brownies when I got home and not feel a lick of guilt while I ate them.

Stick Girl flailed under me, fighting like a chicken about to have her head cut off. I considered lying down on top of her face and suffocating her with my boobs, but that sounded messed up, even to me. Her teeth looked sharper than mine, so, yeah, even with a thick sweatshirt on, I wasn't letting her near my cleavage.

After a few inventive curse words and some moves that would have made a high school wrestling coach proud, I pinned Carameena's arms to the ground above her head.

A masculine grunt of pain made me look over to where Farranen had been grappling with the other fae.

He'd removed his cloak when I hadn't been looking, and it lay discarded among the fallen leaves. Dirt and twigs clung to his clothing and hair, and blood stained the collar of his shirt. As I watched, he used the back of his hand to wipe his face as more blood ran from his nose. The two fae continued to circle each other, their boots crunching through the leaves as they both waited for an opening to gain the upper hand.

My stomach clenched at the thought of Farranen being hurt. I had to remind myself that he'd cut the head off another fae without breaking a sweat. Stick Guy didn't stand a chance.

I was so caught up in watching the guys, that I forgot about Carameena. She'd been lying like a dead log trapped beneath my weight, and once she realized my attention had been diverted, she arched her back while twisting her arms with a strength backed by adrenaline-fueled desperation. She nearly managed to flip me off, but I had size and gravity on my side. She wriggled one arm free and drove her pointy elbow into my forearm like it was a pickax and she was mining for precious metals.

Son of a bitch!

I don't know if she had some fae superpowers and could smell my healing wounds, or maybe it was just dumb luck, but she nailed the deepest laceration on my arm like it had a target painted on it.

That bitch!

I screamed, the harsh ragged sound staining the crisp night air. My fingers went numb, and I lost my grip on the writhing mass of limbs under me. Suddenly unbalanced, I toppled forward, landing on my face in the muck. I spit dirt and blood out of my mouth along with a few curses. I was going to hack that skinny bitch into firewood. Hopefully Farranen would let me use his sword.

Leaning on a fallen tree for support, I kept my reinjured arm clutched against my chest. I couldn't see any new blood soaking into the sleeve of my hoodie, but it stung like a fresh wound under the bandages.

"Theodo—" My head jerked up as Farranen gasped.

When the stick fae had dismissed me as a threat, they had turned their efforts to where Farranen stood with his back to a tree. They hovered just out of reach of the sword he held with a steady hand while he held his thigh with the other—

Oh, no, no, nonono—

The hilt of a dagger protruded from his left thigh. The blood drained from my face and then rushed back in a hot wave as anger darkened my vision. How *dare* they. I wasn't just going to chop them into kindling, I was going to turn them into fucking toothpicks.

"*No!*" I yelled, not quite sure what I was saying no to. I scooped up a rock the size of my fist and hurled it left-handed at the male. It missed its target by five miles but got the attention of the female. She hissed and moved toward me.

"Theodora, run!" Farranen took a step toward me, falling back against the tree when his injured leg gave out.

Screw that. I wasn't leaving him to this pack of jackals.

I picked up another rock; this time aiming for Carameena. Again, it fell short of its intended target, but it stopped the female's advance.

"Please!"

I looked over her shoulder and met Farranen's stark gaze. His eyes pleaded with me to listen, and I realized I was distracting him. My mere presence was putting him in danger; I was probably the reason he had a knife lodged in his leg.

Damn it. I didn't want to leave him behind while I ran for safety. Logically, I knew I couldn't do anything for him, but every cell in my body was screaming that it was wrong, so fucking *wrong*, to abandon him.

"*Run.*" This time it was an order, and I obeyed.

I ran.

Chapter Ten

Big girls are not built for jogging.

There's just too much jiggling and bouncing for it to be comfortable. Without a workout bra? Forget about it.

Since I had no idea how to maintain the steady pace needed for long distances, I flat out sprinted through the trees. My shoulders rebounded off errant tree trunks, while straggly branches reached out and yanked at the hair that had fallen out of my braid. My lungs sucked in air like an industrial-grade vacuum as I blindly ran toward what I hoped was my cabin.

I shot frequent glances over my shoulder, hoping to see Farranen but fearing I'd find another psycho fae, freshly escaped from Fairie and hunting me. Leaving him behind made me feel like the lowest form of pond scum, the kind even leeches wouldn't go near.

Hugging my throbbing arm tight to my chest, I tried to ignore the stitch in my side while I scanned the trees for familiar landmarks. There were a lot of generic trees, but nothing that let me know I was headed in the right direction.

The moon was obscured by clouds, so I couldn't even orient myself by its position.

Something to my left moved, and I came to a stumbling halt. I knew it was too small to be a person, so I held perfectly still and watched as a skunk waddled out from behind a tree. A shiver went down my spine as it stared at me with beady little black eyes. I was no expert, but I didn't think it was normal for a wild animal to make such intense eye contact. Not wanting to piss it off and get myself sprayed, I held perfectly still until it disappeared around a large pine tree.

That was close. The whole encounter had left me more than a little spooked. And not because I wasn't wanting to take a tomato bath. Something about the skunk seemed off. This deep in the woods, I shouldn't have been able to see him as well as I had; he'd practically glowed. He'd been bright enough for me to clearly make out the double stripe pattern down his back and between his eyes. I'd even been able to see his missing right ear—which reminded me of the dead skunk I'd dragged out of the crawl space beneath my cabin.

But the skunk I'd buried was dead, and couldn't possibly be wandering around the woods...Could it?

With a frustrated growl, I took off running again. There would be time to contemplate the mysterious skunk later, once I knew Farranen was safe.

A small sob tried to break free from my chest, but I clenched my jaw shut and blinked back unshed tears. I would not cry. I was not helpless. I would...I would go back to the cabin and get my shotgun.

Yes, that would work.

It was a plan, and having a plan was better than not having a plan.

Someone stepped out in front of me, and I didn't have time to stop before I careened face first into him. My poor nose bounced off a hard chest, catching the slightest aroma of roadkill slathered in cheap cologne on a hot day, before I braced myself against a tree. I looked up, ready to tell him to watch where he was going, but the words died on my lips when I saw his face.

The short narrow nose, framed by dark brown eyes and narrow cheekbones, was exactly as I remembered it. Every hair was neatly trimmed in a stylish cut, the dark mahogany soldiers all gelled in place as if their lives depended on it. Even the smirk on his lips was familiar.

"Will?" His name left me in a whisper, as if I didn't have enough breath in my body for the simple syllable.

"Hello, Theo."

****

Sucker punched. Dumbstruck. Bushwhacked. Blindsided.

They all apply to the moment you come face-to-face with someone you never thought you'd see again. It was like getting hit in the chest with an emotional two-by-four.

The moment was surreal. All the things I'd regretted not saying, all the things I'd wished I could do over flitted through my mind and disappeared just as quickly.

My heart knew this man. Remembered every single anniversary that we'd celebrated, and even the ones we forgot. Every Valentine's Day when he'd bought me a new sweater or earrings. But not flowers, he never bought me flowers. I'd even asked him about it once, and he'd said, "Someday, Theo, someday I'll bring flowers, and it will really mean something."

Oh, my God. The rose.

I had dismissed the rose someone left on my front porch as a mistake and promptly forgotten all about it. Now I wondered.

"The rose?" I asked hesitantly.

"Yes. I knew you'd see it for what it was."

His proud smile faltered and then dissolved into annoyance when he realized I didn't know what I was supposed to see the rose as. It had looked like a plain old red rose to me. If it was a message meant to let me know he was still alive, he would have been better off leaving a card that said something like "Hey honey, I'm not dead—surprise!"

"You are my sunshine?" he coaxed.

His eyes were so full of expectation that I said the first thing that came to mind. "The song?"

"Yes!" He looked relieved, like he was worried I would be too stupid to figure it out. And I guess I was, since I still didn't get it.

"You were humming it when I left for work that day. The last day…"

"The last day I saw you?"

"Yeah." He looked uncomfortable already, so I didn't tell him that I couldn't remember what song was stuck in my head that day. I'd been writing, so the radio had just been background noise.

The urge to throw my arms around him and hold on forever was strong. It took all my willpower to stay where I was.

I wanted to say that I was looking at a stranger, that this couldn't be the man I'd fallen in love with in high school, that time had changed him into someone I didn't know anymore.

But it wouldn't have been true.

I didn't run to him, because it was *me* that had changed. I wasn't the same woman I'd been six years ago. That woman, that naïve, idealistic woman, was gone. All the hurt and confusion from his disappearance, all the guilt from my failure to find him, had hardened that woman into who I was now.

I had a million questions, but I asked the only one that really mattered. "Where were you?"

He sighed, and the expression on his face was remorseful. Not the blank-eyed look of someone haunted by trauma, just the mild contrition I'd always seen when he'd been caught in a lie and was forced to admit the truth.

All the nights I'd spent worrying, thinking about so many horrible situations that could have possibly befallen him, suddenly seemed like a giant waste of time. Wouldn't there have been some sign, some physical indications if he'd been kidnapped or recruited into a terrorist organization or abducted by aliens? I would have been able to tell, right?

"I had to go away for a while. But I'm back now, Theo." He quirked a smile that I had once found charming. Now it just made him look evasive.

"You just left." My voice cracked, and something inside me broke right along with it. "You didn't even say goodbye."

"I'm truly sorry I had to leave like that. It wasn't supposed to happen that way." He tucked his hands into the pockets of his slacks and pursed his lips. He must have realized I wasn't going to throw myself at him. Evidently, this wasn't the welcoming reception he'd been expecting. Poor Will.

He scanned the surrounding forest with

apprehensive eyes, and I wondered if he was avoiding my gaze. He'd always been a good liar, as long as he didn't have to make eye contact. "We should go; it's not safe out here."

My injured arms, the stich in my side, and the stinging cut on my lip from falling, all came rushing to the forefront of my awareness. Damn it—I needed an ice pack and a drink.

But that's not what got my feet moving. There were still two angry fae on my tail, and Farranen was hurt, or worse. Knowing he was in danger lit a fire under my ass like nothing else could. I brushed past Will, stumbling as fast as I could in the direction of my cabin.

"Where are you going?" Will fell into step behind me without any of the huffing and puffing I was doing. Good to know he'd made time for improving his endurance while he'd been gone. It had always been about his priorities.

"Home."

"Wait—what's the hurry?" He tried to snag the sleeve of my hoodie, but I shrugged out of his grip.

"My—" I was going to say friend, but that didn't even begin to describe Farranen. My fae? That would be hard to explain, even if I'd felt inclined to. Which I didn't. My crush? Yeah, that's not something you can tell your husband, even if it were true. I settled for "My first-aid kit is there. And the shotgun."

If he was surprised that I was talking about retrieving a firearm, he didn't give any indication.

"Okay…How can I help?"

The offer caught me off guard, and I looked back to see if he was joking. His eyes were confused but sincere, and they made my heart hurt. I didn't want to fall right back into thinking that he would be there for me if I needed him.

"Just stay with me?" I asked, doing my best to keep my emotions in check.

"You got it."

And before you go getting the wrong idea, you should know that I didn't ask him to stick around for emotional support. No, it was much more self-serving than that. I wanted him with me in case those stick fae came after me; there was strength in numbers, and I wasn't stupid enough to think I was any match for the fae by myself.

The lump of shame grew in my chest, but it wasn't enough to make me leave Will behind. Sometime soon, when I was done running for my life, I was going to have to make time for some serious self-improvement. I didn't like this cold, selfish person I'd become. Throwing someone else into a dangerous situation, just to save my own bacon, wasn't who I wanted to be.

We navigated around the thick underbrush until Will stopped and grabbed my hand. "This way."

I looked in the direction he was pointing. "How do you know where I live?"

"Broken Road? Cabin number five, right?" He made a cocky gesture, and I frowned. "It wasn't that hard to track you down, Theo."

Whatever. The hows and whys didn't matter right now, not when Farranen needed me to hustle my butt. I headed in the direction Will had taken.

I was getting lightheaded, and I had to focus on putting one foot in front of the other. When was the last time I'd eaten? I doubted Will had any snacks stashed in the formal overcoat he wore. But even if a juicy stuffed turkey had stuck its head out of his back pocket and waved to me, I would have been too mortified to ask. Will had always frowned upon my hearty appetite, so I'd gone out of my way to avoid eating in his presence. Old habits die hard.

"Almost there," he told me.

I looked around at the never-ending landscape of trees and brush, wondering how he could tell we were getting close. I'd lived here for over a year, and I still had no idea where we were.

Abruptly, the forest was interrupted by a gravel road, and I sighed in relief at the first real sign of civilization I'd seen since leaving home. A large dark blue, or possibly black, sedan was parked about twenty yards away on the shoulder of the road. It sat in a puddle of moonlight, like it had a giant spotlight shining down on it. A shiver ran down my spine; that was a weird place for someone to park a car.

"This doesn't look right." I didn't realize I'd stopped walking until something shoved me between my shoulder blades, and I stumbled out into the middle of the road.

"Hey—" I tried to protest, but my words were cut off abruptly as an arm wrapped around my throat from behind. Will's too-strong cologne invaded my nose, making me dizzy as he pulled me against his chest, so that I was effectively trapped in a giant bear hug.

"You cheating *whore!*" He spat the words next to my ear. "I can smell him on you."

My head throbbed as if it had its own heartbeat. Some of my anger was for the man strangling me, but most of it was directed at myself. I was pissed that I'd let someone put me in this helpless situation again. First Ozzy, now Will. I never should have turned my back to him.

I clawed at the sleeve of his coat, but he didn't seem to notice.

"Move it." He dragged me toward the car.

I kicked my feet, but the loose gravel offered no traction under my runners. "Will—"

He tightened his grip around my neck, cutting off my plea. "Shut. Up." Frustration colored his words, giving me a perverse sense of satisfaction. I had no intention of making this easy for him.

He pointed a key fob at the car, and the trunk popped open with the taillights flashing. Good things did *not* happen to women who were transported in the trunk of a car. I jammed my elbow across Will's forearm, causing him to lose his grip on the keys. They jingled merrily as they fell and disappeared into the gravel, leaving only the sound of his harsh breathing and the scuffle of my shoes.

"*Fuck!* Theo! I'm doing this for *us!*"

Somehow, I doubted that.

I was getting really fucking tired of men thinking they knew what was in my best interest.

"All you had to do was wait!" He grunted as my head banged against his chin. "Fuck this."

Part of me wanted to shrink away from his rage, knowing that once his anger reached a certain level, he wouldn't be able to restrain it anymore. He was like a grenade, and my perceived disobedience had pulled his metaphorical pin. In the past, I'd always chosen to duck and cover while the dishes and drywall took the brunt of his tantrums.

I was tired, *so* fucking tired of having no control over anything. Instead of cowering and waiting for the explosion, I decided to take the damn grenade and shove it down his throat. Maybe I'd get caught in the fallout. I didn't really care.

I doubled my efforts to get free, and my struggles were rewarded with a furious string of curses that would have made a sailor blush. My vindication was short-lived.

The arm that had been crushing my airway disappeared, and I greedily gulped air down my burning throat. This was the second time in less than an hour that someone had tried to choke me. If I survived, I might look into deep sea diving since my lungs were getting used to going long periods of time without oxygen.

Will spun me around, his fingers digging into my shoulders as he pulled me closer, until we were nose to nose. His smile was grim, and if I were not so scared, I would have tried to slap it right off his face.

"I wanted to do this right, but you've given me no choice."

Before I could ask what the hell he was talking about, he opened his mouth and the dim rays of moonlight flashed across two long pointy fangs.

Will struck, sinking them into my bruised neck, and I opened my mouth to scream.

Chapter Eleven

My consciousness returned in lazy waves.

The throbbing of my joints, the sharp pounding in my skull, and the dull ache across my arms were all present and accounted for, but sometime during my involuntary nap, they'd faded to background noise. I took a deep breath, and the pain in my abused neck flared up like I'd poured acid on it.

"Damn—" My voice was the same kind of raspy that was associated with the phrase "three packs a day."

Cracking my eyelids open, I was grateful that the room was dimly lit. And even more grateful to see that I wasn't in the trunk of a car or an unmarked grave.

The room was large for a bedroom, with only two twin-sized mattresses pushed up against opposite walls, and an empty walk-in closet without a door. The carpet was thick and had probably been ivory colored and expensive when it was new. Its pattern and texture were made for hiding high traffic wear and tear, but time and a lack of cleaning had left it a few shades darker than the tan paint on the walls.

Where two windows should have been, giant pieces of plywood had been screwed to the wall. They completely blocked any outside light, so I had no idea what time of day it was, or how long I'd been knocked out.

The only other color in the room was the dark

brown of the stains that had pooled on the mattresses and floor. My stomach roiled when I realized the same-colored stains were splattered across the walls and ceiling. It didn't take a genius to realize they were blood.

Memories of seeing Will and the subsequent attack came rushing back to my frontal lobe, and I sat up. I needed to get the hell out of here. Wherever here was.

I wobbled to my feet unsteadily. My nose was grateful to put some distance between it and the moldy bed I'd been lying on.

Did Will really have fangs? Maybe I'd dreamt that part. Or I'd hit my head and imagined it.

My fingers sought out the tender spot on the left side of my neck. The skin was raw, and I could feel two jagged tears that itched as I probed them. Blood had dried on the chest of my sweatshirt, staining the bright pink fabric an ugly burgundy. I had definite confirmation that Will's new dental upgrade wasn't a product of my imagination.

Had he been attacked by a fae like I had? If Will was a changeling, Farranen was going to shit a brick. I hoped that I'd stay alive long enough to see the expression on his face when he found out.

The sudden reminder that Farranen was wounded, or possibly dying, kicked my butt into gear, and I shuffled toward the bedroom door.

"It's locked."

I froze halfway across the room, as the pile of rags on the other mattress sat up. Now that I was closer, I could see that it was actually a woman lying under a grungy blanket. She looked like a cancer patient with an addiction to heroin. Her skin was so pale it was nearly translucent, and the hollows in her cheeks were so prominent, I could have used them as teacups. Plain brown hair hung listlessly around her shoulders in tangles. Fear and hopelessness had dulled her eyes to lifeless brown pools of mud.

There were about a dozen sets of puncture marks around her neck; some had scabbed over, but some were still fresh and had trails of blood dried around them.

Living as a hermit had dried up my previously extensive vocabulary of greetings, and I had no idea what to say to the poor woman with the bite marks that matched mine. The fact that my husband was probably responsible for her suffering was a huge elephant in the room that I didn't want to acknowledge.

After a minute or seven, I was the one to break the silence.

"I'm Theo."

She looked at me as though she didn't understand English. Or maybe I'd grown a second head. Who knows? With the week I'd been having, anything was possible.

When she didn't answer me, I returned to the task of checking the door. And, yeah, she'd been right. It was locked.

A quick sweep of the closet turned up a handful of dust bunnies, so I moved on to the plywood blocking the windows. They each had a few dozen thick screws holding them in place, and had been drilled in nice and tight. Prying at the edges of the wood earned me a few broken fingernails, but it failed to improve my chances of escape.

"There's no way out." The woman's eyes followed

me as I ran my fingers over the baseboards. I wondered how long she'd been here to sound so resigned.

"There's got to be a way." Optimism wasn't really my thing, but I tried to sound cheerful. Maybe I could pry one of the baseboards loose and use it as a weapon when Will came back.

"He only opens the door when it's time to feed."

"Okay, well, the next time he brings food we can make a run for it. I'll go for his knees—"

"He doesn't bring food. We *are* food." She gestured at her neck.

My mouth fell open, and I had one of those holy-shit-is-she-joking-because-I-don't-think-she's-fucking-around-but-I'm-going-to-sound-like-an-idiot-if-I-go-along-with-it moments, where I was hesitant to give actual words to what my brain had come up with.

"Vampires." Thank God, she beat me to it. The slightest hint of a smile ghosted over her lips, and then it was gone just as quick as it had come.

My jaw would have hit the floor, but my mouth was already hanging open. It's a good thing there weren't any flies in here, because I probably would have inhaled one by now.

"Vampires?" I dredged up every ounce of cynicism that I had, thrusting it into the word like a weapon.

She pointed at her injured neck, with the universal expression for *Duh* on her face.

I had a brief moment of wanting to argue with her, but that would be a pointless waste of time. After my violent introduction into the supernatural world, it would be stupid to deny that anything but humans and fae existed.

"Vampires, huh." I slumped down onto the carpet,

since it looked cleaner than the mattress. "Wait—*vampires?* Like, plural? More than one?"

"Yeah—just the one guy comes in here, but I can hear them out there arguing sometimes."

Damn. How were we going to get past multiple vampires? My whole plan involved catching Will by surprise and then running as fast as I could. You'd think a book nerd like me could come up with something a little more sophisticated. Something that Robert Ludlum would concoct for Jason Bourne to execute, involving nothing more than a shoelace, a hairpin, and a stroke of luck.

I checked the pockets of my hoodie, but I came up empty-handed.

"Do you have anything we can use as a weapon?" I asked.

She shook her head, making her limp hair brush across the bloodstains on her skin.

"What's your name?"

"Vanessa."

"Well, Vanessa, I think our best chance is to make a run for it." I eyed the exhausted way she slouched against the wall. "Can you walk?"

She shook her head again and tugged the blanket down to show me a pair of handcuffs around her wrists. A separate chain linked them to another pair around her ankles.

Fuck.

"Maybe I can carry you."

A sad laugh escaped her lips. "It's too late for me."

"It's never too late," I told her, determined to throw her over my shoulder as if she were a sack of potatoes if I had to.

"He'll be back soon. If you're going to go, do it now."

"I can't just leave you here." I studied her; something familiar about the woman itched at the back of my brain. "How long have you been here?"

She shrugged. "A couple days, maybe more."

"What happened?"

Another shrug. "I was leaving work, and someone grabbed me from behind. I woke up in the trunk of his car, and he dragged me in here."

"Could you tell where we are?"

"It was dark out; I couldn't see much. We're upstairs. The staircase is to the left and leads straight to the front door."

The conversation lapsed into silence, both of us lost in our own thoughts. I was missing something important here. Oddly enough, it was the blood-stained hot-pink bra strap hanging off her bony shoulder that ended up jogging my memory.

"Hey! You're the waitress!" I hadn't recognized her without all the makeup, but that expensive-looking push-up special had been right at my eye level the night I'd been too drunk to drive myself home.

Damn it! That meant Ozzy had been right about Will. Not that I'd had any doubts about his innocence since he'd used my neck for a chew toy. Still, I had been trying to keep an open mind about the whole thing. I mean, this could have been an isolated incident. I'm not saying it was something I could forgive, but I had been holding onto a tiny shred of hope that I didn't have to add "serial killer" next to "ex-husband." And, yeah, I had already mentally slapped a big fat X in front of Will's name.

That bastard! I wondered if I should apologize to Vanessa for his ghastly behavior, even though I wasn't responsible, or even aware of it until now.

I wanted to crawl under the filthy blanket with her and wallow in misery while I examined every single memory I had of the asshat I'd been married to. I wanted to go over them with a fine-tooth comb, and pick them apart until I could pinpoint the exact moment things had gone wrong. See if, maybe, I could have prevented this from happening.

I shut off that line of thinking before the betrayal choked me. I'd have time for the pity-party later. Complete with ice cream and cake. Lots and lots of cake. But right now, I had to get Vanessa out of here before Will came back.

After a short discussion weighing the pros and cons of me piggy-backing Vanessa out of here, I lost the argument. My conscience didn't like the idea of leaving her behind, but I would get help and come back for her as fast as I could. It would be stupid to think I could get her down the staircase and out the door unseen.

"I'll be back," I told Vanessa, attempting to sound confident, like the heroine in one of my novels.

"Just go." She waved me toward the door, like I could sweet-talk the lock open with my sparkling smile and winning personality.

It was a fairly modern door, and when I rapped on it with my knuckles, it sounded hollow. *Now or never*, I thought.

Raising my foot, I kicked the door as hard as I could, putting every bit of my weight into the move instead of relying on my pathetically small supply of leg muscles. The impact jarred all the way up to my hip, and I rebounded back, landing on my butt.

Why the hell wasn't I wearing steel-toed boots yet? Even hiking boots would have been better than sneakers.

The pain from my potentially broken toes was forgotten when I saw the hole in the door. The first layer of glorified cardboard was smashed in, and there was nothing past the hollow center, except for another paper-thin layer on the other side.

I hauled myself to my feet, grateful that whoever had built the house had cheaped-out and gone with particle-board doors instead of a traditional slab of solid walnut.

Using my hands to tear chunks of the thin particle board off, I made a hole big enough to fit through. Glancing over my shoulder at Vanessa, I tried to contort my lips into a reassuring smile. It was probably more creepy than encouraging.

"I'll be back with help as soon as I can."

She tipped her head in acknowledgement, the forlorn movement louder than any words would have been. I hoped the sight of her huddled motionless beneath the blanket, as her wide hazel eyes tracked my movements, wouldn't be my last memory of her.

Knowing that the clock was ticking until Will's inevitable return, I busted through the second layer of the door with my heel, then ripped away the damaged chunks of board like a claustrophobic gopher who'd been in hibernation for the last six months.

I wriggled through the hole I'd made. And by hole, I meant the entire lower third of the door.

Whoever had done the decorating in the bedroom, must've also had a hand in the hallway. Plain walls painted in another neutral shade, this time dirt brown, were interrupted at regular intervals by dingy white doors and trim. There were enough of them for me to upgrade the house to a mansion in my head.

The well-traveled carpet, also uncommitted to any particular color family, spread out in both directions. I went left, as per Vanessa's directions, and soon found myself at the top of a prom-night-worthy staircase. The banister, unlike the shoddily crafted doors, was solid wood and curled downward, while the ceiling above soared at least two stories high before coming to a majestic peak. A glass and black wrought iron chandelier, aged with dirt and cobwebs, was a work of art that dominated the lofty space. Half the bulbs were burnt out or smashed, but they threw off enough light that I could probably make it down the stairs without falling.

I was halfway down the stairs when the sound of voices reached me. I froze, waiting for an exclamation of "She's getting away!" When nobody immediately noticed me, I let out the breath I'd been holding, and I continued my not-so-stealthy glide downward, keeping my back against the wall where there were fewer creaky spots to step on. The third-grade version of me would have been proud of my *Nancy Drew* moves.

The foyer came into view, its large black and white tiles checker-boarding the floor beneath a decade's worth of filth. Across the fifteen-foot space was a set of double doors with boards nailed over the glass inserts. There had been no frugal-minded considerations made here; those suckers were the real deal. Winged black hinges were bolted to substantial slabs of timber that could have sustained a whole family of beavers for a month.

I'd been on the receiving end of Will's angry words too many times not to recognize the indignant pitch from where I stood on the bottom step. When his tirade was interrupted by a woman's voice, I wanted to stay rooted to the spot. She sounded pissed, but it was the condescension in her tone that intrigued me. I'd never had the backbone to deal with my husband during one of his tantrums, but this woman obviously did, along with a set of titanium balls from what I could hear.

"…Too much attention to us—"

Someone grabbed me from behind, and my startled shriek cut off the eavesdropping session before things had even gotten good.

A hand roughly pushed me, and I stumbled over the last stair and fell onto the cold tiles. The man moved to stand over me, and when I didn't immediately move, he scowled and grabbed my wrist. Dragging me like a bag of wet laundry, he hauled me through an arched set of doors that was set along the same wall as the stairs.

His hand was like a vise, and the bones in my arm ground together, but I was actually grateful in a weird, warped way that he hadn't manhandled me around in a giant bear-hug. I'd found myself in that position too many times this week, and I didn't think I could stomach the vulnerability again so soon.

I kicked and clawed at my captor, even though I knew it wouldn't make much of a difference. Still, I wanted this jerkwad to know I wasn't going down without a fight, and it helped to hold my panic at bay.

The man unceremoniously dumped me like last week's trash. I scrambled to my feet and found myself surrounded by a half dozen men, including my furious husband.

Ex-husband, I reminded myself.

The dark room was lit only by a handful of wall sconces. They were erratically placed but hinted at the vastness of the room. More plywood decorated the tall walls; some were haloed with the faint glow of sunlight.

"What have we here?" The woman's voice was regal, as if she were royalty addressing her court. After some shuffling of feet, the semicircle of men parted so I could finally put a face to the voice.

She was short like I was, but that's where the similarities ended. Delicate and petite, she was wrapped in a well-tailored royal-blue pants suit. The cream-colored shirt underneath her blazer perfectly matched the string of pearls around her throat. The sharp click of her black heels on the tile was dainty and deafening at the same time. Her blonde hair was cut just below the ear and framed a jaw that was hard with irritation. She stared down her too-pointy nose at me, like she'd found a fly in her organic vegan soup.

Next to her, I looked like a hobo in my orange kitten pajamas, bright pink sweatshirt, and mud-caked runners. All the rolling around on the ground and being transported in a car trunk had pulled most of my hair free from the braid, and I could still taste dried blood on my lip.

Woefully underdressed was putting it mildly.

"Marissa, allow me to introdu—"

"I found her sneaking around on the stairs." The man who'd dragged me in had interrupted Will, and I'd have snickered if the situation had been less lethal.

I wasn't stupid enough to think any of these men

were human. Their pale skin and dark hollow eyes, along with the meticulous measures taken to keep out any errant rays of daylight were all good indicators that I was standing in a room full of vampires.

"Who are you? How did you get in here?" She fired the questions at me as if the words were ammunition and she wanted to draw blood.

"I'm Theo," I answered her first question automatically, but I was drawing a big blank on the second. Did she mean, how had I escaped? "I kicked the door in."

Her cold blue eyes assessed me, and she clearly reached the conclusion that I wasn't capable of what I'd claimed. Whatever. Let her underestimate me.

"Check the house for other intruders," she hissed.

One of the men scampered off to do her bidding. It might have been the same one that grabbed me on the stairs, but it was hard to tell since they were all similarly dressed in black pants and black shirts. Will was the only exception, with his wrinkled white button-down dress shirt. But, hey, at least they had matching bloodstains, like they were all wearing the uniforms of a '90s boy band. With a little smudge on this guy's chin, another streak on the back of that guy's hand, they all looked like little boys playing with war paint.

"You picked the wrong house to break into." Her lips, painted scarlet red, twisted with cruel satisfaction. She should have gone with a darker shade, so that my dried blood would blend in better once she was done sucking me dry.

"I didn't break in!" Was she joking? I didn't know her well enough to tell. "I don't even know where we are!"

Everlyn C Thompson

She tapped a well-manicured nail against her chin while she studied me. "Liar. You trespass on my property—"

"*He* kidnapped *me!*" I jabbed my finger in Will's direction but didn't take my eyes from the she-vamp. I knew who the biggest threat in the room was.

She spun her head toward Will, in one of those smooth inhuman moves straight out of *The Exorcist*.

"William."

He took a step forward, ignoring the dangerous tone in her voice. Or maybe he was just too stupid to recognize it for what it was.

"Marissa, this is the woman I told you about. She'd be the perfect companion for us—"

"I said *no.* You haven't earned the right to sire your own line."

Will ramped up the pleading whine in his voice. "*Please,* Marissa, I love her! She'd make a magnificent addition to our family!"

In a move faster than I could track, she wrapped her hand around Will's neck and lifted him into the air. "I decide who to turn! You've already called too much attention to us; I will not allow you to endanger my brood any longer!"

Man, I wished I had some popcorn. The show was just getting good.

Chapter Twelve

The missing vampire returned, skidding to a halt and drawing everyone's gaze.

"What did you find?"

"The doors and windows are still boarded up tight, she didn't get in that way. And I found something in one of the upstairs bedrooms..." He took a step back, like he was nervous that Marissa was the type to shoot the messenger if she didn't like the news he brought. I can't say I blamed him. "A body, chained up and drained. I could smell the blood from others too."

"You brought a human here? Into *my* home?" She was deceptively calm, her blue eyes locked onto Will like she was just waiting for an excuse to rip him a new asshole. "Is this true?"

"We are superior! Why should we hide from *them*?" I recognized his righteous anger for what it was: a deflection of the wrongs he didn't want to admit. Even in undeath, his MO hadn't changed.

"Because they outnumber us, a thousand to one!" she snapped. "How long until someone comes looking for the body upstairs? Or this one?" She gestured to me and I wanted to point out that I was still alive, but it seemed kind of premature. That little fact could change at any second.

The body they were referring to must be Vanessa. My heart squeezed painfully, and I forced my thoughts away from the poor woman who'd been counting on me to bring back help.

"They're already looking." Seven sets of vampire eyes turned in my direction, and I wished I had kept my mouth shut. Oh well, it was too late now; in for a penny, in for a pound. "The PIMPs." I pressed my lips into a tight line to keep any snickering to myself. What a stupid name.

One of the male vampires helpfully volunteered, "The Paranormal Intelligence Maintaining Peace Agency."

"Pish; those idiots wouldn't know how to find their own asses, even if I drew them a map." Marissa waved away the notion with a careless hand.

"They've already linked over twenty missing women to him." Marissa's glare went all the way down to the marrow of my bones. Why the hell wouldn't my mouth stop talking?

"You know this, how?"

"They came to warn me. In case he came looking for me."

Her gaze was shrewd, and I tried not to fidget. "And these PIMPs are looking for *him?*"

"Yes." I knew Ozzy wouldn't stop looking until he found Will.

"And the rest of my brood?"

What the hell was a brood?

Marissa rolled her eyes at my bewilderment. "The others I have sired! Do they search for the rest of us?"

I tried to think of anything Ozzy might have said about other vampires, but I was drawing a big blank. He had plenty to say about the fae, but he'd given me the impression Will was working alone. Then again, he'd been pretty vague about the whole you're-being-stalked-by-a-monster-but-I-won't-tell-you-what-kind situation. My only education about the existence of vampires was courtesy of Will and the fangs he'd violated me with.

"No—just Will, as far as I know."

"Good." She snapped her fingers and held out her hand. A brief pause filled the air, like she was waiting for someone to high-five her, but then one of the vamps handed her a knife.

My heart thundered in my chest, and I had a moment to wonder why she'd need a knife when she had a perfectly good set of fangs to rip out my throat with.

"No! Please don't!" Will threw himself in front of me, blocking my view of Marissa. "She could be useful! I'll sire her myself—"

"You are too young and too weak to sire anyone!" She slanted her brows contemptuously at Will before turning her frosty gaze on me. "Why her? She is no use to my brood. Too plain, too tame for my tastes."

"We can wait a few weeks, get her back to a reasonable size." Will was rambling now, the words falling from his lips faster than I could keep up with. "I'll get her down to any size you want. I'll share." He turned his pleading eyes to the men gathered around us. "I'm just saying what you've all been thinking, that another female in the brood would be—"

"Enough!" Marissa tried to cut him off, but Will's whining was like a runaway train; it wasn't going to stop until it ran out of steam or hit a brick wall.

"She's really good, so eager to please in the bedroom—"

"Hey!" I exclaimed. My cheeks heated with embarrassment and fury that he'd talk so candidly about our sex life. I wanted to strangle the jerk for revealing things I'd considered private.

"*Enough!*" The knife in Marissa's hand streaked upward in one smooth motion, sliding through the flesh of Will's throat and effectively ending his tirade of begging. He gasped once before his skin parted, the wound gaping like a second mouth. The arc of his blood that sprayed upward caught me by surprise, splattering across my face and chest.

Will's body slumped to the ground. A good wife would have knelt on the filthy floor and held his lifeless body or screamed in grief or done *something*. I wasn't a good wife. I just stood there, gaping like a fish out of water.

"Ugh, I'm tired of his griping." She handed the bloody knife to one of the men. "Get rid of the body." He moved efficiently, wiping the blade on Will's pant leg before tucking it into his belt.

"You." Marissa pegged the man standing closest to me with a glare. "Get rid of the one upstairs."

He spun on his heel and left, followed closely behind by the man dragging Will's body.

My breath stuttered through lips that had gone numb, and I tried to blink away the blood that clung to my eyelashes. My mouth tasted like old pennies, and I resisted the urge to spit. I doubted that the homicidal vampire would appreciate me hocking a loogie at her feet.

"And you..." Her blue eyes were colder than an iceberg as they traveled the length of my body. "What to do with you..." She trailed a sharp pointy nail down her face while contemplating me.

"I—" I shut my mouth, since I had no idea what to say.

"I am not interested in having another woman in my bed. I have no doubt my fledglings would welcome the opportunity, but *I* am their sire and my tastes do *not* run that way."

My head was pounding, making it hard to grasp what she was saying.

"Are you going to kill me?" If she was, I hoped she'd just get on with it. The smell of blood was making me nauseous.

"I haven't decided yet."

Using my sleeve, I wiped some of the sticky blood off my face. "Well, could you hurry it up? I'm not getting any younger here." Getting snarky with a pissed-off vampire probably wasn't the smartest thing to do. I couldn't help it; an empty stomach brought out my bitchiness.

To my surprise, Marissa chuckled. Which was infinitely better than her killing me for the sass.

"You have big balls for a human. I can see why William wanted you."

"Uh, thanks?" A backhanded compliment was better than a formal announcement of my impending murder, so I tried to sound grateful. "So, I guess I'll just see myself out then…" I took a step toward the door, and my foot slipped on the trail of Will's smeared blood. My ankle twisted to the side, and strong hands caught both my elbows before my butt hit the floor. My sneakers squeaked across the floor as I struggled to regain my balance, while shrugging off the two male vampires who held me between them like I was a rag doll.

"Let go!" I funneled all my exhaustion and frustration in the words, while giving the vampires my haughtiest glare.

"Hmmm, this is quite the predicament that William has put us in. I have a strict no-killing policy for my brood," she mused. "Yet, here you are, with knowledge of our kind and a bite to prove it."

She eyed the bite mark on my neck, making it throb.

"I won't tell anyone." My promise sounded small in the large room.

She waved a well-manicured nail indifferently. "I know. I can smell the fear and desperation rolling off you."

Gross. I wanted to ask exactly what aroma was associated with fear and desperation, but I doubted she'd humor my curiosity.

"No, it is the PIMPs that concern me. Even though I was unaware of William's...*activities*, as his sire, I am still accountable for his actions."

Shit. Why did I tell her about Ozzy? So stupid, Theo!

"If I kill you, there will be nothing to lead them to me."

"If I disappear, they'll know it was Will." I thought back to what Ozzy had said about him stalking me. The memory of seeing a man watching me in the parking lot at the Boot Scoot surfaced, and just as quickly, I realized it must have been Will. In all likelihood, it was probably Will I'd seen lurking in my driveway too.

"They know he took Vanessa." Marissa's eyebrows rose in confusion, and I quickly added, "The waitress.

The woman upstairs in the bedroom."

My brain felt sluggish as I fumbled to piece together a strategy that didn't end up with me dead. "Leave the bodies somewhere I can lead the PIMPs back to. I'll tell them Will attacked me." I pointed at the bite marks on my neck for emphasis. "Then I was forced to kill him in self-defense. They won't have any reason to keep looking, so you'll be safe. Case closed."

Assuming they didn't already know about the rest of Will's "family," but I chose not to mention that particular fact.

Marissa tilted her head, contemplating my hastily made plan.

Sweat broke out on my forehead, and my entire body ached. My anxiety ratcheted up another notch. I might pass out before anything was decided.

One of the vamps behind Marissa caught my eye. Running his tongue over his fang, he smiled hungrily. I was guessing that, if Marissa gave the order for my death, she wouldn't need the knife. I glanced back and forth nervously at the other men in the room, but they all waited stoically for their sire's decision.

"Yes...That might work."

I nearly fell over as my relief made my knees weak. Good thing my elbows were still locked in their vise-like grip, or I'd have fallen on my face.

****

It turned out I was pretty good at planning a fake murder.

Technically, the murder part was true, since Will really was dead.

But the rest of the details were fabricated, so as far as I was concerned, the whole situation fell into the category of "fake murder."

I'd suggested Will and Vanessa's bodies be left at the abandoned Gas & Go east of Tamarac so that no humans accidentally stumbled across them before I could tell Ozzy where to find them. After leaving my fingerprints all over the bloody knife, I handed over my dirty sweatshirt to the vampire tasked with dumping the bodies and evidence at the "crime scene."

I took the keys for Will's vehicle, so that I could drive myself home and tell Ozzy that I took the car after escaping from the gas station. I'm pretty sure the trunk still had my blood in it, making my story that much more believable.

After a tentative truce was reached, I high-tailed it out of there as fast as I could.

The good news was that it was still daylight outside; it was probably about one o'clock in the afternoon judging by the sun's position. The bad news was that I had no idea where I was.

The exterior of the house looked just as neglected as the interior. The dark blue paint was sun-faded and peeling from the rotting siding. Broken glass littered the ground under the boarded-up windows, along with shingles from the roof. It had probably been a decade since the grass had seen a lawnmower, and the overgrown driveway was only identifiable by the fresh tire tracks leading in.

I hadn't gotten a good look at the car last night, but in the overcast daylight it was impressive. It was some kind of luxury sedan, all black with tinted windows, a far cry from the practical import that Will had left abandoned downtown when he'd disappeared.

Five other expensive vehicles were lined up on one

side of the yard. I recognized the high-end SUVs, but the three sports cars were mysteries.

How could they manage to afford such nice cars and clothing, and why did they choose to live in an abandoned building? Later I'd have time to ponder the financial logistics of vampire broods, but right then I needed to focus on getting home before I passed out from starvation and blood loss.

It took me three hours and five wrong turns before I made it back home. Once the driveway had spit me out onto a rural range road, I realized I was slightly east and a whole lot north of Tamarac. The quarter of a tank of gas got me home with only fumes to spare. I doubted I would have been able to flag down another motorist for a ride looking the way I did. If I'd had my wallet, I would have stopped on my way through town to fill up.

I parked the borrowed sedan at the end of my street and put the keys in the cup holder, but I didn't get out of the car.

I felt a million years old. I wasn't even sure if my shaky legs would support me if I tried to stand.

There were so many things I needed to do. Food and a shower were pretty high priorities. *I should probably put some antiseptic on the bite on my neck,* I thought. Who knew what kind of germs vampires might have? The bandages on my arms would have to be changed too.

None of that had seemed important on the drive home. All I'd been able to think about was Farranen. Was he okay? Would I be able to find my way back to where I'd left him? Would he even be there anymore? It was nearly sunset; a whole day had passed since I'd left him.

What if those creepy stick fae were still in the woods, watching and waiting for someone like me to go running straight into their trap? Every time I closed my eyes, I could see the pained look on Farranen's face and the dagger sticking out of his leg as he shouted at me to run.

I never should have run.

Guilt swamped me, burying me alive in an avalanche of emotions. God, I didn't have time for this. Farranen was out there. Injured. Possibly dying. I had to get my shit together and find him.

But I needed to be smart about this. I would be no good to him if I passed out.

What would Farranen do?

I hadn't known him long, but I had no doubt that he'd have found a way to help me if our positions were reversed.

Throwing open the car door, I nearly had a heart attack when something huge and hairy jumped into my lap.

"Gah, *Dog!*" I pushed at him with weak arms, and he willingly backed away from the car so I had enough room to stand. New pains made themselves known as I tried to stretch out my cramped muscles after hours of inactivity. Dog whined as I let out a series of groans; his sad doggy eyes followed me as I lumbered up the driveway and across the porch steps.

"Oh, for heaven's sake!" I looked at the door, with its three dead bolts that I didn't have the keys for. I'd given them to Farranen when we'd left last night, since my pjs didn't have any pockets.

"Fuck." It was pitiful as far as cursing goes, but there was no one around to hear but Dog, so I didn't care. "Fuck, fuck, fuck."

I banged my forehead against the door a few times, just because I had no idea what else to do. The solid *thunk* sound that my banging made let me know that the door was the old-school solid wood kind, not a cheap door-crasher special like the bedroom door I'd broken. Out of sheer habit, I reached out and turned the doorknob and nearly fell over when the door opened.

"What the hell?" I cautiously peered inside. I *knew* that I'd locked the door before I left. Someone had obviously been here recently, and since Farranen had my only set of house keys, I had to assume it was him.

"Hello? Farranen?" Dog followed me inside as I drifted from room to room. The cabin was empty, but there were scuffs of dried mud on the floors and a smear of blood on the edge of the kitchen counter like someone had gripped it after coming through the back door.

If Farranen had been here, he hadn't stayed. My disappointment was short and swift, but at least I knew he'd made it out of the woods alive.

After raiding my fridge, I wolfed down a bowl of cold pasta, cottage cheese straight out of the tub, and some sliced deli chicken. I was too hungry to look at the expiry date on the chicken; it still smelled good, and I didn't really want to know if it was past its prime.

My arms protested when I tugged my pj top off over my head. Since my sweatshirt had taken the majority of Will's blood, my top was fairly clean but the bottoms weren't salvageable. Dog wandered into the bathroom as I picked at the tape and gauze on my arms. He lowered himself to the floor and put his head on his paws, like it was no big deal to watch a crazy woman in her panties swearing at the twigs and leaves matted in her hair.

"Enjoying the show?" I asked, immediately feeling stupid that I was wasting perfectly good sarcasm on a dog.

It took me two rounds of shampoo before the water ran clear. Little pieces of dead leaves and dirt built up over the drain, and I scooped them into the bathroom garbage when I was done. Once my hair was snugly wrapped in a towel, I threw on a pair of panties and a nightshirt. My brain felt like it was running on autopilot as I opened the first-aid kit and went through the motions of disinfecting the cuts on my arms. They were healing faster than I had anticipated, and they only required a few bandages to cover the shiny raised lines. The purple bruise where the fae bitch had elbowed me was new, but overall, I no longer looked like I'd tangled with a lawnmower.

I was forced to use the mirror to inspect the bite mark on my neck, which was something I'd been putting off since I got home. The skin around it was torn and had turned an angry red. It would be just my luck to survive the change, only to die from an infected vampire bite.

My reflection stared back at me as I wondered, was this what Will had seen when he looked at me? Wide hazel eyes with tired dark smudges under them, skin too pale to be pretty, and thirty pounds that hadn't been there six years ago? Had he really meant it when he said he still loved me?

I didn't know what to think.

I didn't want to think at all; I just wanted to sleep.

Chapter Thirteen

The click of the back door shutting jolted me from a deep sleep, the soft noise far more effective than a bucket of ice water. I'd been too edgy for a good sleep, my dreams a tangled mess of worry and uncertainty.

"Theodora?" Farranen's voice accompanied purposeful footsteps across my hardwood floor. His silhouette filled my bedroom doorway a second later, and the only light came from the faint glow of his sword.

"Thank the heavens," he murmured before he crossed the room with quick strides and engulfed me in his arms. The familiar scent of pine and cinnamon surrounded me, and my eyes heated with tears.

"Do the fae really believe in Heaven?" I asked, keeping my face pressed against his shirt.

He let out an uncharacteristic snort of laughter and squeezed me tighter. I tried to think of something sarcastic to say, so I wouldn't have to tell him how worried I'd been.

"Where were you?" He cupped the back of my neck, his hands cold from being outdoors, and I shivered at the wave of magic that slid into me as soon as our skin touched. It eased through me, like dark wine and thunder, touching every single ache and hurt in my body.

"You weren't here, so I went back and searched the

forest. Your trail ended at the road; I saw your blood. I thought…"

Shadows cut harsh lines into his face from the glow of the sword lying across my blankets; hopefully he couldn't see the tear that was rolling down my cheek. I hated that he'd been worried about me. It was such a foreign concept to think that he'd cared enough to track me through the woods with an injured leg.

"How's your leg?" I asked, steering the conversation away from my encounter with Will. I wasn't ready to talk about the vampires yet. I just wanted to enjoy having Farranen next to me for a few more minutes before reality came crashing back in.

"Fine. Nearly healed."

"How is that possible?" My eyes slid shut as the magic caressed its way through me. I hadn't realized until now how hollow I'd felt without it. This must be how addicts felt; I was going to be in for a world of hurt when it was time to say good bye to my fae and his magic.

"Some fae have healing magic; mine is especially strong."

"Oh, that's handy. What happened to the stick fae?"

"Who?"

"The crazy fae that came through the gate. The ones that looked like sticks."

He smiled in amusement, and I dug my fingers into his shirt so I wouldn't be tempted to reach up and touch his full lips. "Ah, the brownies. I returned them to Fairie for trial."

"They're lucky you caught them. I was going to chop them up into firewood."

"I had no idea you were so fierce; I will be sure to remain in your good graces."

I couldn't tell if he was teasing me or not, so I chose not to say anything and just enjoyed running my fingers over the soft fabric of his shirt. When he shifted on the bed and released me, I tried not to look disappointed.

I scooted back on the mattress as he lifted his sword until it disappeared over his shoulder, taking all traces of light with it. There was no point in asking how he was making it glow; he'd just give me a vague answer about it having something to do with fae magic.

Fabric rustled, and then a cool draft flowed against my heated skin as the blankets were lifted. "What are you—"

His body slid in next to mine, and then the covers were back, sealing out the cold air again. My hands automatically sought out his shirt, but all they found was his bare chest. "Oh, my God. You better not be naked."

He pulled me closer, tucking my head under his chin and settling one of his hard thighs between mine. "Just take the magic, Theodora," he grumbled into my hair.

"You, sir, are taking liberties ill-suited of a gentleman."

He sighed in exasperation, and I shut the hell up and let the magic lull me to sleep.

****

The biggest drawback to hanging around with fae and vampires, aside from the constant life-threatening situations, was the total lack of a daily schedule. I didn't own a watch, and my internal clock was so messed up, I never seemed to know what time of day it was. Or even what day of the week it was.

It's been pointed out to me that, some mornings, I can be bit of a grumpy bear when I first wake up, but today I was absolutely giddy as I stretched. Just slap a yellow sun on my belly, and you could call me Sunshine Bear. I had no idea how long I'd been asleep, but it must have been a while; my body felt gloriously rested for the first time in days. A lot of that was due to the fact that Farranen had spent the night next to me.

I opened my eyes and smiled, until I saw the dark look on his face.

"What's wrong?" Apprehension tightened my chest, making it hard to breathe.

"Who did this?" His fingers ghosted around the bite marks on my neck. The wound was still full of angry bees; the bandage must have come off while I was sleeping.

"Uh, it's kind of a long story." I fought the urge to pull the covers over my neck; I hadn't done anything wrong, even though the angry look on Farranen's face said otherwise.

"Tell me who it was." The demand in his voice ticked me off; he could have asked nicely instead of sounding like a bossy jerk.

"My husband." My words created the reaction I was hoping for. Farranen couldn't have looked more shocked if I'd announced I was moving to a nudist colony.

"He's—"

"A vampire? Yes, but he was human when we were together. The whole vampire thing is new."

"Where is he?" His eyes glowed brighter as his

aggression ramped up and he contemplated a dozen different ways to kill Will.

"Dead." His silence was satisfying, in a narcissistic kind of way.

"You're sure?" He sounded hesitant, like I might be upset over the death of a man who'd kidnapped me. Although, Farranen didn't know about the kidnapping, so maybe he was just concerned that I'd fallen into a grieving widow headspace.

"Yep," I told him cheerfully. "I had a front row seat for the whole thing." I mimed swiping a knife over my throat. "Oh, speaking of my ex-husband's dead body, I should call Ozzy so he can deal with the mess. Do you have a cell I can use? I lost my mine."

His frown grew at the sudden shift in direction our conversation had taken. He knew I was leaving something out (a lot of somethings actually), but he didn't know what.

"I need to go home to shower and change. I will bring my phone when I return."

"I thought you said cell phones don't work in Fairie."

"I am not going to Fairie."

I averted my gaze when he stood up and pulled his clothes back on. FYI, he was still wearing the black boxers that I'd seen him in before, but I only noticed because I tried to sneak a peek at his thigh to see if it really had healed. Honest.

"Then where are you going?"

"I have a temporary property on this side of the gate, as well as a permanent dwelling in Fairie."

My curiosity soared, and I immediately pictured a cobblestone pathway leading to a cozy fairy tale cottage—a covered front porch next to arched double doors, a sharp-peaked roof, and dormers covered in cedar shakes. I could practically smell the smoke that curled from the slightly crooked chimney. I'll bet there was even an old-fashioned push mower in his shed.

Of course, my stupid brain leapt to provide a visual to go with that happy thought.

Farranen with his long hair tied back, muscles rippling on his shirtless torso, as a fine layer of sweat reflected back the midafternoon sun.

My hormones must have had some input on putting that predictable image together.

"Theodora?"

I jumped when Farranen knelt in front of me and touched my hand. "Sorry, what?" What had he been saying before I got lost in my daydreams?

"I will return soon." He looked like he was going to say more, but, after a long pause, he stood and left without looking back.

****

After applying another layer of antiseptic cream to the bite on my neck, I raided the fridge for the quickest edible thing I could find. My tastebuds were willing to take a hit for the team if it meant getting food in my belly faster. Toast with cheddar cheese and sliced tomatoes might not have been the breakfast of champions, but it definitely hit the spot.

Dumping my plate in the sink, I wandered outside to sit on the back porch steps. The sun had just gone down, and the smear of pink and orange clouds fading into darkness was beautiful.

I didn't want to call Ozzy and deal with all the vampire crap.

I wanted to bake a cake and then curl up on the sofa with a good book. I missed the self-imposed privacy I'd previously taken for granted. Being alone had felt safe, like hiding behind solid brick walls. It was the perfect place to hole up and lick my wounds after losing Will.

In a small way, I'd just lost him all over again, and I'd rather deal with this second wave of grief in private.

The crunch of footsteps on dried twigs broke through my inner musing, and I looked up expecting to see Farranen. I let out a little squeak of shock when I recognized the red hair and thick shoulders of the PIMP agent.

Ozzy stopped about ten feet from the steps and held up his hands in a gesture of surrender. "Hey, Theo. I'm not here to cause any trouble."

Yeah, like I was dumb enough to fall for his I'm-just-as-soft-and-innocent-as-a-marshmallow routine.

"What do you want, Ozzy?"

"I just wanted to check on you, to see how you're doing." He narrowed his eyes at me. "And don't call me that."

"You mean, you wanted to see if I'd grown any claws or fangs yet? Maybe ripped the throats out of some humans, just for fun?"

"No, but if you had…You know you could tell me, right, Theo?"

I almost laughed at how much he sounded like a bad afterschool special. Instead, I told him, "I'm good. No claws or fangs."

"Would you mind if I took a look at your wounds?"

I hesitated, acutely aware that I was unarmed,

while he was probably packing enough heat to set off a metal detector from three hundred yards away. And while I wouldn't mind showing him if it meant he'd go away and leave me in peace, a big part of my brain was saying that I shouldn't let him get any closer.

Maybe I was overly suspicious; but after the week I'd had, could you blame me?

"Leave your coat and weapons on the table."

He raised an eyebrow, like maybe I'd managed to impress him. Or maybe he was just thinking of all the ways he could hurt me without the weapons. Either way, he didn't protest as he stripped off his leather jacket and methodically lined up three handguns and five knives on the table.

I wondered if it was casual Friday at the PIMP office; instead of his usual wrinkled slacks and dress shirt, Ozzy was wearing worn black jeans and a dark red T-shirt. He did a slow spin, showing me that he was no longer armed.

"Okay, come see." I tugged at the edges of my bandages until they came free. My first-aid kit had seen more action this week than a discount hooker, and I was grateful that I'd run out of the name-brand bandages. The cheap knock-offs took less arm hair with them when I ripped them off.

The old steps creaked as Ozzy took a seat next to me.

"You're healing faster than you should be." His tone was carefully neutral, without a trace of accusation.

"Yes." I stared him straight in the eye, wanting him to know that I wasn't scared. I was still human, and therefore I had nothing to fear from him. PIMP laws didn't apply to me.

"Have you noticed anything else unusual?"

"Like what?" I asked in exasperation. Every aspect of my life was unusual these days.

He gave me a patronizing look, so I snarked, "My backyard has become Grand Central Station. Every fae in the neighborhood traipses through like they own the place." I thought back to all the furry visitors I'd had in the last week. "Not to mention the animals; it's like a traveling zoo around here now."

"What animals?" he asked in an odd voice.

"A dog, a cat, and a skunk. Oh, and a deer on the road." The dog was my own fault since I kept feeding him, but the other three had been unsettling. Not because I was a city girl and unaccustomed to wildlife, but from the way they'd stared at me with such a bizarre intensity, as well as the slight glow that had seemed to radiate from them. The skunk had been especially freaky, since it looked just like the one I'd found dead a few days earlier.

"Did you touch them at any point, Theo?"

"Touch them? Yeah, I petted the dog a few times." Who wouldn't want to pet Dog? For a scruffy stray, his fur was ridiculously silky.

"Oh." I didn't like the way he said it.

"What 'oh?' Why does it matter?"

"Did the guardian explain that if you survive the transition, you'll have ankou magic?"

"Yes." I remembered him saying something along those lines.

"Theo, the ankou are considered the grave reapers of the Fairie realm." Well, that made sense, since they certainly looked the part. "It requires a significant amount of magic for them to bring a person through the veil, but smaller less-sentient creatures, like animals, tend to manifest on their own when they can sense ankou magic." He studied me, like he was hoping for a reaction. When I didn't obligingly give him one, he ran his hand through his hair in frustration. "Ghosts, Theo! The ankou can see ghosts!"

"*Ghosts?*" No, Dog couldn't be a ghost. Ghosts couldn't inhale a steak in less than two seconds. Ghosts didn't take naps in the shade outside, and then use their sad doggy eyes to guilt me into sharing my cake.

"But you said you touched them, so they couldn't have been ghosts." Ozzy slanted me a smile that wasn't remotely reassuring. "Now, let me see your injuries."

I was expecting some sort of warning, or maybe veiled threats regarding the possibility of my humanity ending, but instead he gently took my arm in his hands and continued to study the claw marks. Leaning in closer, he inhaled deeply, and just when I was thinking about pulling away from him, he licked my arm.

"What the *hell?*" I yanked my arm back, disgusted and outraged.

I shot to my feet and put some distance between us. A slight breeze wafted over the moisture, cooling it against my feverish skin.

"Sorry, it was the easiest way to check." He sure didn't sound sorry.

"Check for what? Whether or not your PIMP buddies will be smart enough to find where I bury your body?" Anger was a whole lot easier than freaking out from fear.

"I needed to be sure you're still human."

"So you *licked* me?" Well, I sure as hell didn't

think that was an official CSI investigative procedure.

Ozzy smirked, and two enormous white fangs pressed into his bottom lip.

Oh, fuck.

Ozzy was a vampire.

How in the world had I missed *that*?

If I'd been at the top of my game, I would have been able to connect the dots sooner.

Clearly, I'd been putting all my energy into minor things like survival and healing and not dying, rather than using it to power my depleted brain cells.

It made sense that Ozzy was a vampire, since he'd been hunting Will, who was also a vampire.

After a long silence while I wrapped my mind around the fact that I was sitting next to a vampire—a freakin' *vampire!*—my mind shifted out of first gear into fifth.

"Can you turn into a bat? How many vampires are in your brood? Are there any women, or is it all dudes? How often do you have to drink blood? Are all the PIMPs vampires? Why do you need so many guns when you have..." I gestured at his fangs. "*Those*?"

"Theo, can we focus on what's important for a second?" Geeze, apparently the grumpy-pants vamp didn't like being on the other side of the interrogation table.

"Right. Of course. What were we talking about again?"

Ozzy let out a long-suffering sigh and raked his hand through his hair.

"Hey, your head healed!" There was no sign of the damage from when I'd hit him with my hammer. "Is that like, some kind of super vampire healing? Can every vampire do that?"

"*Theo*—"

"Sorry! Just curious."

"Has Will tried to contact you?"

Just like that, all my interest in snooping through Lifestyles of the Rich and Undead dried up. I tried to paste a blank look on my face.

"When did you see him?" Ozzy zeroed in on my unease like a shark on chum.

"I ran into him last night." I spoke slowly, choosing my words with care.

"Are you all right? Is that what happened to your lip?" His eyebrows dipped in concern, and I tried not to panic under the intense scrutiny.

"He put me in the trunk of his car and took me—" Oh, crap, I wasn't supposed to mention the abandoned mansion in the woods. "—to a gas station. He might have been squatting there. It's east of town." Mostly true statements, since the squatting part was hypothetical.

"And he just let you leave?"

"I escaped." Also true. "He killed Vanessa. Her body is there." The sorrow I heard in my own words was genuine. She deserved better than to be used like a disposable human juice box.

"Was there anyone else there?"

"No." Another truth, since I was referring to the Gas & Go.

"Do you know where he is now?"

"Dead," I answered, keeping my fingers crossed that I wouldn't have to go into detail. "My escape included an incident that involved his throat and a sharp pointy knife."

"Damn, I'm glad you made it out all right, but I was hoping to get some answers out of him."

I shrugged and stared at my dirty running shoes. If I looked traumatized enough, maybe he wouldn't press me for details on how I'd supposedly killed Will.

Ozzy stood and checked his phone. "Well, I need to get over to that gas station to see what I can find."

I tried not to look too relieved that he'd kept the interrogation minimal. I quickly rattled off the location of the bodies, and he texted the address to someone. Another PIMP agent? I wondered if they were all vampires.

"Let's get you inside so I know you're safe before I take off." He offered me a hand and pulled me to my feet, but instead of letting go, he tugged me forward until I fell against his chest. A sharp pinch tugged at my neck, and I pounded my fists against his chest in panic.

"Hey! Let go!" I protested.

He stepped away and waved a scrap of fabric in my face. "He bit you?" The snarled words cut through my anger faster than any blade could have. My fingers moved to cover the bite mark, but it was too late. He'd already torn off my bandage and seen the evidence for himself.

I didn't bother to answer his question, since he already had the answer.

"Did you take his blood?" he asked.

"What? No!"

"Think carefully. He could have forced you to drink it if you were unconscious or drugged. Is there even a chance that you might have had some?"

"No!" Memories from Marissa's mansion replayed through my head like a movie on fast-forward. I remembered waking up in the bedroom, then escaping down the stairs, and finally Will's execution. No drinking blood that I could recall.

"Even a sip, Theo; just the smallest smear of blood transferred by a kiss…"

"No. And I certainly didn't kiss him!" The thought of kissing anyone with my split lip was painful and disgusting—which made me think of the foul taste of rusty pennies in my mouth after I'd watched Marissa slit Will's throat. And the fountain of blood that I'd been doused in.

Oh, shit.

Ozzy must have caught the panic on my face, because he was quick to mask his worry with a bland expression. "Tell me, Theo. I can't help you if I don't know what happened."

"I…" Fuck. Fuck, fuck, fuck. I was a terrible liar. There's no way I'd be able to pull something believable out of my ass. "I…I think you should go." He seemed sincere, but I had no idea what the protocol was for someone who'd accidentally ingested vampire blood. He'd already tried to lock me up for being attacked by a fae, and I doubted that, just because it had been a vampire this time, it would be any different.

I needed more info before I knew who I could trust.

Disappointment darkened his eyes when he turned away.

"Hey, Theo?"

"Yeah?" I asked, wrapping my arms around my middle apprehensively.

"How did you know her name was Vanessa?"

"Uh, Will must have mentioned it."

He nodded once before disappearing into the

darkness.

I stood outside until the temperature had dropped low enough that I shivered, trying to figure out why I had so much guilt after our conversation. Technically, I hadn't lied so my conscience should be clear. Still, the idea of misleading an agent of law enforcement had my tummy tied up in knots. He'd caught my slip up about Vanessa's name; what else had I missed?

Chapter Fourteen

Dog showed up while I'd been lost in my thoughts. His sad yellow eyes said that clearly I was an idiot for standing outside in the cold, when I had a nice warm cabin and kitchen full of food available.

He was probably right, though I wouldn't admit it out loud.

I invited him in and opened a can of tuna that he promptly inhaled. Thoughts of Will continued to haunt me, and I desperately wished I'd thought to buy a new phone so I could call Katie. She'd be able to provide me with a much-needed woman's perspective.

Taking an apple from the bowl, I wandered into the living room and flopped onto the couch. I'd always appreciated how quiet and empty the place was, but tonight it just felt desolate.

"I watched a woman slit my husband's throat open. I didn't even try to help him; I didn't even cry."

Dog let out a tiny whine that I'd like to think was sympathetic. Or maybe he just wanted more tuna.

"He wasn't a great husband. Sometimes I wonder if that's because I wasn't a very good wife."

Dog crept closer, like he was listening to my teary admission.

"He bit me. I think I got some of his blood in my mouth. Am I going to turn into a vampire?"

Dog tilted his head; apparently, he didn't have the

answer for that one either. Or maybe he didn't know what a vampire was. Although, with the way he'd consistently avoided Ozzy, maybe he did know. Animals were supposedly more sensitive to the supernatural than humans.

I sighed and didn't bother wiping away the tears that were rolling down my face.

My body felt empty without Farranen's magic. Little twinges of my own magic flickered inside me, but who knew how much longer that would last. Once they were gone and I was just a normal human again, he wouldn't have any reason to see me.

It was a depressing thought, and it made my heart feel empty too.

Dog jumped up on the couch and put his head on my thigh. After a short internal debate with myself about whether or not it was smart to let myself befriend an animal that would eventually leave, I thought, *screw it.*

My fingers sank into the silky fur behind Dog's ear, and he didn't protest. I let my hand wander and was surprised to feel the fine bones of his shoulders and ribs beneath his soft coat. I knew he was thin, but this was more than just being underfed. This was from being starved.

"You poor guy," I murmured. "How about I go bake us a cake?"

Considering the week I'd had, a cake was justified.

****

I had always subscribed to the belief that women take longer to get ready than men. I mean, with the time it takes to blow-dry and style their hair, then apply however many layers of makeup, it's easy for a lady to spend an hour or more to make herself presentable. And don't forget the vast number of wardrobe choices that must be made.

Thankfully, none of that was really a priority for me. I usually just let my hair dry naturally and threw on whatever was clean. Fifteen minutes tops, and I was showered and dressed. My crappy water heater may have had something to do with the short amount of time I spent under the spray.

I was just pulling the cake out of the oven when Farranen walked in, two hours after he'd left.

Two. Hours.

I really hadn't pegged him as the type to waste time primping.

Still, who was I to judge?

"Hey! I didn't realize you lived so far! You could have just showered here, and I could have thrown your clothes in the washing machine."

I filled the sink with soapy water to wash my hand blender. Yeah, I take my cake pretty seriously. Only freshly pureed, ripe pineapple went into my fruit cake.

"Theodora." I glanced over my shoulder at the serious tone in his voice, the one that made him sound remote and stony.

"What's wrong?"

Another man followed him through the back door into my kitchen, forcing me to back up to make more space for all three of us in the small kitchen.

He was slightly shorter than my fae, with long, dark brown hair and even darker eyes. He carried himself with the same regal self-assuredness that Farranen had.

"Hello." While doing my best to sound polite, I

shot Farranen a *what the hell!?!* look.

"This is Augustus of the Light Court, one of the queen's knights."

"From *Fairie?*" I tried not to sound shocked that someone from another realm was standing in my kitchen. I mean, besides Farranen. Him, I was used to.

Gus didn't even bother to acknowledge my question. "Your presence is requested by the queen. I will escort you through the gate and accompany you to her court."

"Now?"

"At your earliest convenience." Something in his eyes told me my earliest convenience better be right now.

Right, of course the queen would want to meet when most normal people would be brushing their teeth and crawling into bed for the night.

I looked down at my black yoga pants and white sweatshirt with NERDY BY NATURE printed across the chest right next to a mustard stain. "Should I change?"

His steel-gray eyes took in my attire, and apparently, he wasn't impressed. "I would recommend that you do."

"I will help you choose something suitable." Farranen strode toward my bedroom, and I was forced to follow or stay with Gus. Not wanting to find out if the knight was big on small talk, I hurried into my room and shut the door.

"What the hell is going on?" I demanded.

"I felt Augustus cross over on my way here. I was able to intercept him and find out his intent. Rumor of a changeling has reached the queen. At this point it's just supposition, probably created by the brownies I caught yesterday, but she has tasked him with an official investigation.

"To deny your existence would only delay the inevitable. By bringing you forward myself, I will petition for your guardianship. If Augustus suspects I was purposely hiding my knowledge of you, I will be put to trial."

"*Were* you hiding me?"

"Yes." The concern in his eyes was as comforting as his brutal honesty. "Think me selfish if you must, but the fae are a cold desperate lot. The possibility, however small, of new blood would be too tempting for some to resist. I would not be able to guarantee your safety there."

He pulled the only dress I owned from my closet. It was a plain green knee-length sundress I'd worn to a wedding ten years ago. "Put this on."

I doubtfully eyed the thing like it was going to sprout fangs and bite me.

"Theodora, please. We don't have much time."

Something in his voice scared me, and I took the dress.

"Turn around," I said. The man might have no qualms about prancing around my bedroom in his underpants, but I didn't share the sentiment. After he'd turned to face the wall, I stripped off everything but my panties. "Okay, what do I need to know?"

"You cannot lie. The queen will know if you try. You can omit facts, but every word you speak must be the truth as you know it."

That shouldn't be too hard to do, since I sucked at lying.

"Do not eat or drink anything. Fae food has…unpredictable outcomes on humans."

I pawed through my dresser drawers for one of my pretty lacy bras. Okay, my only lacy bra.

"Don't trust anything you see. Fae can glamour anything or anyone."

I thought about that, while I shimmied the dress over my head. "Could one of them glamour themselves to look like you?"

"Of course."

"We should have a secret password, so I know that it's really you. Can you zip me up?"

His fingers were cool against my skin as he slid the back of my dress closed, and they did nothing to match the heat in his eyes when I turned around.

"Bagel," I blurted out, desperate to break the tension that was winding its way around us.

"Bagel?" The bright green in his eyes slowly dimmed back to the dark forest color I was used to.

"For our secret word," I explained.

He took a step back, and his smile was slightly relieved. Or maybe I was just seeing my own relief reflected back at me.

"A good choice for a password, as there are no bagels in Fairie."

"Great. So, bagel it is." My mouth kept moving, rambling without my permission as Farranen's eyes drifted lower, taking in every inch of my body, all the way down to my bare toes.

"Do you have shoes?"

"Yeah, probably in my closet." I skirted around him, glad to be out from under his appraising eyes. The way he'd looked at me…It was stunned and possessive, but I'd also seen a streak of longing before he'd lowered his gaze.

I nearly dove headfirst into my small closet to hide the flush that his presence always seemed to cause. Not to mention the fact that my nipples that were suddenly noticeable through the stretchy fabric of the dress. I grabbed a pair of black sandals with jeweled straps that were hiding next to a box of old CDs. By the time I had finished hopping around to get the damn shoes on, Farranen's calm stoic mask was firmly back in place.

"Okay, I'm ready." Well, as ready as I'd ever be.

"Wait."

I froze next to the door.

"One last thing. Your magic has changed."

"What? Is it gone?" That didn't sound right; I could still *feel* it in me. The subtle buzz was stronger than ever with him standing so close.

"Not gone; it is growing faster than I thought possible." A hint of smile touched his lips. "I noticed it last night, but I did not think to question it in my exhaustion."

"Okay, that's good. Right?" I'm not sure when I'd jumped on the magic bandwagon, but the idea of losing the magic made my chest ache.

"Yes, very good." The emotionless mask slid back into place; he was going to say something I didn't want to hear. "I need to know; after you were bitten, did you drink any of Will's blood?"

Fear slithered into my stomach and congealed into a cold lump. The importance of his question settled over my shoulders like a heavy blanket.

"It was an accident," I whispered.

The muscles of his jaw tightened, and the small

amount of worry that he quickly hid spoke volumes about the kind of trouble I might be in.

"I suspected as much. The process is much simpler than the change; any blood exchange with the undead can pass on the magic that animates them."

"Am I going to turn into a vampire?"

"I believe it would have happened already, if you were."

I recalled Marissa's words. *You are too young and too weak to sire anyone!*

"Will's magic was too weak to sire anyone."

Farranen got a funny look on his face; I'd probably said too much. I hadn't planned on hiding anything from him, but this wasn't the time to tell him about my encounter with Marissa.

"How do you know that?" His suspicion was nearly tangible, and I wished I'd phrased it differently. Or kept my mouth shut in the first place.

"I'll tell you later?"

The stiff set of his shoulders guaranteed it wouldn't be a conversation I would enjoy.

"Okay, then, I guess we should go. Mustn't keep Gus waiting."

He was staring at me again, but this time he was watching the same way a man stares at an old car, the kind that used to be a classic but needed work. Like he was assessing whether painting over the rust would cut it, or if he'd have to replace the fenders completely.

"The queen must not see your wounds from the vampire. Your familiarity with the other supernaturals in this realm would not endear you to her."

I looked down at the flat red lines peeking past the edges of the bandages on my bare arms and wished I could hide them too. "I might have a knit sweater…" It wouldn't match the dress, but neither did the shoes, so it probably wouldn't matter.

"I have a better idea." He held out his hands, and I didn't have to think twice before giving him mine.

His magic flowed across my palms and up my arms to envelop the wounds like warm sparkling sunshine. My eyelids slid shut, and I couldn't hold back a little sigh of pleasure. His magic hovered briefly, before it shot up past my shoulders and then continued down my back. It was suggestive and intimate, and it made my heart flutter, in a way like I imagined sharing a smile with a secret lover in a crowded room would. I bit back a gasp as the magic traveled lower, and I couldn't be sure, but it felt like it paused at the swell of my behind before traveling down to my toes.

"There." Farranen announced, the husky timber of his voice making me think the sensual vibes I was picking up weren't totally one-sided.

Opening my eyes, I was shocked to see my plain sundress had changed from sage green to a deep forest green. When I moved, bright green tulle flashed beneath the skirt that was now fuller and shorter. The thin spaghetti straps that had done nothing to conceal my bra were gone; the neckline that previously hovered just above my cleavage, now covered my entire neck and half my throat, concealing the bite marks.

"Wow." I fingered the wounds that were no longer visible, my arms were also covered in snug fabric all the way down to my wrists.

"Fae glamour," Farranen explained.

"Neat trick." I smoothed the lines of the dress over my body, admiring how the fabric hugged my curves instead of clinging to them.

"It is more fitting for an audience with the queen."

"It's the same color as your eyes." The dress made me feel beautiful, but not nearly as much as the flames in his eyes did. The intensity was too much; I was going to melt.

I looked away first.

It was a sign of my weakness, but it was either that or burn from the heat.

"We should go," he scraped out on a gravelly pitch.

Yeah, good idea.

Chapter Fifteen

It's a good thing that I hadn't taken the time to do something fancy with my hair.

Traipsing through the woods, wearing heels in the dark; it's like I was just asking for a broken ankle. Actually, for a klutz like me, wearing heels *anywhere* opened up the possibility of bodily harm. I was glad I'd done my hair in a simple French braid while I'd been waiting for the cake to bake. The braid added a touch of elegance, yet it didn't get snagged on stray branches as I fought to stay upright.

Gus led the way, with me in the middle, and Farranen bringing up the rear.

Something glowed in the near darkness ahead of me. If I squinted hard enough, I could just barely see the outline of a sword sheath at Gus's hip. A quick glance back showed me the same light halo where Farranen's sword was tucked away. Maybe fae glamour wasn't as foolproof as I'd been led to believe.

"*Oh*—" My heel sank into a soft spot in the dirt, and I pitched sideways. Farranen's hand gripped my upper arm, preventing me from another fall, and I smiled with gratitude and embarrassment. Instead of releasing me like he had the previous ten times, he pulled me closer, lifting me off my feet.

"Hey!" I exclaimed. His right arm slid behind my knees, supporting me until I was cradled against his chest. The idea of it might have sounded nice, but I knew firsthand that nothing kills a romantic vibe like being carried by a man who suddenly realizes that you're too big to sling around like a doll. All the macho dries up and gets replaced with a heap of holy-shit-this-heifer-weighs-a-freaking-ton.

Only, this time, none of that happened.

"Walking was taking too long. Would you prefer a piggy-back ride?"

"No," I said, but I conceded.

The rest of our journey through the brush passed much quicker now that I wasn't slowing us all down.

Before we'd left my cabin, Farranen had used his glamour to split his simple white shirt down the front so that it gaped open, showing off the shallow dip between his pecs. A delicate gold chain laced back and forth through the fabric, holding the two sides loosely together. Gathered ruffles adorned his neck and wrists, reminding me of something that the duke would wear.

His cloak was longer, billowing around us and brushing the ground as we walked. Intricate gold embroidery swirled around the bottom, edges, and hood. When I looked closer, the pattern of vines and leaves seemed to be slowly moving. A giant green emerald nestled in a bed of gold twigs sat at the hollow of his throat, holding the edges of his cloak together.

When I'd raised an eyebrow in question at the sudden wardrobe change, he'd stiffly told me, "The queen will expect me to wear the traditional guardian's uniform. I find it impractical and only wear it for formal occasions."

"It's more practical that these heels," I pointed out.

"Touché," he acknowledged with a nod.

Farranen returned me to my feet once we reached the clearing with the hawthorn tree. I immediately missed having a tangible connection to his magic. I briefly considered brushing against Gus to see if I'd feel the pull of his magic, but his surly expression made me chicken out.

The men walked toward the spot where I had seen Farranen disappear the last time we were here. Gus gave us a nod over his shoulder before he stepped *into* a flat section on the trunk. His entire body disappeared with his cape fluttering behind, the tree appearing to swallow him whole, in a really creepy magic trick.

"Whoa," I breathed. I had the same sense of awe as watching Farranen's sword disappear, but on a much larger scale.

I moved closer, wanting to touch the tree where Gus had been, but Farranen grabbed my wrists and spun around me to face him.

"Theodora, do you trust me?" He'd dropped the stony expression to reveal compassion and a touch of anxiety.

"Trust is earned," I answered automatically, then offered a small smile to soften my honesty. He'd already earned my trust, and we both knew it.

Ugh. I didn't want to be that girl. You know, the one that would blindly put her faith in others; the girl that was so stereotypically naive that she would willingly serve her heart on a platter for any old Joe.

"I need you to do whatever I say. Augustus is allowing me to escort you while in Fairie, so I will do my best to get you through this unharmed. Do not agree to anything without consulting me."

My mind got a little distracted when he said escort.

I assumed it meant something different in Fairie.

His fingers slid lower until they were laced with mine. "We must go."

I nodded and let him tug me toward the tree. A quick glance showed me his face was an impassive mask again. I realized that he used it like armor.

He lifted a single booted foot and stepped through the gate in one fluid motion. I had a brief moment of panic as he disappeared, and then I was forced to follow or let go of his hand.

A short burst of light made me squint, and I had the sudden sensation of walking through a waterfall. Only, instead of water, a warm magical curtain like honey cascaded down, parting wherever it touched my body. Another step, and we left the magical veil of light behind.

My eyes took a moment to adjust, and Farranen's fingers slipped through mine as I squinted at the unfamiliar surroundings.

We were still standing next to the hawthorn tree in a small clearing, but the forest beyond was nothing like the boreal forest we'd left behind. Tall trees with gracefully twisting limbs bowed overhead, creating a canopy of leaves still at the height of their life cycle. Vibrant and green, they looked like late spring or maybe early summer growth. I was unfamiliar with the species of trees; some had small clusters of flowers in different shades of pink and purple, while others had fist-sized fruit dangling low enough that the aroma of their sweet flesh reached me from across the clearing.

A canopy of stars hung overhead, shining far brighter than anything that existed on Earth, making flashlights or lanterns unnecessary.

I had so many questions. Why was there no moon? Did the queen live in a palace? If so, was it far from here? Would it be okay to take off my strappy heels and go barefoot?

I opened my mouth to ask, but the look Farranen shot me was a clear warning not to.

Gus was already waiting for us on one of the four paths that led into the trees. It was wide enough to walk beside Farranen as Gus led us farther and farther into the forest. This time, I didn't have any problems with my heels sinking into the ground, and I was able to walk smoothly across the thick grass.

Okay, that was a lie. I managed to not fall on my face. It was a win, and I was happy to take it.

The silence of the woods was eerie. Not spooky or creepy, but just kind of subdued, as if all the insects and animals had sensed our arrival and were holding their collective breath. I could feel them watching, even though I couldn't see anyone.

The trees ended at a giant stone arch covered in ivy. There were symbols carved in the rocks, but I couldn't understand them.

Two guards were positioned on either side of the entrance, dressed similarly to Gus. Their soft gray shirts had gold buttons down the front. Polished black boots that rose to just under their knees sat on top of black pants that were snug enough to be called tights. Their cloaks were a prissier version of Farranen's, made from a midnight black fabric that flowed from their shoulders but ended at their elbows. Deep hoods cast shadows that obscured their faces, but I could see enough to know these fae would be able to pass for human.

Their hands moved to the swords strapped to their

belts as we approached, but they made no move to draw them.

Gus strode though the arch without acknowledging the guards. Farranen inclined his head to each of them as we passed, receiving almost imperceptible nods in return.

The grass gave way to a cobblestone path that widened enough to be considered a road. Buildings and then animals behind fences emerged as the trees were spaced farther and farther apart. I recognized cows, chickens, warthogs, and cougars, but others were clearly native to Fairie.

Multiple times, my eyes caught small movements as someone peeked around a building or tree, but when I turned my head to see, they ducked out of sight.

I tried to mimic my escorts and keep my gaze straight ahead, but I wanted to see *everything*. I mean, this was a *whole new realm*, and all I wanted to do was explore every inch of it. To keep myself grounded, I pictured the empty swirling pit of Lebolus's face, until the urge to wander off disappeared.

****

We walked for at least a half hour without anyone stopping us.

I'm pretty sure that, if I got lost and had to find my way out of here, I could follow the trail from my bleeding blisters back to the gate. While I appreciated the beautiful dress Farranen had glamoured for me, the shoes sucked. The tiny little straps that crisscrossed my feet and ankles were pretty to look at, but definitely not made for nature walks.

The castle was more Gothic than fairy tale, not that I knew exactly what a Fairie castle should look like. I had done some research on mid-sixteenth-century European castles for my novels, and they had a lot of similar features.

Built from large gray slate blocks, the four square corner towers swept upward to impossible heights. Tall narrow windows were topped with stained glass that arched gracefully into sharp peaks at the top of each tower. Flying buttresses spread from dizzying heights, while intricate carvings darted around the large supports. The roof was made up of at least a dozen peaks, all culminating at different heights and capped with sharp arched windows, bordered with dark gray marble insets.

From what I could see, there were balconies at four different levels; the largest was about five stories up, spanning two thirds of the way across the castle.

The overall effect was majestic and terrifying.

As we approached, two large wooden doors swung inward. They were each easily twenty feet wide and forty feet high, and I couldn't even begin to guess how much they'd weigh. You could drive three full-sized RVs side by side through those suckers without having to worry about scratching the paint.

Four guards stood abreast, blocking the large hallway as we stepped inside. Three were the same height and stature as Gus, but the fourth was a woman. Her flaming red hair was tucked into a tight bun at the top of her head, and its red was the only real color in the monochrome room.

"Augustus of the Light Court, Gray Knight to the queen, requesting an audience with Her Highness," Gus announced. His voice bounced off the black and gold marble floors, before ricocheting up into the ribbed vaulted ceilings and away.

"On what business?" the tallest of the guards asked. His blond hair and blue eyes stood out in sharp contrast to the scar that ran from his cheekbone to chin, which effectively split his top lip but not the bottom. He was the only guard to spare me a second glance, even though it was more of an appraisal for a possible threat than it was him actually checking me out.

"Confidential investigation. Queen's orders."

"She'll receive you in her private chambers." His quick response made me think he'd been expecting our arrival.

The four guards parted ranks, and Gus swept past them without any further comments. Farranen gave them a brief nod as we followed. My heels sounded as though my feet were jackhammering through concrete as I struggled to keep up with the men's brisk pace.

We passed three staircases that were architectural masterpieces, each covered in thick crimson carpet and as wide as the North Saskatchewan River. I lost count of the turns we took as Gus led us deeper into the castle. Most of the doors we passed were closed, but a few that were ajar were lit by the flicker of firelight. The low murmur of voices inside ceased as the shadowy figures within caught sight of our entourage.

Just when I thought my feet wouldn't carry me another step, we stopped. I'd been subtly sneaking glances at the paintings on the walls, wondering if they'd been painted by a human or fae, so I failed to notice when Gus came to a halt. Farranen grabbed me by the elbow, stopping me with my nose an inch from the gray knight's back.

I wanted to shoot him a grateful look, but he

remained facing forward with that awful blank look on his face that made me anxious.

Gus uttered something I didn't understand, then the stones on the wall next to us swirled and spun until they'd blurred into something that looked liquid. I was staring, but I didn't care. The shimmering motion was hypnotic, like a mirror made of mercury.

Pulling a small knife from his belt, Gus slid the edge along his finger until blood welled and slid down to pool in the palm of his hand. He held it out toward the wall, until it disappeared inside the swirling light.

Magic prickled across my skin, and I tried not to flinch as it probed at me. It was a lot like when you met a new dog and they felt the need to poke their wet nose in every crook of your body. Slightly uncomfortable, but mostly just awkward.

The silver light on the wall faded to something like frosted glass. Movement on the other side hinted that we weren't alone.

So far, Gus had just ignored me, but now he looked back over his shoulder and gave me a look that could best be described as a carefully concealed leer. My stomach did a little flip flop, but I hid it with my disdainful bitch face. Something about this guy just rubbed me the wrong way.

The circle of magic on the wall grew until it was the size of a large door, and Gus strode through with the confidence of someone who'd done it a hundred times. When I hesitated, Farranen rested his hand on my lower back; the slight touch was enough to remind me I wasn't in this alone. Throwing my shoulders back, I stepped into the glassy doorway and hoped I wouldn't find myself in a room full of ankou fae.

Chapter Sixteen

The woman in front of me had to be the fae queen.

Magic coalesced around her like a swarm of flies buzzing around roadkill in the summer.

Striking purple eyes coolly appraised me from a pale, perfectly shaped oval face. Her delicate blonde eyebrows rose to match the inquisitive tilt of her lips. Thick waves of golden hair that gradually faded to sage green hung around her shoulders and down her back.

A midnight-black dress covered her dainty frame from wrist to ankle, the tight bustier displaying the full extent of her cleavage to anyone who cared to look. I'm pretty sure I could see the darker skin of her areola from where I was standing.

I approached the large dressing table where she sat, while the two men flanked me on either side.

Gus and Farranen both dropped to one knee, and a surge of panic hit me since I had no idea what the proper etiquette for a human addressing the queen of the fae was. Should I kneel too? Drop into a curtsy? I'd never done one, so it was highly likely that I would fall on my face…Not exactly the first impression I wanted to make.

I quickly scanned the room, but there was nobody else around to give me any hints.

Thankfully, I was saved from any further indecision when the queen leveled an imperial look at my escorts and told them, "Rise."

Her eyes raked over me skeptically. "This is her?"

"Yes, Your Highness," Gus answered.

Feeling like a bug under a microscope, I tried not to fidget. The magic in my body was like a second heartbeat, sending little shocks of static electricity crackling through my veins. My hands itched to reach for Farranen, knowing any contact with him always helped calm the magic, but everything in his frigid expression and stiff body language told me that would be a bad idea.

"Come here, little one." The queen held out a hand, and I realized she was talking to me.

Oh shit.

I really didn't want to get any closer, but I didn't want to look like a petulant child by refusing either. I took the few steps across the crimson runner, and then I put my hand in her waiting palm with all the carefulness of someone handling a live virus.

She inhaled sharply as soon as her smaller hand took possession of mine. It felt a little like sticking your finger in a light socket—warm and buzzy and *so* strong. Her magic was like Farranen's: a current that was luminous and alive. I wanted to immerse myself completely, do a big ol' cannonball into the deep end and never come up for air.

"Oh my." Her body gave a little shudder before she released me, and I immediately stumbled backward until I was standing between the two men again.

"Who are you?" she demanded softly. Her slight astonishment was gone, but I could easily recognize the cold calculating smile she was giving me for what it was; she was deciding how best to use me. Knowing she was searching for any weakness on my part, I kept my shoulders back and my gaze level. And yeah, I sucked in my belly, but I'd been doing that since I'd been forced to put on the dress.

"Theodora Edwards." I was insanely proud that my voice didn't shake.

"Theodora Edwards...*What* are you?"

"Human." I had to force myself to say it with confidence.

"True...But that is not all." She sent Gus a pointed look and flicked her fingers in my direction. "Augustus?"

The giant fae grabbed me by my elbow, and his magic zinged across my skin with all the grace of a landslide. It plowed across my senses until I could taste the cedar and metal that he smelled of. It was potent but held none of the sensual vibes that I'd felt from Farranen or the queen. Thank God.

"Hey!" I shouted. Gus released my arm just as I moved to yank it from him, sending me tumbling backward into Farranen. My entire body felt overly sensitive, and the familiar strength of my guardian's arms was a balm on my frayed nerves.

"She has magic..." Shock replaced Gus's formal tone, and I wanted to shudder as he raked his eyes over me as if seeing me for the first time.

"Yes?" the queen drawled, obviously wanting to hear more.

"It's fae, but there's something else there too." Looking confused by his own words, he reached for me again, and I tried to shrink back out of his reach.

"Enough," Farranen told Gus. The thrum of tension radiated from where he touched me, and I was grateful he hadn't pushed me away. "You'll only succeed in frightening her more."

"Tell me, Guardian, how you came to be in possession of a human with fae magic?" The queen's words interrupted Gus from making another grab for me.

"One of the dark fae passed through my gate unsanctioned," Farranen explained. "Before I could capture him, he attacked Theodora. As her injuries were a direct result of my negligent actions, I swore unto her an oath of protection. She is now under my guardianship."

The queen tapped a delicate finger on her thigh as she studied Farranen, like she was looking for flaws in his story. "She is human, yet she has magic."

"Yes, I believe she has begun the change."

The queen sat up straighter, and her eyes narrowed in disbelief. "Impossible. There hasn't been a changeling in centuries." She stood, revealing that she was shorter than I was. If I took off my heels, we'd probably be the same height. "There are none left with the power to sire. Who did this?"

"Lebolus."

"Bring him to me."

"He was lost to psychogenic atrophy. I was unable to return him to Fairie in his state without endangering more humans."

Something akin to grief crossed her face but disappeared with a blink. "Another of us lost." She seemed to be talking to herself.

We waited while she paced back and forth, her dainty slippers filling the silence as they whispered across the carpet. When she finally came to a halt, her shark-like gaze landed on me, and I probably wasn't going to like what she had to say.

"The loss of Lebolus is unfortunate; however, it appears he has left us a gift in his stead. Augustus, gather three of your strongest men. You shall attend her until we know if the transition is successful."

Oh, heck no. I wasn't going anywhere with Gus. The smirk on his face made me want to throw up. I opened my mouth to protest, but Farranen spoke first.

"I am oath-bound as her guardian and will not leave her unprotected until I am released from her service."

I turned around and met his level gaze when he formally asked, "Theodora, do you release me from the life debt I have sworn unto you?"

"I…" I searched his remote expression, hoping for a clue how to answer, but I came up empty-handed. Before we'd come through the gate, he'd told me to do exactly as he said. But this wasn't an order to follow, he was expecting an answer.

The fae were skilled at twisting words until I didn't actually know what they were talking about anymore. I tried to replay the exact wording he'd used, and my best interpretation was that he was asking if I wanted to be handed over to Gus or stay with him.

Not a hard choice to make. Just the thought of having to touch the douche behind me made me uncomfortable. The thought of not seeing Farranen again…That made me more than uncomfortable.

"I do not." I tried to mime his serenity while my insides were vibrating with anxiety. I caught a brief flash of approval in his eyes before he turned back to the queen.

"Very well, Guardian. You may attend the human. Take any three of my court to assist you. Choose carefully; if there is even a small chance that she may turn, you'll need those with the strongest magic."

"Of course, my queen." Farranen inclined his head respectfully.

"She is our first hope for new blood in ages! You cannot expect a guardian of the gate to attend her—" Gus spit out the words bitterly, and I involuntarily took a step back. The dude was pissed.

"Do you question my decision?" The queen's voice was deceptively sweet.

"No, my liege—"

"Do not forget your position and power were bestowed by me, Gray Knight, and I can just as easily take them away." Her eerie eyes glowed a brighter shade of purple. "The guardian's power has surpassed even yours, though he fails to flaunt it."

Gus bowed, nearly bending in half as he addressed her. "My apologies, Your Highness."

She waved a hand negligently, and the swirling power in her eyes faded away. "Accepted." She primly took a seat on her dressing chair and pinned Farranen in place with a piercing look. I had a good forty pounds on her, but damn, the tiny bitch was scary.

"You will keep me updated on your progress. If she truly has the potential to become a changeling, you will do everything in your power to see her through the transition. This precedes your duties as guardian of the gate. You may close the gate when you are otherwise engaged for long periods of time attending her."

Farranen gave a slight bow in acknowledgement, and a small wave of his magic flickered against my awareness when his cloak brushed my leg.

I felt like I'd dodged a bullet until Gus opened his big mouth. "I formally petition to assist the guardian."

"No." Farranen shot the knight a look that men only get when they don't want to share their toys. "I will choose fae with the strongest magic, but only those that Theodora is accepting of. Humans are notoriously chaste, and any sexual disharmony will jeopardize the possibility of her magic taking hold."

Wait, what is he talking about? Sexual disharmony? I knew I was blushing but couldn't stop. He couldn't possibly be talking about picking out sex partners on my behalf, right? Because, that wasn't going to happen. I opened my mouth to tell him exactly what my thoughts on the subject were, but he shot me one of the same looks he'd given me when we'd stood next to the hawthorn tree.

He'd asked if I trusted him.

Now, he was asking me to trust him again.

I shut my mouth but started a mental list of all the adjectives I was going to use when I told him he was an ass. Then we were going to have a nice long, probably awkward conversation so he could outline exactly what his attending my change entailed, down to the last tiny detail.

"Any three of your choosing will be sufficient." She turned to Gus. "Your petition is denied."

She rose abruptly, and I caught a flash of skin before her dress settled into place. Looking closer, I realized her bodice was made of thin layers of lace, all combining to give the illusion of a solid black fabric. The slight hints of her lean body were effectively more erotic than if she'd been naked.

"Farranen of the Light Court, you have served me and my court with honor and diligence, and in recompense for your service, I charge you with this human's transition. I don't have to tell you how significant it would be to our people to have the power to make changelings again. You will share her bed and give her your seed for thirty nights. If you are unable to make her with child, I will transfer the task to others who have already proven virile by fathering young."

Her words were followed by a harsh snap of magic that settled into my bones. It wove its way around me, and the answering tug from Farranen's direction was immediate. My stomach dropped, landing somewhere in the vicinity of my knees, and I struggled to comprehend what had just happened. Did the queen just order Farranen to have *sex* with me? That wasn't possible, right? She couldn't just tell someone to do that, could she? I was human; I didn't have to obey her.

"Thirty nights is hardly long enough; the change may not come upon her for several more days. Her body is still recovering from the initial attack, and she may not be fertile for days or even weeks after the transition is complete."

"True..." The queen eyed my chest, and my traitorous nipples respond immediately. Her eyes slid lower behind her thick lashes as the weight of them traveled over my belly and hips. My face heated even further when she stopped at the apex of my thighs. Moisture pooled, making my panties damp. The sensual vibes she was putting off threatened to smother me.

"Sixty nights should be more than enough. She is lush; the perfect vessel to give new life to my court."

Her casual talk of impregnating me with a fae baby

was like an arctic wind that immediately chased away any desire I'd been swamped with. She couldn't have known, but her remarks had hit a sore spot. I had no uterus. No hope of being a mother. The emergency hysterectomy had saved my life, but it killed any chance of me carrying a child.

I should tell her, but then she'd have known that I was useless to her even if I did survive the change. There would be no advantage in keeping me alive, so I kept my infertility to myself.

"My queen." Farranen gave a low bow before grabbing my elbow and propelling me toward the door.

****

As soon as we stepped through the gate on the Earth side, Farranen led me to the tree root shaped like a bench. It wouldn't be long until morning, but my dress wasn't equipped for the chilly night air. The temperature was just above the freezing mark; I could see little patches of fog through the trees.

"Sit," he ordered. I sat but only because my feet were begging to take off the tiny torture devices cleverly disguised as shoes. He knelt and carefully unwound the narrow straps from around my swollen ankles.

"Can't you just unglamour them?"

"I must remove them first, or it may cause more damage."

The impartial façade he'd held all night finally fell away, but the expression he wore now scared me even more. His anger I could deal with, but the way his lips tilted down and the tightness around his eyes betrayed the worry he tried to hide.

I let my body droop forward, like I was exhausted

as I leaned closer to my guardian. "Can they still hear us?" I whispered.

"No. The gate is shut, and there are no fae nearby."

He successfully removed one of the shoes, and I hid a wince at the red welts circling my foot.

I thought about what the queen had said. I was trying not to jump to conclusions; maybe I had misinterpreted what I'd heard.

"How come it sounded like everyone was talking in English? I thought you said that you use glamour for everyone on this side to understand you."

"I added a translation glamour when I did your dress."

"Oh. Thanks."

The second shoe came off, and he handed me the pair before scooping me into his arms.

"I can walk," I protested.

"You should have told me that the shoes caused you pain."

I snorted; he must not be familiar with ladies' footwear. "Most women's shoes are painful."

"Then why do you wear them?" He sounded genuinely perplexed.

"They look pretty."

He made a disgusted sound. I wanted to point out that he'd been the one to choose the two-inch pointy-heeled nightmares, but I didn't think it was worth arguing over.

"I can walk." I said it again half-heartedly; my body was relaxing against the heat of his, and I was content to let him carry me.

"Fae are far stronger than humans; it is no burden to carry you."

"Oh." My conscience eased a bit, knowing that he wasn't going to need a chiropractor after hauling my heavy ass around.

"It is…enjoyable having you in my arms." His admission gave me a warm fuzzy feeling, even though he sounded like he'd rather be having a root canal that talking about his emotions.

As much as I wanted to snuggle into his embrace, my mind kept going back to what the queen had said. I needed to tell Farranen about my hysterectomy, I just wasn't sure how to bring it up.

"Interesting attire for an early morning stroll." Ozzy's distinct baritone voice cut through the companionable silence that had been slowly building. He rolled the last syllable out so it came out sounding like *st-rrrrrrollll*, turning the innocent word into something mildly indecent.

Farranen came to sudden stop and lowered me back onto my feet. He didn't draw his sword, but I got the feeling he wanted to. His right hand hovered at waist height, while his left was wrapped firmly around me. And I wasn't complaining, seeing as I wasn't sure whether Ozzy was here for a checking-up-on-Theo visit, or a hauling-Theo-away-in-handcuffs visit.

"What do you want?" I demanded. Yeah, it was easy to fake bravado with my hands clinging to Farranen's cloak.

Ozzy took a step closer and inhaled deeply. "I can smell her from here. Vamps fall under PIMP jurisdiction." His smile was predatory. "She's my concern now."

"I am *not* a *vampire!*" I exclaimed, sounding completely offended.

199

Farranen's fingers tightened around my waist almost painfully, but I didn't mind a bit. "She's under a direct charge by the queen. Royal fae ruling trumps any primitive legislation by your agency."

"All vampires are—"

"Theodora is under my guardianship; any and all of her involvement with the fae is strictly confidential. The agency may address any concerns it has with me."

"Bullshit." Ozzy planted one hand on his hip, while the other slid through his hair in frustration.

"On my word, you have my oath," Farranen said. A little snap of magic accompanied his fancy words, and Ozzy must have felt it too, because every muscle in his body tightened, sending off waves of aggression that made me cling tighter to the fae next to me.

The two men stared at each other longer than I thought necessary, but I was too chicken to break up their little pissing contest.

Ozzy was the first to look away. "Fine, but this is on you, fairy. If she does anything—"

"Understood." Farranen swept me back into his arms, effectively dismissing the pissed vampire. I wrapped my shaking arms around Farranen's neck and pressed my chin into his shoulder so I could watch the path behind us. I wanted to be sure Ozzy didn't follow us back to my cabin.

Chapter Seventeen

The sun was just rising when we got back to my place.

Farranen carried me straight into the bathroom and insisted that I wash and bandage my feet. After changing into some comfy yoga pants and a tank top, I shuffled out of my bedroom in search of something to satisfy my hunger.

Two plates loaded with sandwiches and sliced fruit were waiting on the table.

"I thought you might be hungry."

I jumped at the sound of his voice. I'd assumed he'd left for the day.

"Ah, thank you." He pulled my chair out and waited until I'd taken a seat before sliding into his own.

"Here, this should help keep you warm." He handed me a pair of socks, the kind that had a red stripe around the top and made me think of sock monkeys. They were too big for my feet, which was perfect, because they didn't rub my blisters like my own socks would have.

"Where did you get these?" I asked as I gently rolled them up.

"I ran back to my place for a quick shower and grabbed them."

The fact that his hair was damp, and his formal clothes were gone had escaped me until now. The plain white T-shirt and low-slung jeans he wore were startlingly modern on his body. *Wow,* I thought. He could have just stepped out of the cover of a men's health magazine.

"You weren't gone very long," I said, just so I didn't say what I was really thinking.

"It is convenient to maintain a dwelling on this side of the gate."

That made sense, since he wouldn't want to be wandering around the woods all day. "Is it close by?"

"Yes. Two houses to the south."

His easy admission surprised me, and I choked on my sandwich.

"What do you mean? Two houses to the south of where?" I demanded once I was able to breathe again.

"Here." He took another bite before clarifying, "Cabin number three."

"Wait—we're neighbors?" I put down my sandwich, unable to focus on the crispy bacon, lettuce, and tomato layered thickly on perfectly toasted bread. "For how long?"

"I purchased the cabin when it was built in 1960."

"But I've never seen you before the whole, you know, attack in the woods."

"The fae must remain unnoticed in this world; I use glamour when I am around humans."

It was odd to think that I'd been exploring the woods for the last year and hadn't seen him. But he'd probably seen me. Like a freaking stalker. I hadn't even known he was there.

My anger at the queen's highhandedness returned. Combined with the humiliation of hearing Farranen talk about me like a breeding mare, my emotions coalesced into a giant seething ball of bitchiness.

"I know you must have concerns about our audience with the queen." Apparently, he wasn't as completely heedless of a scorned woman as most men were. I most *definitely* had concerns.

"I had to make certain concessions so that I could maintain my guardianship over you," he explained.

"*Concessions?* Is that what it's called when you agree to be someone's baby daddy?"

"Would you rather I left you in Augustus's care? Or perhaps one of the dark fae? Their sexual proclivities are far more extreme than any human."

I wanted to spent the next few minutes contemplating exactly how extreme Farranen's sexual proclivities were, but I quickly shut down that line of thinking and focused on my anger instead.

"I'm not having sex with someone just because the queen of the fae tells me to!"

A stony expression settled on his face, and I wondered what emotion he was hiding from me. I didn't like that he remained aloof in a conversation in which I was so emotionally invested.

"There is a way out of this that does not require you to have intercourse with me." His words were flat, but the magic leaking from him felt despondent. Was it because the queen was using him as a stud to make babies? Nobody had asked his opinion on becoming a father. The fae seemed to regard procreation as a wondrous gift, so I'd assumed he would be excited at the prospect of playing a part. Maybe Farranen wasn't interested in being shackled by family life; there were plenty of human men that weren't.

Or was it possible my venomous rejection had hurt

him?

It hadn't occurred to me that he'd actually *want* to have sex with me. I mean, sure, I'd definitely been fantasizing about it, but realistically it wasn't likely to happen. He was on the same level as a Greek god, while I was…Well, I was *me*.

Short and chubby, too plain to ever be considered beautiful, with none of the hair and wardrobe know-how that other women used to transform themselves into something desirable. I wasn't terrible, but I wasn't anything special either. Men like him didn't typically settle for women like me.

Tall and slim with perky boobs was what men wanted. I didn't own sexy lingerie or evening gowns; hell, I practically lived in yoga pants and sweatshirts.

Like I said, we weren't on the same level. Not even on the same playing field, really.

Farranen stood, interrupting my melancholy thoughts to take his empty plate into the kitchen.

"Finish eating; you'll need your sleep." If he was trying to sound ominous, he'd missed the mark by a country mile. To my ears, it sounded more like an unspoken promise of good things to come. Physical things.

Good Lord, why didn't my libido have an off switch?

"So, we don't have to, you know…" I gestured vaguely in the direction of my bedroom.

"No, you can sleep easy knowing I have no plans to seduce you…" He paused, and I heard the unspoken *yet* as he stalked closer to where I hovered next to the table. "My orders are in regards to the next sixty *nights*. Seeing as it is now eight o'clock in the *morning*, we are free to do as we like."

"Oh." That was a handy loophole. If Fairie had lawyers; he would have made a good one.

He took another step closer, putting himself closer into my personal space, and the cold expression on his face cracked to reveal a simmering heat. "However, as I am oath-bound into your service, it is entirely your right to request my assistance with anything you desire. *Anything.*" He slowly reached out and caressed my hips, tugging me closer until there was less than an inch of space separating us. The intense way that he stared at my lips was making me think that *anything* didn't refer to taking out the garbage or sweeping the floors.

I had a moment of doubt that I was possibly misreading the situation, and then his fingers tightened, gently pulling until the distance between us disappeared. He lowered his head until his lips were level with the curve of my ear and whispered, "You truly have no idea the effect you have on me."

The reverential way in which he spoke revealed that I wasn't imagining the chemistry between us, but it was the hard ridge of his arousal pressed against my belly that completely convinced me.

A needy sound escaped my throat, and I pressed myself harder against the evidence that said he desired me in a way that I hadn't been wanted in a very long time. My hands clutched at the front of his shirt; his heart was racing as fast as my own.

"Can we—"

"Yes." He silenced me with a chaste kiss, barely pressing his lips to mine before pulling away. His thumb brushed across my lower lip, and the emotions shining in his eyes ranged from endearment to fragile hope.

Did he really doubt that I wanted him?

Any woman would be crazy not to.

I let my hands wander until the soft hair at the nape of his neck filled both my palms. Being this close, the laundry soap on his clothes teased my nose, but it couldn't hide the comforting scent that he naturally exuded. Fresh clean pine and a hint of cinnamon. I raised myself onto my toes, hoping he'd meet me halfway.

He crushed his lips against mine in a bruising kiss. The sudden softness of my breasts rubbing against his hard chest made me sigh, and he swiftly took advantage of the opportunity to slide his tongue past my lips. Holy hell, the man could kiss. I clutched his neck tighter, wanting to get closer, but I was already stretched as high as my short legs would go with the blisters on my feet protesting fiercely.

As if he could read my mind, Farranen palmed my butt and dragged me upward, tortuously slow, so that every inch of his erection ground against me as he lifted me higher. The kitchen table pressed against the backs of my knees, and my weight settled onto its scarred top. My legs parted instinctively to cradle his lean hips, and then the wonderful friction of denim over hard flesh nestled against my lady parts.

I moaned, and he rocked against me in response. My fingers dug into his shoulders, urging him on when he ground himself against me harder. Thank God I'd put on a pair of thin yoga pants; every stitch in the fabric of his jeans, every tooth on the strained zipper as his cock tried to break free, stood out in glorious detail. My whole body trembled, and my panties grew damp from the sensations threatening to take over.

"Let go," Farranen whispered against my jaw while his hips continued to rock against me. "Let go, and I'll catch you."

His words relaxed the last bit of tension I'd been holding onto, and I shifted my hips higher. The familiar magic that wound between us intensified into an intimate caress that only heightened my awareness of where our bodies touched.

Oh, there. God, yes—there!

My back arched, and I screamed as every muscle in my body tightened painfully. The orgasm washed over me in a sudden hot wave, and I clung to my guardian as I rode out the intense sensations that left me shaking and covered in a thin layer of sweat.

Cognitive thoughts slowly returned as the last lingering spasms of my release faded. I opened my eyes and found Farranen staring down at me with such affection that I stopped breathing for a few seconds. Had anyone ever looked at me like that before? No, definitely not.

His smile faded a little, and he ran his thumb across my cheek. "Why do you cry?"

I didn't want to tell him that he'd made me feel more loved in a week than my husband had in almost a decade. His look of adoration would probably dry up as soon as I told him about my infertility.

"Just tired." I gave him a half smile and hoped he'd leave it at that.

"Of course. We both need rest." I hoped that wasn't a code word for sex. While I had enjoyed the incredible orgasm, I wasn't someone who could sleep with a man without becoming emotionally involved.

Farranen must have sensed my apprehension as I got into bed, because he left his jeans on before climbing in next to me. The light kiss he pressed to my forehead was G-rated, and the tension in my body melted away as he held me against his chest.

We both politely ignored his giant hard-on trapped between us.

****

I think we can all agree that I'm not a morning person—or an early-afternoon person as the case was today. Dog appeared to be the only one who didn't get the memo.

"How did you get in here?"

He gave me a friendly tail wag from where he sat on the end of my bed, not bothered at all by my testy tone. I rolled over and buried my face in my pillow so I wouldn't say something rude. My pillow smelled like spicy pine trees, and a little bit of my grouchiness melted away. I could easily have stayed there, cocooned in my warm blankets and Farranen's scent for another hour, but my stomach reminded me that it was being neglected.

Dog watched as I gingerly walked to the kitchen and started a pot of coffee. He gave me a sympathetic whine, and I told him, "You're lucky dogs don't have to wear heels."

I sat down at the table and fired up my laptop. It was positioned at the opposite end of the table from where Farranen and I had—yeah, never mind. I wasn't ready to pursue that particular thought until I had a respectable amount of caffeine in my body.

After putting a pot of water on to boil to make some hard-boiled eggs for an early-afternoon breakfast,

I filled a mug with coffee and carefully carried it to the table. I added sugar and vanilla until the mug was filled to the brim, and then I carefully slurped some of the hot liquid perfection.

All of my remaining bad attitude faded away as I immersed myself in the tale of the duke and Priscilla. The duke had just issued a challenge to another man who, due to his own desire to wed Priscilla, was caught spreading false rumors about the feisty beauty.

Breakfast had come and gone by the time the scrape of the back door opening dragged me from my fantasy world.

Farranen came in, bringing with him a draft of air that hinted at autumn's impending arrival, and the first thing I was aware of was his cold, impersonal expression that was firmly back in place. The second thing that caught my attention was the traditional fae clothing he wore. My hormones immediately mourned the loss of the faded jeans that had clung to his backside like a lover. Knowing that something was amiss, I eased myself to my feet.

"Theodora." His tone was uncomfortably formal. "I bring forth an official appeal for your audience with esteemed members of the queen's court."

"What? Do we have to go to Fairie again?"

"No. The queen has opened the gate to males of both courts, so that they may be close at hand during your transition."

"Why?" Judging from his dour expression, I was missing something important.

"Her Highness wishes to increase your chances of a successful change by allowing any eligible males the opportunity to pursue you."

"What do you mean *eligible* males?"

"Any male with the ability to procreate."

"I thought that none of you could *procreate* anymore."

"The queen has deemed all males with the physical ability to possess a female, in the manner needed to beget a child, as eligible."

"Great. So anyone with a penis? And she expects me to date them?" My voice rose in outrage. Dog whined and crawled farther under the kitchen table. "Wait...We *are* talking about dating, right? Because I *know* you're not talking about a booty call—"

"No!" Farranen held out his hands in supplication as he hurriedly clarified, "They wish to court you. You may reject their official requests for audience—"

"Fine. Hard pass on the audience thing."

"Theodora..." His voice softened around my name, making me lose a little of the outrage that I was holding. "While I have no desire to allow another fae near you, humoring the queen's wishes will keep her content, giving me more time to find a way to free you from the fae realm and from under her rule."

"Fine. Polite pass?" I huffed.

He shook his head wistfully, and I hung mine in defeat.

"When do I have to do this?"

"The T'Holly brothers wait at your leisure."

"They're *here?*"

"Yes. Shall I show them in?"

I looked down at my ugly gray sweatshirt with a cartoon squirrel hugging a book and the words I LOVE BOOKS. "Can I change first?" Not that anything I owned was much better, but at least then I could have found something I hadn't slept in.

Farranen considered my frumpy attire, and I heard a smile thread its way through his words. "What you wear will matter not."

Before I could figure out if that was meant to be a compliment or not, he'd opened the back door and let two men into my cabin. They were both shorter than my guardian, but still much taller than I was. Their matching navy cloaks were long and formal, probably chosen to perfectly contrast the chestnut brown of their hair. Lacy silver leaves were embroidered around the collars, and small ruby-colored jewels were clustered like berries between them.

"May I present Daphorus and Elvinian of the Light Court. Sons of T'Holly of the Light Court." Farranen introduced them with all the flair of a bored waitress. All he needed was a hairnet and a notepad for taking orders.

The brothers bowed in perfect synch, their long cloaks brushing across their over-polished boots. Identical sapphire blue eyes studied me with ill-concealed eagerness. Was I supposed to bow in return? I needed to take a fae etiquette class. Thankfully, they both rose before I could ask.

"My lady, it is an honor." The brother with the slightly crooked nose, Daph, addressed me with a smile. "We are humbled by your consideration."

While Daph continued to prattle on, I glanced to where Farranen stood, off to the side with his back straight and his arms folded across his chest. His face was composed into an expression of feigned boredom, but there was a tic in the muscle of his clenched jaw. A small chink in his emotional armor that would have been easy to miss if I hadn't been looking. I caught his eye and shot him a how-much-longer-do-I-have-to-put-up-with-these-fools-in-my-kitchen? look.

The corner of his mouth tilted up in a brief smile, and I hoped he wouldn't let me suffer much longer before sending the T'Holly brothers away.

"...is of considerable wealth. Our branch is the eighth wealthiest in Fairie, and our lineage can be traced back seven generations. The T'Holly bloodlines are extremely strong, as you can see; our father was able to produce two male sons, as was my grandfather, and great-grandfather before him."

I nodded, feeling like the brothers were exhibit guides, taking me on a dull museum tour. My attention, which had wandered, was brought back to the men in front of me as they both suddenly unclasped their cloaks with a flourish and dropped them to the floor. I made a very unladylike noise as their bare chests were revealed.

Elvie picked up the conversation, smoothly continuing on from where Daph had left off. It made the whole thing sound rehearsed, like it was a business presentation.

"...well skilled in satisfying many females, although we've never had the opportunity to bed a human woman." His nimble fingers slid into the drawstring waistband of his pants. His pants looked like expensive silk, and they slid down to his ankles without a sound.

"Hey!" I averted my gaze to the side, only to find the second brother as naked as the first. "Oh my God!" *What the hell!* A furious blush heated my cheeks, and my temper climbed to epic heights. I didn't like strangers in my personal space, *especially* strangers with their ding-dongs hanging out.

I slapped a hand over my eyes, but not soon enough to avoid having an image of Daph's fully erect cock seared into my brain. It thrust proudly from a dark thatch of curls, its smooth head and shaft blushing as fiercely as my face.

"We'd be happy to demonstrate our virility—"

"Pants!" I gestured wildly at the fabric pooled at their feet. "Now!" I peeked through my fingers and immediately regretted it. Despite all of his posturing about satisfying women and his strong vigor in bed, Elvie's member stood at half-mast. It's a good thing I had no intention of taking him up on his offer, because it didn't look like his manhood would have been up for it. Ha—pun intended.

His half-inflated weenie was something I could have gratefully gone a lifetime without seeing.

"My lady, if you'll just give us a chance—"

"*Pants!*" I shrieked, unable to look away, as Elvie urgently tugged at his mostly soft penis.

Dog whined from under the table; apparently, he didn't appreciate the lewd display of male anatomy either.

"Look, brother, I've not seen one of his kind before."

Daph's condescension toward my dog only lowered my opinion of him further. Dog might be scruffy and a little rough around the edges, but he had better manners than either of these two pompous fae.

"Gentlemen, the lady tires of your games. Theodora has humored your attempts to woo her and kindly rebuffs your attentions." Farranen's voice was a welcome distraction.

"Wait! My brother's greatness truly lies in his stamina; if the lady were to spend but a minute, I'm sure he would rouse to his full potential. This infirmity is most unlike him—"

"Not happening." Aversion dripped from my words like acid, but no one paid me any attention. Farranen and Daph were locked in a staring contest, while Elvie tried unsuccessfully to coax an erection from his sleeping cock. I actually felt sorry for the guy; the pressure from his brother was obviously making the situation worse. He continued to jerk with one hand, while the other cupped his balls and squeezed with a desperation that looked painful.

"Please, the stress of being in a new realm has cast Elvinian in a poor light. His sexual appetites usually exceed my own; I am sure—"

"The lady bids you good day, gentlemen. You are dismissed." The edge in Farranen's voice hinted that he was one step away from throwing their naked asses out the door.

"Perhaps I could offer myself unaccompanied, until my brother is able to join us?" The last thing I saw, before I turned and ran for my bedroom, was Daph's elegant hand as it reached down and grasped the base of his cock, offering it as if it were a bouquet of flowers.

I really didn't care for flowers.

Chapter Eighteen

Rage and humiliation bubbled up in my chest, until they coalesced into tears. I was furious that I'd been forced to hide in my own house. *My* house. I considered grabbing the shotgun from its hidey-hole and physically enforcing my right to privacy, but I didn't want to risk getting another eyeful of the naked T'Holly brothers.

Someone knocked on the door, and I stopped pacing back and forth when Farranen let himself in.

"I didn't say you could come in."

"I apologize. May I come in?"

I eyed him suspiciously. His expression was calm, and I couldn't tell if he was being a smartass or serious. I avoided answering his question by asking one of my own. "Are they gone?"

"Yes."

I tried to gather my chaotic thoughts, but after a few moments all I could come up with was, "What the *hell* was *that?* They dropped their drawers in my kitchen! Who *does* that?"

"They were attempting to win your affections. Displaying their ability to sexually please you is no different from offering a gift of monetary value." He shrugged a single shoulder, as if it were no big deal that I'd just had two naked men attempt to seduce me.

"That's…*not* okay!"

"It is the way of the fae."

"How could you just let them waltz in here and treat me like some kind of floozy?" Another hot tear ran down my cheek, and I angrily swept it away.

Farranen's face darkened, and he stalked toward me. "Do you think it is easy for me to stand idly by while others of my kind conspire to win your heart?" His hands were tender where he gripped my shoulders, not matching the fury of his words.

"I don't know," I answered honestly.

"I'd rather face a flock of greckle demons unarmed than watch as another spoiled male from an elite bloodline seeks to possess you. And make no mistake, to most of them, you are just something to possess. After hundreds of years, the sudden appearance of a female in the middle of the change is a novelty they cannot resist. To make you with child would be an even greater prize for them."

It was no secret that my new popularity had nothing to do with me personally, but hearing Farranen throw it out there like that hurt me more than I was prepared for. More angry tears slipped out, and I wrenched myself free from his gentle grip.

"So, what? Should I invest in a revolving door to accommodate everyone that will be stopping by to flash me their junk?"

"I am sorry I have put you in this situation."

Sorry couldn't erase the indignity of being talked at as if I were a street whore.

"How much longer?" I asked. My anger was fading, leaving me weary.

"They will continue to vie for your affections, until you choose one or more."

"Yeah, I figured that. I meant, how much longer

until we know if I'm going to change or stay human?" Dying was a possibility too, but I didn't like saying that out loud.

"Each transition is unique to the human. Lebolus's strength played a part in how deep he was able to sow the seeds of his magic and how fast they took root. The more potent the magic of those who attend you, the faster your own magic should grow. It will also depend on your own strength; the harder your body fights the magic, the longer it takes."

I had no control over any of those things, and it ticked me off that I had no say in the matter. "This is bullshit."

"Agreed."

Did he have to be so damn agreeable? It would be easier if I had someone to blame for this whole mess, but logically, I knew it wasn't Farranen's fault.

"There are ways to dissuade them from calling."

"Really? How?" And why was he just telling me this now?

His tone was carefully neutral as he explained, "Should your magic fade, they'll lose interest once your permanent humanity is evident. That's one option."

"Okay. That sounds good." Really good, actually, except for the part where Farranen would go back to protecting the gate behind a layer of glamour, and I'd never get to see him again. That part would suck big hairy balls. Maybe the second option would be better.

"What's the second option?"

"Announcing that you've chosen a courtier would deter others."

I paced again, struggling to understand what he was saying.

"So, let me make sure I have this straight. I'm either going to die, fight off the magic and stay human, or turn into a changeling."

"Correct," he answered stiffly.

"Okay, so if I stay human, life will go back to normal, and I'll never have to deal with courting or the fae again. The queen will have no power over me?"

"Yes."

"And if I turn into a changeling, then what? I'll be stuck in this awful cycle of men showing up at my door until I finally choose one of them? And what exactly does courting involve? Is it like dating? And why are they showing up now? Aren't they just wasting their time since we don't even know if I'm going to change?"

"Yes, but they hope to secure the chance to court you, should you change, and their early arrival may help to advance the transition."

I frowned at him in suspicion, knowing he was being too choosy with his words for that to be the whole truth.

"How would they be able to advance the transition?"

"During the final phase of the change, a single male may not be able to meet your demands."

"For magic? Like what I've been stealing from you?"

"What is offered freely cannot—"

"Be stolen. I know." We shared a small smile before he steered the conversation back to more serious matters.

"The final phase of the change requires sexual pleasure to bond the magic to your soul."

"Sex?" I squeaked and had a brief flash back to my fourth-grade sexual education class.

"Yes, one or more will need to attend to you multiple times over a short period." He kept his gaze steadily on the floor, and I was glad that I wasn't the only one finding this awkward.

"That's why they showed up at my door? Hoping to get in on the action?" I could taste the bitterness of the words on my tongue.

"Any intercourse during your transition is believed to strengthen you and prepare you for the final phase, increasing the likeliness of success."

I glared at him while he continued to study the hardwood. "You *knew* this but didn't tell me?"

"I thought it unnecessary to burden you with knowledge of something that may not come to fruition."

"You *ass.*" I stomped out of the room and grabbed my keys from the peg on the wall. "When *were* you planning on telling me? Before or after you let some random male climb into bed with me?"

"Theodora—"

I whirled around so that I could face him. I needed him to see the honesty in my eyes so he'd know I meant every word I said. "I'm going out. Don't be here when I get home. Take your magic, and don't come back." Tears choked my throat, cutting off my tirade before I could truly get started.

"Theodora, don't do this. Without my magic, yours will fade." Farranen's expression was pained, but I forced myself to maintain eye contact.

"Good. I don't want it anymore."

Farranen flinched as if I'd physically slapped him.

Great—now I could add remorse to the party of rioting emotions I was already working to suppress.

Unable to stand seeing the pain in his eyes any longer, I grabbed my muddy sneakers and my wallet, and I marched outside. I held the truck door open long enough to scan the yard for my damn dog, but he was nowhere to be seen. His disappearing act was probably for the best; he deserved better than my foul company right now.

****

Standing in the parking lot of the Shop 'n' Save, I tossed the plastic grocery bags onto the passenger seat in my truck, indifferent to the fact their contents were getting banged around. Broken cookies tasted just as good as whole cookies. And I'd bought a pile of them.

What can I say, I'm an emotional eater. Shopping in such a confused mental state meant a lot of impulse buys. I was next to the open passenger side door, contemplating cracking open the box of cinnamon buns and weighing the likelihood of being able to drive without getting cream cheese frosting on the seats, when someone approached me from behind.

I spun around, ready to face anything from a troop of girl scouts to a pack of hell hounds. My paranoia seemed a bit unnecessary when I saw that it was just one man with a superficial smile.

"Good afternoon." He inclined his head but didn't break eye contact, since he was so much taller than me.

"Afternoon," I replied.

A trickle of uneasiness crawled up my spine when he didn't say anything else. I wondered if Hannibal Lecter had had a grandson, because he'd probably be putting out the same friendly-but-in-a-creepy-serial-killer-sort-of-way vibes. I couldn't point to one specific thing that was alarming; his black dress shirt and slacks were neatly pressed and expensive looking. His cufflinks and matching buttons appeared to be made of a black metal that absorbed the fading sunlight rather than reflecting it.

I would have guessed that he was about my age, mid-thirties at the latest. His sleek black hair hung an inch above his wide shoulders, and it looked as if it had been cut straight across without any thought to style. His nose was aristocratic and added a touch of elegance to an otherwise harsh face. His cheekbones looked sharp enough to cut steel.

"May I assist you with your purchases?" He gestured to my bags waiting in the shopping cart.

"Uh, no thanks," I told him, suddenly aware just how deserted the parking lot was.

"All right…Then I'll be on my way." Despite his words, he continued to linger. I wanted to load the rest of my food in my truck, but I was afraid to take my eyes off him.

A cold gust blew through the lot, funneled by the buildings on both sides, and I shivered. The sudden drop in temperature matched the stranger's blue eyes, and I found myself unable to look away. The pale color of his irises glittered like hard diamonds; if I squinted, I could actually see the tiny little fissures that split the individual facets of his eyes. They were beautiful and deadly, the same way a chocolate truffle laced with cyanide would be.

When I finally blinked and was able to look away, the parking lot was a lot darker than I remembered it being. How long had I been standing there daydreaming about diamonds and poisoned chocolates?

The man was still standing there, closer than before, and I automatically took a step back until my back was pressed against the truck. His left eyebrow was arched in surprise, and his smile no longer seemed as threatening. It looked genuine this time, but I didn't know him well enough to say for sure. Definitely less fake though.

"Merry meet, my dear." He inclined his head once more, then he spun on his heel and walked away. I watched until he turned onto the street and disappeared around the corner.

Okay—that was super weird.

Where had he come from? I recognized the only three cars in the parking lot as belonging to two locals and the grocery store cashier, so he hadn't parked here; he clearly wasn't shopping. All he'd done was offer to help me with my bags, and my overly skeptical brain had spun it into something sinister. I was finally paying the consequences for living like a hermit for so long. From now on, I was going to live with my feet firmly in the land of the living. No more fae magic, no more vampires, and no more imagining danger lurking around every corner. I was going to rebuild my life; it wasn't too late to start over.

I finished unloading the shopping cart and jumped in the driver's seat of my truck.

Getting my social life back on track would be a good first step, and I knew just where to go.

****

Country Customs was closed. Damn it! Stupid small-town business hours.

I didn't realize how much I'd been looking forward

to seeing Katie's friendly face until disappointment settled over me like an itchy wool sweater on a hot day.

I banged on the window, hoping that maybe she was working in the back of the store, but the lights stayed off, and nobody came to the door. Behind the glass, a mannequin without a face watched while I debated my options.

I could try to find Katie's place, but I'd never actually been there, and I didn't have a cell to Google her address. Did they still print the white pages? And where the hell would I find one after hours in downtown Tamarac? I couldn't recall seeing a pay phone, but then again, I'd never needed one.

My other option was to head home to my empty cabin. Maybe I could bribe Dog into binge-watching some TV with me. My fruit cake was still in the fridge, but I could whip up something rich and chocolatey. Maybe brownies. I wondered if Dog had ever tried brownies.

The wind tried to pull my hair from the messy bun I'd tied it in, and I huddled deeper into my sweatshirt for warmth. It was only six thirty, but the sun had already set. The air smelled like rain. I should head home; if it rained, the roads would freeze into solid sheets of ice.

Screw that. I knew Katie lived on the west side of town, and last winter she'd complained about having to park in her driveway because she didn't have a garage. It wouldn't take long to cruise over a few streets and look for her silver sedan. Maybe I'd get lucky.

I smiled, pleased to find myself genuinely eager to spend time with someone else, rather than wanting to just sit at home, alone with a cake. I could see the door to my social life opening up before my eyes, and it was a glorious sight.

Something slammed me into the side of the truck, knocking me off balance and pinning my hands behind my back. I screamed until a hand smashed my head on the driver-side window.

"Who did you tell?" a man's voice hissed against the side of my face.

I struggled against his hold, knowing he was bigger and stronger, but not willing to let him think that I was intimidated. I hurled every four-letter word I could think of, plus some I invented on the spot.

Mentally, I ran through the growing list of men that I'd pissed off enough to attack me. It was longer than I'd like to admit.

I knew it wasn't Ozzy; this guy didn't have the height or broad shoulders that the PIMP agent did. Definitely not Will, since I'd seen him die with my own eyes. Not Farranen either; my body would have recognized his immediately. Maybe one of the T'Holly brothers? Perhaps I'd insulted their honor and they wanted revenge? But no, I didn't feel the familiar buzz of fae magic.

"Get off!" I shouted, just as he released me. I fell backward, and I landed on my butt on the cold curb. Quickly scrambling to my feet, I found my attacker locked in Farranen's hold, with the edge of a dagger pressed to his throat.

"Are you unharmed?" Dark green eyes traveled over every inch of my figure. "My lady?"

"Ah, yeah…All good." I was still out of breath, but aside from the lump on my head, I wasn't injured. Emotionally, I was a hot mess, but I doubted anyone cared about that but me.

So much for a nice, safe, normal life.

Farranen threw my attacker against the hood of my truck and frisked him for weapons. I stepped closer and tried to figure out where I'd seen him before. He continued to glower at me from beneath a tangle of messy brown hair. His black jeans and navy windbreaker were unremarkable, doing nothing to jog my memory.

"Theodora is under my protection; to trespass against her is to trespass against the queen."

The guy growled and tried to break free, but my guardian slammed him back against the truck. When Farranen pulled out a pair of handcuffs and snapped them in place, the man hissed and bared his fangs.

"Whoa! He's a—" I shut my mouth and looked around before whispering, "A *vampire.*"

"Yes, and I am most eager to find out what business a vampire has with you."

Oh, shit. The vampire wasn't the only one in the hot seat. I still hadn't told Farranen about my deal with Marissa. As soon as I thought the words, I realized where I'd seen my mystery attacker before. He was one of the vampires in Marissa's brood.

Chapter Nineteen

The bench seat in my truck wasn't made for traveling long distances with two large men.

I sat behind the wheel, crushed between the door and Farranen's hard body. The vampire was strapped into the passenger seat with his hands behind his back, and he had a look of near hysteria on his face.

High levels of male testosterone, combined with my own anxiety created a heady blend of pheromones that made me lightheaded. It was too cold to crack the window; even with the heater blasting, I was still shivering from being outside without wearing a coat.

I kept my eyes peeled for wildlife, since I still wasn't sure if the deer from a few days ago was real or a spectral product of my supposed grave-reaping magic.

We made the twenty-minute drive in fifteen, which probably accounted for some of the vampire's nervousness.

I filled my arms with as many grocery bags as I could carry, and I trudged up the stairs. The front door opened without a key, but I didn't feel any of the wariness that walking into my dark cabin should inspire. Knowing that Farranen was behind me chased away any lingering fears I had of someone lying in wait to ambush me. Seriously, good luck to them. Random burglar versus the guardian of the gate? Yeah, I know who I'd put my money on.

It took two more trips to gather everything from the bed of my truck. Most of the bags had split open during the drive, and groceries had scattered everywhere. By the time I had put the food away, Farranen had tied the vampire to one of my dining room chairs and was standing over him with a detached expression to hide the fact that he was actually pissed.

"Theodora, would you join us?"

Oh, crap—it looked like hiding in the kitchen was no longer an option.

"Merrick was just telling me an interesting story about how you two met."

Double damn. Judging from the vampire's swollen eye and bleeding lip, he was even less enthusiastic about sharing that particular tale than I was.

My guardian turned his dark gaze to me, and I tried not to squirm under the scrutiny. Did the fae have some sort of mind-reading powers? Why hadn't I thought to ask sooner?

"Okay, so I mentioned that I ran into Will the other night and that he sort of ended up dead. But I may have left out the part where he was part of a brood that wanted to kill me because I knew that Will had been kidnapping women and killing them. So, I agreed not to tell Ozzy about the brood, and they let me go. End of story; we all lived happily ever after." I smiled gingerly, hoping that my rambling story had made sense.

"She lies." Merrick's tone lacked the aggression from before.

"I do not!" I exclaimed.

Farranen looked at me with a raised brow, and I quickly did a mental recap of what I'd told him.

"Just out of curiosity's sake, what part do you think I lied about?" I asked.

"You told the PIMP agency about us."

"I did not!"

"Liar." He spit a mouthful of blood on the floor, and I glared at him. Who did he think would clean that up? I was going to have to find a pair of rubber gloves before I went anywhere near it. I wasn't taking any chances when it came to vampire blood. Farranen smacked the vampire across the back of his head.

"I didn't tell *anyone* about your brood. Not even him." I gestured to the angry fae.

"Then explain how they found our nest, mere hours after we let you go!"

"I have no idea!" I hadn't even told Ozzy about the gas station and bodies until the next night.

"Who found your nest?" Farranen stepped in, sounding like a parent breaking up an argument between siblings.

"The PIMPs." He spoke with such vehemence that I had no doubts he spoke the truth.

"What happened?"

"They came as soon as the sun set. Noah and I were heading out to hunt."

"To hunt...humans?" I interrupted.

"No, squirrels." His tone was sarcastic, making me feel like an idiot for even asking. "Marissa only lets two of us hunt each night. I was getting dressed upstairs, and I heard them break through the doors. They used some of those flash-bang things, and then they were shouting at everyone to get on the floor." He swallowed, making his Adam's apple bob up and down.

"The ceiling in the bathroom was rotting, so I

228

clawed a hole in it until I could climb into the attic. The windows up there aren't boarded, so I smashed one out and ran."

"What happened to everyone else?" I took a seat at the table.

"I went back the next night. All four of my brood-mates were dead. Marissa was gone, but she is still alive; I would have felt it if she'd been sent to her true death."

"Wait, I thought the PIMPs are like supernatural law enforcement? Why would they slaughter everyone?" Maybe I was missing something. Marissa had seemed super concerned about keeping her brood under the radar, so why would the agents kill them on the spot?

Farranen turned toward the back door, and I expected to see someone there, but the door stayed shut.

"I am being summoned to the gate."

Damn, I didn't want him to go. I still hadn't apologized for my part in the argument we'd had. I was still pissed that he had thought I'd be okay with casual sex, but I wasn't ready to cut him out of my life completely.

His eyes were dark with remorse, and I was relieved that he wasn't happy with the way we'd left things either. "I will return as soon as I can."

I nodded and watched him walk away.

"Hey, wait! What about him?" I looked over at the vampire bound to my dining room chair.

"The ropes are enchanted to hold his kind."

I eyed the flimsy rope doubtfully.

"Do you still have the shotgun?"

"Yes."

"Good. It will make you feel safer until I return."
He disappeared out the door before I could object.

"Soooo…" I had no idea if I was expected to play
guard or hostess while Farranen was gone. "Do
vampires eat real food?"

"Yes." He studied me for a few seconds, like he
was faced with a complex puzzle. "Blood sustains our
magic; food sustains our bodies."

"Oh. Do you like cake?" I was famished, but it
would be impolite to stuff my face in front of him
without offering to share.

"Yes, I do." He wiggled his fingers where they
were tied to the arms of the chair. "But unless you plan
to feed me like a child, I don't think I can hold a fork."

He had a point. I hadn't forgotten that he'd
attacked me earlier, so I wasn't about to give him any
pointy objects that he could use as a weapon. It had
been stupid to make the offer.

"Sorry, I didn't think that through."

"It's understandable."

Another awkward pause; it might have been
minutes, or even hours. Merrick was the one to finally
break the silence.

"You're not what I expected."

"What were you expecting?"

He shrugged. "Will made you sound like a demure
little thing, a typical housewife. I had no idea why he
wanted to drag you into our world." He smirked but not
in an unkind way. "I think I get it now. He never
mentioned that you're fierce and resourceful. You went
toe-to-toe with Marissa and didn't back down. You're
bold for a human woman. And pretty, but that's why
Marissa didn't like you to begin with."

"Um, thanks?" What a weird back-handed compliment.

"She doesn't like having other females around. We can hunt them, but we aren't allowed to bring them back to the nest." He looked lost in his own thoughts, so I stayed quiet.

"Did Will tell you about his first death?" Merrick asked.

"First death?"

"When his human life ended."

"No." He'd been too busy shoving me in the trunk of his car, and I'd been a little preoccupied with being kidnapped, so the subject hadn't come up. I'm sure he would have mentioned it if we had a chance to sit down for coffee together.

"Marissa found him in an alley. Shot in the leg and bleeding out. We usually stay away from situations like that because they often attract too much human attention. It's safer to find someone willing to drink from, and then send them on their way." He shifted uncomfortably in the chair. How long it had been since he'd fed? His lean frame and gaunt eyes suggested it had been a while.

"We both knew the wound was fatal. Marissa offered to sire him, and he accepted. His first death came that night. Marissa caught him trying to return to his old life a number of times. He was punished." I didn't want to know what kind of disciplinary measures had been used to keep my husband in line, so I tried to change the subject.

"So you think the PIMPs took her?"

"It had to be them."

"Okay, let's say it was them. Why would they take

her, but kill everyone else?"

"I don't know." His shoulders slumped, the hopeless look on his face tugging at my compassion. I'd worn the same expression myself after Will's disappearance.

"Do you have a cell phone?"

His eyebrows furrowed in confusion. "Yeah, in my back pocket."

"Can I borrow it?"

"Sure."

Giving him a wide berth, I circled his chair and approached from behind. True to his word, the top of a sleek black phone poked out of his jeans. It didn't take much wiggling to free it, and I was relieved to see that the battery was half full and there were two bars of service. Living in the middle of nowhere meant service was intermittent at best. I carried my new treasure into the kitchen and fished around in a drawer until I found Ozzy's business card.

"Who are you calling?" Merrick called out.

"Ozzy. I'm going to see if he knows what happened to your brood—"

A huge crash came from the dining room area, and I nearly dropped the phone in surprise. I couldn't see the table from where I stood, but the scuffling sounds meant the vampire was either loose or would be shortly. I grabbed my sharpest paring knife from the wooden block on the counter. I know, I know, most people would grab the biggest knife, but I wasn't carving a turkey. I needed something that would cause a lot of damage; I didn't have much room to maneuver in the small cabin.

Merrick stalked around the corner with the magical

ropes hanging from his arms and chest. The chair was absent, so I assumed that he'd smashed it into little pieces.

Farranen should be happy to know that, technically, his enchanted ropes had worked since they hadn't been cut and the knots were still tied. I doubted he'd see it as optimistically as I did. He was going to blow a gasket when he found out I'd let Merrick escape.

"Hey, Ozzy! It's Theo, could you come to my cabin? Like, *now?* Great! See you soon!" I chirped the words happily before shoving the phone into my pocket, all the while keeping my knife hidden from the ticked-off vampire. "Ozzy's on his way."

"You're bluffing." He prowled closer, flexing his arms to maximize his reach within the confines of the rope.

"Nope. He'll be here any second now."

He smelled the air, his anger turning to confusion as he zeroed in on where I stood. "You smell like a vampire." His eyes narrowed as he considered me. "But not."

I didn't have anything to say about his bizarre claims, so I stayed silent.

"What *are* you?" He was close enough to reach me now, and the tips of his fangs glinted in the weak lighting when he curled his lip in thought.

"Just Theo," I told him truthfully.

"I'm sorry, Theo, but I must feed so I can find my sire. I'll try not to take too much."

He tried to grab me, moving quicker than I thought possible, but I was anticipating it and slashed at him with my knife.

"Get the hell out of my house," I snarled and made another slashing motion.

Desperation darkened his eyes, and my heartrate responded. This was bad. Really, *really* bad. I hadn't drawn any blood yet, but it was only a matter of time until the knife found its mark.

"I must find her," he offered as explanation, as if that made it perfectly all right to use my carotid artery like a juice box.

"Find someone else to snack on," I told him.

He lunged again, this time managing to seize my wrist holding the knife. He twisted, and I screamed but didn't release it. My knee shot up and connected with his male goods, giving me a brief moment of satisfaction to know he'd probably need an entire excavation team to retrieve his testicles from where I'd lodged them.

Then it was my turn to really scream, one of those furious shrieks that let the entire neighborhood know I was frustrated and scared but wouldn't go down without a fight. Anticipating another knee to his crotch, he used the full weight of his lanky body to keep me pinned against the counter.

His chest was smothering my face, making it hard to breathe. I didn't want to die surrounded by the stink of his plastic windbreaker and unwashed body. My hands were trapped between us, and I grunted with the effort of trying to shove him away.

Something ripped, and all the air rushed out of my lungs.

Merrick cursed and backed away.

"What the—" I forgot what I was saying when I saw the blood on his hands. He looked as shocked as I did, like he had no idea what the sticky red stuff was.

Oh my God, did I stab him? I hadn't meant to. I just wanted him to keep his fangs to himself.

I trembled and fell to my knees on the old linoleum floor next to my abandoned knife. I was so cold. My limbs tingled, and I couldn't feel my body anymore. Everything was numb—except for my hands. Those were still warm because they were covered in blood.

Something slammed into my back door, making Merrick jump. It sounded miles away, but the impact vibrated through the floor.

I held up my hands, hypnotized by the way the glossy red liquid slowly rolled off my fingertips. *Drip...Drip...Drip...*

Another crash resonated, followed by the sound of something splintering.

Irritation broke through the fog my of shock. Couldn't I get through a single night without something in my cabin breaking? I couldn't afford to hire a handyman to help with the constant upkeep, and more repairs were going to eat into my writing time.

Merrick shrieked, sounding like a terrified school girl instead of a fully grown vampire, and bolted toward the front of my house. He was in one hell of a hurry to get to the front door. Or possibly the bathroom, since it was in that direction too. Did vampires need to use the bathroom? I'd have to ask Ozzy once I finally got around to calling him.

The back door burst open, slamming into the counter and eliciting a small gasp from me. I watched as a huge shadow blocked out the starlight before stalking into my kitchen on enormous black paws.

I smiled tiredly when Dog's yellow eyes turned in

my direction.

"Hey. He went that way." I gestured with my chin toward the living room. If the vampire was injured badly enough, maybe Dog could catch him and bring him back.

Farranen was going to be pissed that I let him get away.

Dog turned back to the front of the house and growled. Had he always been so big? It looked like he'd grown overnight and was now the size of a pony. My perspective on size must be off, since I was staring up at him from the floor.

After another growl that was loud enough to hurt my head, Dog padded over and curled up next to me. His fur was gloriously warm, and I gratefully buried my hands in it. I'd have to give him a bath tomorrow to get all the tacky blood off, but right now I didn't care about the prospect of corralling him in a tub of soapy water; I just wanted the comfort of his nearness.

He whined but didn't pull away.

I tried to ask him if he'd ever tried brownies before, but my mouth couldn't form the words.

Something was wrong, *seriously* wrong. Alarm bells rang in my head. I should get up. I tried to get my feet under me, but the floor was slippery with blood.

The lights in the kitchen dimmed, and the room tilted. I gripped Dog harder, grateful he was there so I wasn't alone.

Being alone was way overrated.

Chapter Twenty

A deep rumble surrounded me.

I could feel it in every breath as it slowly worked its way into my bones. It was comfort and devotion and belonging, and it expected nothing from me in return. The sound was more tangible than a hug, but less substantial than the wind.

I sighed and let myself sink deeper into the darkness.

"*Theodora!*"

I ignored the voice that wanted to pull me from the safety of the rumble. I sighed again and burrowed into the warmth as it shifted around me.

"*Stop, you'll kill them both!*"

Something bright flashed in the dark, and I struggled to turn away from it.

"*Theodora!*"

More voices intruded, too low for me to understand. I just wanted to be left alone.

The rumble vibrated through me, telling me I wasn't alone.

"*Let her go.*"

The magic living inside me fluttered, and instinctively recognized the familiar magic of my guardian close by. I reached out, but my hands couldn't find him.

"*Back off, you're only upsetting him more.*"

I wanted his magic. Needed it. It called to me. I tried to shrug off the vestiges of sleep that clung to me, making my body too heavy to move. Sounds of a scuffle broke through the haze, and I finally succeeded in prying my eyelids open.

"Step aside, or on my oath, I'll—" The threat died on Farranen's lips as I looked around.

I had to squint against the glare from harsh fluorescent lights, but I was able to confirm that I was in my kitchen. The odd angle of my cupboards told me that I was on the floor.

The loud rumbling continued, and I was stunned to discover it was coming from Dog. I was draped over his shoulders like a scarf, and he'd curled his lower half around my legs.

"Shhh," I whispered. I wanted to run my fingers through his soft fur to sooth him, but it was stiff and matted.

"Theo, look at me." The near panic in Farranen's voice turned Dog's low rumble into a deeper growl. The hair on the back of Dog's neck stood straight up, and tension coiled through his muscles.

I focused on my fae where he stood next to the broken door. Like a medieval knight without armor, he loomed larger than life with his sword held straight out, pointed at the heart of another man.

I wanted to ask him to shut the door; it was so damn cold in here. My magic stuttered and ebbed. It must not like being so cold either.

"Fare…" Farranen's name faded on my lips, and I didn't mind the way it sounded. I couldn't think of a man fairer of character, so the nickname felt right.

"Tell your friend we mean you no harm." He

lowered his voice to a calming cadence. Knowing he was nearby was comforting, and with the vibrations from Dog's chest, I was slowly being lulled to sleep.

"Theodora!" Farranen called. I wrenched my eyes open.

Farranen put his sword away and turned to Dog with beseeching eyes. "She is injured. You must let us help her."

I wanted to tell Dog that it was okay, that Farranen would never hurt me. He must have sensed my thoughts because his growl faded to a nearly inaudible resonance beneath my cheek.

My fae approached cautiously, keeping his hands in plain sight. My magic had faded to background noise, but it leapt the moment Farranen's hand made contact with my face.

I tried to smile in gratitude as his warmth enveloped me and chased away the chill that had taken over, but my face contorted into a grimace as feeling rushed back into my body.

"My lady…Theo…" His voice was hoarse with emotions that I didn't understand.

I let out a strangled sob as pain dug its fingers into my stomach.

"Let me see." Farranen rolled me onto my back, forcing me out of the fetal position I'd been curled into. My muscles screamed in protest at being moved after spending so long in one position. I whimpered and tried to snuggle back into the softness of Dog's body as hands poked at my belly.

Coarse words in a language I didn't understand belied the ease in my guardian's efficient prodding. He was upset, but he wanted me to think he wasn't.

"Ow," I told him.

"I know. It's not that bad." His tone said otherwise.

"Here." The man standing over Farranen's shoulder unclasped a chain from his neck and removed his black cloak. He was either a big cosplay fan, or he was fae.

Farranen settled the cloth over me, and the scent of starless winter skies and fresh snow rolled over me to mingle with spicy pine trees and blood.

The fae who lent me his cloak knelt next to me, and his glittering blue eyes teased my memory for a second before he reached out and touched my arm. Fae magic blossomed under his hand and swept through me, caressing and gentle as it explored every inch of my body. It was like Farranen's, but more direct.

"You," I whispered. There had been something off about him when he'd approached me in the parking lot, but I hadn't been able to put my finger on it. He must have been glamoured.

"She needs a healer." The fae continued to study me like I was an interesting bug, but I wasn't going to complain since he was still sharing his wild-tasting magic.

"S'okay…Just tired," I slurred.

Farranen leaned in close enough that his hair brushed across my jaw. "I will take you to the healer in my realm; she is powerful and will help you."

I wanted to politely decline and crawl into my own bed. Fairie was the absolute last place I wanted to go. My sweatshirt was soaked in blood, and I hadn't done laundry since I'd worn my only dress. My feet still hadn't recovered from the misery of wearing heels last time, and I was in no rush to do it again. And, to be perfectly honest, I was terrified of having any more men drop their pants in the hopes that I'd take their cocks for a test drive.

I should get up and get one of the fresh steaks that I'd bought for Dog. He deserved a whole plate full of steaks for scaring off Merrick. As far as I was concerned, he could have everything in the whole damn fridge.

Farranen lifted me gently into his arms, and I cried out at the sudden movement.

"I can fetch the healer and bring her here," the stranger suggested.

"No. The vampire may be lurking close by for a second chance. She will be safer in Fairie."

"Very well, I will escort you to the gate. Then I will return and hunt the bastard down."

Farranen murmured his thanks, and then the only sound came from the soft footfalls of the men as they bustled me through the sleeping woods.

I clung to my guardian. Not just the thick fabric of his shirt, but the pulse of his magic. I hung onto it with hope and desperation, terrified that it too would fade as my own already had.

****

Fairie's best healer, Eddesta of the Dark Court, looked like a cross between a spider monkey and a walrus.

"More tea?" she asked.

"Please."

Eddy shuffled on heavy legs to the tea cart and refilled our cups. Her face was flat with a pointy chin, and it was covered in a fine coat of short white hair. Tall ears, each with a sharp peak, twitched intermittently, depending on which way she was facing. Her hands and thick neck were a dull gray and looked rubbery, but I knew from experience that they were baby soft. A full-length rose-colored dress covered her ample bust and round belly.

Her orange eyes were the only part that looked remotely human. They sparkled with mirth when she laughed, reminding me of Jolly Old Saint Nick.

"Here you are, my dear."

After spending five days in a magically induced coma, my body was weak but healed. And starving. Like, chew-the-foot-off-my-own-granny-because-I'm-so-freaking-hungry starving. But Eddy insisted I could only have liquids for the first day, so I accepted the dainty teacup and tried to be grateful for the hot drink.

During my brief scuffle with Merrick, my knife had sliced a six-inch gash just below my belly button. I'd been lucky to avoid hitting any organs or intestines, but the knife had severed the muscles, causing me to bleed like a fountain. Eddy said the shiny pink line would scar, but it didn't bother me. It's not like I paraded around in a bikini every day.

And seriously, who stabs themselves with their own knife?

One of the perks of my unplanned nap was that everything had healed; the blisters on my feet, my split lip, the lump on my head, even the bite on my neck was gone. There were scars, but I didn't mind. They were just proof of the things I'd been strong enough to survive.

A formal knock at the door echoed throughout the big room, and I set my teacup down. It wouldn't be Farranen; he'd been sitting in the chair next to me since

I'd woken up this morning and had only left when Eddy ordered him out. He'd looked exhausted, with dark circles around his eyes and fine lines creasing his face. I doubted that he'd gotten much sleep since we arrived in Fairie.

Eddy opened the door, and the fae with the crystal-blue eyes entered.

The healer immediately dropped into a surprisingly elegant curtsey. "My lord."

"How fares our guest?" He stepped past Eddy without acknowledging her. His eyes never wavered from where I lay, propped up by a million pillows and drowning in too many blankets. I felt like prey, caught by the intensity in his gaze as he strode across the room.

He once again wore a black cloak that moved like a shadow in his wake. A small cluster of white opals were arranged in the shape of a triangle, and they adorned the left side of his high black collar. His shiny boots were silent against the stone floor.

"Do you always address people in the third person?" I seemed to recall him doing the same thing at my cabin. In his defense, I'd been too busy fighting to stay conscious to participate in any meaningful conversation.

"My apologies. It is nice to become formally acquainted." His smile was a bit stiff but genuine.

"Right," I said, unable to keep the skepticism from my voice. Did he seriously think I'd forgotten about our chance encounter in the grocery store parking lot? From what I understood, fae didn't just hang out in the human realm for the fun of it. I didn't believe for one second that our first meeting had been a coincidence.

He got one of those looks on his face that most

men get when they're baffled by a woman's behavior but don't want to admit it.

Guilt reared its ugly head; I was acting like a jerk for being snide with someone who'd given me his cloak when I was cold, while he knew full well that I was going to bleed all over it. Perhaps stalking was considered flattering in Fairie?

"Sorry." I rubbed my hands across my face as if I could wipe away my bad attitude. "That was rude; I'm tired and starving, and I shouldn't have talked to you like that."

The bed dipped slightly as he sat next to me. His smile was tentative as he extended his hand and said, "Perhaps we can start over. I am Oakenlief of the Dark Court."

I took his outstretched hand and made a startled noise when he kissed my knuckles.

"Theo…Just Theo." I was proud that my voice didn't waver.

"Healer, a moment of privacy." He made what should have been a request into an order. Eddy quietly retreated to the hall outside.

We sat in silence for a moment, and my eyes kept going back to his right shoulder. The air around it seemed to shimmer, the same way that hot pavement puts off heat in the summer. I squinted and tilted my head until I could see a slight glow.

"You're wearing a sword," I pointed out, and his eyes widened in surprise.

"Yes."

I'm ashamed to admit that I took a small amount of pleasure in seeing him at a loss for words.

He cleared his throat, probably to change the

subject. Typical man.

"I tracked your assailant for two days, but I lost him. I have returned only to check on your health and will be off again as soon as the gate reopens."

"The gate's closed?"

"The guardian has been preoccupied and unable to fulfill his duties."

I caught the words he wasn't saying; Farranen had been too busy babysitting me to do his job.

Lief patted my hand in a soothing gesture. "Worry not. The closure of the gate is temporary and fairly trivial in the grand scope of life in Fairie. He insisted on attending to you personally, allowing no one else in the room, aside from the healer." His slightly perturbed look made me think he'd been denied access as well, and he didn't look like a man that was used to being denied things.

The sudden whisper of magic, *my* magic, hummed through my chest and filled me with excitement. It was like finding a long-lost friend that I'd thought had died. Or like when the stores in Saskatoon stopped carrying Dancing Horse coffee, but then, six months later, I found an entire case of their ultra-light roast on the discount rack. I know, I could have just said I was delighted, but I'm a writer; my brain can't stay away from analogies.

Uncaring of the filmy nightgown I was wearing, I sat up and grabbed Lief's hand. His mouth opened in a surprised little *O* when I tugged at the magic I could feel under his skin. It came willingly, and I welcomed it with my own, loving the way they danced together.

I'd thought my magic was gone. I'd felt the sparkling well inside me dry up and disappear when I'd been laying on the blood-soaked floor with a hole in my belly.

"I thought it was gone," I told him, sounding dazed.

"*My lady…*," he whispered on an exhale. His charming grin morphed into something more—more masculine, more hungry, more carnal. All I could see was the shimmering blue of his diamond eyes as they surrounded my reflection in his dilated pupils.

My body heated under his gaze, and he didn't try to stop me when I pulled away. I quickly tugged the blanket up over my chest so he wouldn't notice my nipples standing at full attention. Was this crazy sudden attraction for a man I barely knew caused by my transition? Or was it something else entirely? Something to do with the fae himself, and the chemistry between us?

Across the room the door banged open, shattering whatever had been building between us.

Farranen stalked into the room, taking in every detail with narrowed eyes. I wondered if I looked as guilty as I felt.

Eddy followed on his heels, looking apologetic as she glanced between the three of us.

"I'm sorry, my lord, I tried to tell him you wanted privacy, but he insisted on—"

Lief waved a hand, dismissing her worries. "It's fine, Eddesta."

Farranen pulled the chair farther away from the bed but remained standing. His stiff posture was making me uncomfortable.

"Did you get any sleep?" I asked softly. His skin was still too pale, his eyes too dark. He didn't just look tired, he looked depleted. I had no doubt that he'd been here while I was in the coma; I could still smell crisp pine trees and cinnamon on the bedding and my nightgown. I was such a mooch—he'd clearly given me more magic than he could spare.

"I am rested, thank you." His polite answer set my teeth on edge. Why was he acting so aloof? This was different than the usual indifference he used to hide his thoughts. This was the pissed-off disappointment that comes with grief.

"Would you like some more tea, Theo?" Eddy's hands were clenched nervously in front of her chest, and I appreciated her effort to distract everyone from the rising tension in the room.

"Any chance I could get some real food?" I asked hopefully.

"You really should wait a few more hours, just to be sure everything is healed—"

"She's not completely healed?" Lief demanded.

"Yes, the wounds are healed, but her body is still weak—"

"She's human. Don't humans rely on food to replenish their bodies?"

"Y-Yes, my lord. I hadn't considered that." Eddy stammered. "I'll send for some immediately."

"There's no need; I will be taking Theodora back to her realm now that she is feeling better," Farranen announced.

I'd feel a whole lot better after a burger and some fries, but I didn't want to sound ungrateful for everything Eddy had done for me, so I kept my mouth shut.

"Good. I will accompany you so that I may cross

through as well," Lief announced.

Farranen's smile was as harsh as his words. "Very well, my lord."

"Why do you call him that?" I asked, looking back and forth between the two men.

"The dark prince prefers the less formal title."

"What? Lief is a dark prince? Like, *the* dark prince?" I didn't mean to sound so horrified, it just kind of slipped out.

"Do you always address people in the third person?" he asked, raising a single brow mockingly in my direction.

"Sorry, it's just—you seem so *normal*." What a sad thing that men with swords, who weren't even human, had become a normal part of my life.

His smile, once again full of charm and elegance, made my heart beat a little faster. He stood, and a brief flash of light haloed him before it shrank down into the shape of a sword hilt over his shoulder. Once the light faded, I could clearly see the leather-wrapped handle waiting for his grip. He winked and told me, "No point in hiding it now."

He disappeared through the door with a silent sweep of his cloak.

Farranen dropped into the chair, lacking his usual grace. Why was he sitting all the way over there instead of next to me? I realized with a sinking feeling that he was intentionally putting physical distance between us. Men only did that to emotionally distance themselves.

"Just say it," I told him. I could tell by the look on his face that he had something to say.

"Theo…"

I hated the way he said my name. He only used my

nickname when he was desperate or caught up in the midst of passion. Since this definitely wasn't what I'd consider a romantic situation, I knew something was wrong.

"Say it," I intoned, my own voice sounding as remote as his.

"Eddesta has discovered an abnormality while treating you."

The blood rushed out of my face, and I was glad I was still sitting. I recognized that tone. I'd heard it from police officers and even from the private investigator I'd hired. Only bad news arrived with that blend of dismal remorse and hesitant sympathy.

Eddy stepped closer, and for once, I didn't appreciate her timid kindness. "You healed much faster than expected, but during my final exam I found...Well, it's what I didn't find actually. You're missing...Oh, Theo, I'm so sorry. You're barren."

I blinked, and it suddenly hit me what she'd discovered.

"I know," I told her slowly, because the sorrow on her face was genuine, and I didn't want to upset her any further. "I had a hysterectomy."

Eddy blanched as if I'd just eaten a live slug in front of her. "You cut out your womb?"

"Yes." I didn't try to explain how debilitating the endometriosis had been. Once I'd become anemic, my heart had worked overtime to keep up with the low amount of oxygen in my blood. As a twenty-year-old, with heart failure looming on the horizon, I'd willingly chosen the surgery.

Judging from her horrified expression, nothing I could say would be a good enough excuse for my self-imposed infertility.

Chapter Twenty-One

Since my clothes were covered in blood and dog fur, Farranen glamoured my useless nightgown into low-riding jeans and a forest green sweater made of the softest wool I'd ever felt. I discreetly checked, and yep, there were silky white panties and a matching bra that fit perfectly. The jeans were slightly stretchy and hugged my curves, and the waistband was low enough to avoid my sensitive new scar. New black boots, that made me look taller without actually adding any height, were buttery soft, and I didn't get a single blister on the walk home through Fairie. The outfit should have made me self-conscious, but instead, I felt like a badass biker chick ready to kick some butt.

Once we crossed the gate, Lief parted ways with a simple "Merry meet."

"Merry part," Farranen answered.

The walk through the woods was dark and somber, matching my guardian's attitude. He refused to be drawn into my first few attempts at conversation, so I concentrated on trying not to break an ankle on the uneven ground. Just because the boots made me look like a graceful warrior woman didn't mean I actually was one.

I used the silence of the walk to mentally prepare myself for whatever awaited me at home. Whether it was finding out that a family of cougars had moved in to my cabin, or that Merrick had returned and burnt the place to the ground, I was ready. All of my preparation turned out to be totally unnecessary.

A brand-new door and frame had been expertly installed in place of the one Dog had smashed. The lock was shiny, and the hinges didn't squeak when I opened it. The smell of new wood and fresh paint made me feel spoiled in a way that was foreign.

The very best part was the giant doggy-door built into the solid wood. It was flexible enough to allow Dog to pass but would keep out any elements that made it past the overhanging roof. A large bolt held a steel beam in place so I could lock it from the inside when I wanted to. If I ever lost my keys, I could easily fit through the space.

I couldn't wait to see if Dog liked it. My heart squeezed a little as I looked around for a giant shadow with amber eyes.

"Where's Dog?"

"Who?"

I cut my eyes to Farranen to see if he was joking, but he looked just as mystified as he sounded.

"Dog. About this tall." I gestured to my hip. "Sad yellow eyes?"

Comprehension dawned on his face and he asked, "You named him *Dog?*"

"Yes." I was getting irritated. "Have you seen him?"

"No. The dark prince arranged for the repairs to your cabin, and I have not left Fairie since you were injured."

"Oh." I looked around the kitchen, noting the lack of mess. The place looked cleaner than it had been long before I'd splashed a few liters of my blood on the linoleum. *I should send Lief a thank-you card or something for taking care everything*, I thought.

I was tired and wanted nothing more than to fall into bed, but Farranen's agitated vibes were making me antsy. I hated the feeling of impending doom that was hanging over us. When I moved toward the fruit bowl to grab an orange, he sidestepped to avoid me brushing up against him.

Okay, now that just pissed me off.

"What's going on?" I demanded.

"Nothing is going on."

"Bullshit! I call bullshit. Pull the fucking stick out of your ass, and tell me what's going on." It was the boots talking. It had to be. I never talked to anyone like this. The new footwear was bringing out my inner shrew.

He clenched his jaw but didn't say anything.

"Don't," I warned him.

"Don't what?"

"Don't shut me out like this. You've had that stupid blank look on your face ever since I woke up. Quit with the distant I-don't-care crap. Tell me what's changed."

He looked at the floor, at the walls, at every damn thing in my cabin except for me. I could see his emotions chipping away at his stony veneer, but they flitted across his face so fast that I couldn't identify them all.

"We have fifty-three nights, unless the queen rescinds her orders." Now he looked at me. His eyes burned bright with furious dismay. "Once she finds out that you're…"

"Infertile." I steadily supplied the word he seemed unable to say.

Now I understood what this was about. My appeal had relied solely on the competency of my reproductive organs. Without a uterus, I was no longer desirable.

I didn't bother to ask what would happen if I still became a changeling; it no longer mattered. I didn't want anything to do with an entire race that judged the entirety of my value on my ability to make babies.

"You should go. Tell your queen now, so this doesn't get dragged out for another fifty-three nights."

Moving toward my bedroom, I took slow measured steps that matched my slow measured breaths, so that the fae that had just smashed my heart wouldn't see my tears.

I didn't think his rejection could possibly hurt this much.

Will and I had mourned the loss of our ability to have children together, but looking back, I realized he hadn't had much of a choice. We were already married, so he would have had to go through the entire divorce process in order to leave and find another woman who still had her uterus. Then again, I'd been the one wanting a family, not him.

I blindly fumbled on the wall until my hand slapped the light switch.

Without another fae around, my magic would wither and die. Another fat tear leaked down my already wet face. Another piece of my life about to be ripped away. I hadn't known I'd mourn for it until I was faced with losing it.

"Theodora, please wait." His strong hands grabbed me from behind, crushing me to his chest.

"Just go," I mumbled. My throat was tight from holding back the sobs I could feel building up in my chest.

"I can't." He sounded as miserable as I did.

Good, I thought. I shouldn't be the only one to suffer.

"Please," he whispered as he brushed his cheek against my hair. "*Please,* Theo. Please."

After a long pause, he gently turned me around so we were face to face. "The healer claims your magic no longer flourishes. It fails to grow, but it does not fade."

I nodded; I'd been thinking the same thing but was afraid to ask what it meant.

"Your magic might linger, but the queen will consider your transition a failure since you remain human."

I nodded again, knowing where he was going with this. I wished he'd just rip the damn bandage off already. At some point, I'd stopped being the girl that wanted the stupid thing peeled off slowly, and now I was a woman who just wanted some closure so she could go back to being alone without the chance of anyone hurting her again.

"I will not be able to disobey if she forbids her court from having contact with you."

I wasn't the only one with tears on my face.

"I understand."

"No," he told me fiercely, "You do *not* understand. The idea of watching you grow ripe with a babe, *our* babe, is something I have longed for. The thought of no longer feeling my magic merge with yours is incomprehensible, but those are things I can survive without. *You* are what I need."

He gave my shoulders a little shake as if he could dislodge the hurt in my heart.

"You, Theodora, are what I need. *You.*"

His lips were hesitant as he leaned down, giving me time to pull away.

He tasted like tears and home.

A small seed of doubt wormed its way into my head. How long could he be content with a broken human? A decade? Maybe two? Sooner or later my shortcomings would drive a wedge between us.

But right then, I didn't care how many more days or hours we had left. Not even a handful of minutes were guaranteed. It would be stupid to fall any further into this. Whatever *this* was.

I kissed him back, letting my entire body relax against his. The feeling of my softness next to his strength was toxic to my self-control. Little nibbles and sucks quickly turned into a desperate dance of tongues and shared breaths.

He lowered his hands, running them over my glamoured sweater, which suddenly felt like steel wool against my skin. His thumbs brushed the sides of my breasts, continuing until they caressed the skin above my jeans. I moaned and rubbed my aching nipples against his chest.

Tired of the clothing between us, I tugged at the clasp on his cloak until something snapped, and the sound of metal bouncing on the floor was quickly muffled by the heavy fabric that pooled around us. I moved on to his shirt, tugging it from his pants and pulling it up until I was forced to break away from his lips or to leave the shirt hanging around his neck. I tossed the offending fabric away, and I tried not to get lost in his impossibly green eyes. I was used to reading the subtle shifts in color that matched his moods, even when he tried to keep his feelings tucked behind a cold façade. Now he hid nothing, baring his vulnerability and passion with every look and touch we shared.

My hands reached for the leather strip that held his hair in a neat ponytail. I wanted to run my fingers through all his beautiful white locks until they were wild and flustered like the way he made me feel inside. I fumbled with the tie because my hands were shaking, and he acknowledged my clumsiness with a smile.

Then, he guided me backward until the backs of my knees hit the bed, and I tumbled onto the soft mattress. I could tell the sheets were perfectly tucked in, nice and tight the way they should be, but I didn't bother getting under them. I was too hot, and there was already too much fabric involved.

My fae toed off his boots, and then I forgot how to breathe when his pants followed. The simple motion was economical, a product of his haste rather than a show meant to tantalize. There was nothing beneath them but the lean ropy muscles of his hips that funneled into a patch of pale hair and his gloriously eager cock.

It had been years since I'd worn jeans, and I struggled with the button until Farranen covered my hands with his own.

"No. Not yet." His voice was hoarse like he had to struggle to get the words out.

He nudged me farther onto the bed and waited until I was settled before crawling over to me. His knees straddled my hips, and I reached for the smooth shaft that bobbed with every move he made. It filled my entire hand, hot and heavy with a pulse of its own. It thrust into my grip once, twice, then a third time before he grabbed my wrist and pulled it away.

"No, not like this." His voice was pained, and I wondered if I did something wrong.

A more confident woman would take the bull by the horns (or the fae by the balls) and know exactly what to do with him. My experience in this department was sorely lacking, so I said nothing and allowed him to wrap my hands around the headboard.

"Don't let go." He leaned forward and placed a kiss on my forehead. I extended my mouth for his attention, but he bypassed it and lifted the hem of my sweater. His fingertips brushed against my newest scar, tracing the line with the lightest of touches. The skin around it was hypersensitive, and my belly tightened as he feathered a kiss across it.

The look he gave me from under hooded eyes made me feel naked and exposed, even though I was still fully clothed.

His body straightened as he rose to his knees with his thick member in his strong grip. The muscles in his forearm rippled as his hand slid from the base of his cock along the shaft until it reached the ruddy head. The smell of spicy pine trees swirled around me, a moment before a thick drop of precum pearled on the tip, glistening against the smooth crown. My mouth watered, needing to know what he tasted like. I arched my back and didn't try to hold back a moan that came out sounding like his name.

His hips pulled back and then thrust. His knuckles turned white as he gripped himself harder with a steady hand, while his other splayed across my belly. His magic churned through me, especially strong where he pressed against my scar.

My jeans were too tight, my panties damp and chafing in a way that was torturous and satisfying. I wanted to be naked as he moved over me, I needed him to be *in* me.

His head fell back, and some of the long white strands of his hair stuck to the drops of sweat on his chest. The large sac that swung in time with his thrusts suddenly drew up between his open legs and his swollen cock grew impossibly longer.

I dug my fingernails into the headboard, refusing to let go until he told me to.

As his hips flexed forward, every muscle in his body coiled and tightened until he uttered a shout that sounded more like a denial than an exaltation. My body tightened in response, and something in the headboard cracked.

Hot streams of his seed shot across my belly and chest, some arcing across the bed to land on the pillows and comforter. Each thrust of his hips brought another surge, and my hips lifted reflexively, knowing that his release shouldn't come until he was inside me, filling me.

His chest glistened with perspiration and his breathing was harsh when he finally released his manhood. It jutted toward me, still erect.

With a shaking hand, he ran a finger through the semen on my sweater and then trailed it across my stomach, following the same path carved by the knife and marking it with his seed. He drew a deep breath, then another and another as if he could find strength in the air around us. When he finally met my eyes, my heart tightened at the emotion that I saw.

Not passion or affection or satisfaction. Just regret.
"Your duty to share your bed is fulfilled."

No.

"My duty to share my seed this night is fulfilled."

No, no, no.

He climbed off the bed, no longer meeting my eyes.

No, no, no!

This wasn't happening. This couldn't be happening. I looked around, as if maybe I was remembering the last few minutes wrong. My body was still clothed, the boots on my feet looking odd in a place where boots shouldn't be worn. Long spurts of semen still covered me, pale against the dark green of my sweater. They cooled on the fragile skin of my belly, and once again my mind protested the wrongness of them covering the outside of my body, because, instinctively, I knew they belonged inside me.

No, please, no.

He bent to pick up his clothes, weariness carved into every line of his body. I realized that I had never asked how old he was. It didn't matter now.

He didn't bother to get dressed. His footsteps were silent as he exited my bedroom. If I hadn't watched him walk out, I probably would have assumed he was still standing at the foot of my bed.

Sobs erupted from my chest in great heaves, and I didn't try to hold them in. No one was around to hear them; Farranen was gone, and I was alone.

My tears burned against my cold skin, but I didn't get under the covers. A mountain of betrayal and anguish was burying me alive, and all I could do is cling to the headboard.

Chapter Twenty-Two

The next two weeks passed by in a blur.

No unannounced visitors came to my door. No one lurked in the shadows of my driveway. No one attacked me with a knife or claws or fangs. Even the parade of animals that may or may not be ghosts had dried up.

Dog and I were truly alone.

I used the time to replace my missing cell phone, and I texted my new number to Katie. She wanted to know when we could have another girl's night out; I told her it would be soon but didn't commit to a specific date.

The first morning that frost covered the ground and the inside of my truck windshield, I drove into town and bought a chainsaw. It was heavier than I thought it would be, and Dog hid in the tree line at the edge of my backyard when I fired it up for the first time. It took me multiple tries to get the damn thing started, and it stank like exhaust once it was finally running. I squealed in triumph after successfully cutting through the first log without losing any of my limbs.

I could smell the possibility of snow in the air, and Dog's coat was getting thicker. It would probably snow within the week. October was early for snow, but I was looking forward to it; I was done with autumn. I spent two days hauling wood back to my cabin and splitting it with an ax. It took four truckloads and three jerry cans of gas for the chainsaw, but my wood shed was finally full.

It took three additional trips into town to find the right part for my broken dryer. I was happy to say I wouldn't have to hang a clothesline in my living room for the winter.

Every muscle from my hips up to my neck hurt in a way that I was proud of. A knot the size of a walnut had taken up residence under my left shoulder blade, and my hands had so many blisters I couldn't comfortably hold a fork. Dog and I had hard-boiled eggs for supper that night.

The cost of continually running the baseboard heaters all winter was astronomical, so I was looking forward to using the small fireplace in my living room. I had a generator for the power outages that the winter storms would bring, but I only had about twenty gallons of gas in the shed. I didn't know how long the gas would keep the generator going during the colder months, so the woodshed gave me a huge sense of security.

Now that the leaves had all fallen, Mrs. Swazle had pointed out the handful of wasps' nests that were visible in the highest branches of the trees. According to her, they were a sign that we were in for a long cold winter. I offered to cut some wood for her, but she had already paid a man from town, and she had more than enough wood to burn steadily from now until next July.

All the wonderful blister bandages from my first-aid kit were gone, used up when the ax handle had rubbed away the skin on my palms. The temporary piece of plywood was gone from my living room wall. Outside, I'd hung new wood siding; it was lighter than the rest of the cabin, but I bought it secondhand so it was cheap. After stuffing new insulation between the wooden two-by-fours, I had screwed in a new patch of drywall. It wasn't perfect; the edges were uneven, and I hadn't spackled or painted over it yet. I probably used the wrong kind of screws; the internet isn't always the best teacher. Still, I was stupidly proud of the fact that I did it myself.

Every time my thoughts turned toward Farranen, I quickly immersed myself in whatever physical tasks needed to be done. There were a lot of them. At night, I found solace in the oblivion of a deep, dreamless sleep that could only be achieved by exhausting my body with hard manual labor. I no longer noticed how the mattress dipped under Dog's growing body. He weighed more than I did, but I didn't make him sleep on the floor. I didn't want to be alone in the bed.

I woke one morning to the steady *ping...ping...ping...*of acorns landing on the cab of my truck; a red squirrel steadily dropped them from the pine trees above to collect for the winter. Last year I'd watched him drag them under my deck, and I hoped he'd find a different hiding spot this year.

After I had finished my coffee and Dog had wolfed down some left-over pork chops, I turned on my laptop. It had been over two weeks since I'd given the duke and Priscilla my full attention, so I parked my butt in a hard dining room chair and dove back into sixteenth-century England.

****

Seven hours later, the soft flapping of the doggy-door dragged my focus from Priscilla's tenacious adventures to my stiff muscles. Dog must have gone out to relieve himself in the backyard.

Chapters twenty-one through twenty-eight had strayed from my original story outline. The duke turned out to be a royal ass who was leading Priscilla on. His bogus attraction wasn't truly for the heroine, but part of a larger scheme to find the missing amulet that had been handed down for generations in her family. Etched on the back of the amulet was the cipher for the mythical scroll that led to the Hunting Hills treasure.

Once the bastard had stolen her priceless heirloom, Priscilla did some investigating of her own and caught up with him, just as he had found the door to the hidden tunnel. Some heated words were exchanged. The duke ended up with his ball sac pinned to the stone wall by Priscilla's hidden dagger, and he spent the rest of his life as a eunuch, while she went on to claim the treasure, which happened to be a grimoire containing a spell that granted her immortality.

What can I say? Writing is my therapy.

I'd probably have to switch publishers. I doubted the ladies at Blushing Hens Press would be able to wrap their heads around the whole paranormal fantasy concept.

My back creaked as I stretched and turned toward the kitchen to see if Dog was hungry for supper, but instead of my furry friend, I discovered a disheveled vampire with stains on his clothing and hatred in his too-bright gaze.

"I can't *find* her!" Merrick growled.

Nothing remotely human stared back at me. This was an apex predator, all teeth and claws and coiled muscles, with insanity in his eyes as he stalked toward me.

"Can't find who?" I asked, slowly backing up.

"Marissa! My sire! *Marissa!*" he shouted. Blood had turned the navy blue of his windbreaker an ugly rust color, and I wondered if it was my blood that he'd been wearing for weeks, or if it wasn't, I wondered whose it was and if they were okay.

"She's not here." I gestured lamely at my boring furniture as if to prove she wasn't hiding behind the old sofa or under the coffee table.

"You will help me find her."

"Okay, sure," I said, in my best convincing voice while remaining uncommitted.

"His blood." Merrick sniffed the air like Dog did when I was making beef and broccoli. "Will. You smell of his blood." His lips pulled back from his fangs, and his smile resembled something that belonged in a horror movie. "Of our sire's blood."

The table was still between us, and I was closest to the bedroom. *If I'm fast, I might be able to get to the shotgun*, I thought. Forget about the knife block in the kitchen—that hadn't worked out so great last time.

I lunged toward the hallway, my slippers skidding across the hardwood. Merrick caught me in a painful bear hug, smooshing my face against his stinky chest. I'd forgotten how damn fast vampires could be. And would it kill him to take a shower once in a while or wash his blood-stained coat? My eyes burned from the stench of sun-scorched roadkill.

"Let *go!*" I shouted.

Where the hell was Dog? He never wandered far from the yard. My heartrate tripled, and I squirmed harder. If this asshat had touched a single hair on my dog's head, I was going to rip off his emaciated arms and beat him to death with them.

"We will be family," he panted. "And you will help me find her."

He dug his dirty fangs into my shoulder, and I screamed every profanity I knew. I'd been under the impression that vampires left two perfectly placed holes when they fed, but Merrick gnawed at my shoulder like it was a chew toy. Tiny black spots clouded my vision when I heard his teeth scrape against my collar bone. All my squirming probably wasn't helping him with his aim.

When I finally tore myself away from him, we were both covered in my blood and breathing hard.

"You're going to pay for that, you stupid motherfucker. This was my favorite shirt." The neck of the navy shirt was shredded, and the flowing white words THIS IS HOW I ROLL and the little white shopping cart full of books were streaked with crimson.

He licked his fingertips like he was savoring a fine wine, and my stomach flipped at the grotesque sight.

"We will be family." He nodded. "Brood."

I didn't bother arguing with the nutcase vampire. I had no idea why he thought we could be a family, but I doubted it would end well for me. The idea was as preposterous as me befriending a bowl of chocolate pudding. Eventually, the pudding would get eaten.

My footsteps were uneven as I backed away; I must have lost a slipper during the struggle. I tried to keep my blood from escaping through the ragged skin on my shoulder with my shaking hands, but I could feel it running down my breast and soaking into my bra.

"You will..." He pounced, knocking me onto my butt and riding my body down to the floor. "...be *mine.*"

My skin crawled as he pulled up his windbreaker, giving me a moment of panic when I thought he was going for the fly of his pants. His filthy fingers bypassed the zipper, but my relief was short lived when he pulled a small utility knife from his pocket. Its handle was dull and old, but when he flicked out the blade, it looked shiny and wicked sharp.

Trapped on my back, with a homicidal vampire about to stab me (again), my traitorous brain went to the one thing I'd been trying so hard to avoid thinking about for weeks.

Farranen.

This is not how I wanted to die, feeble and helpless in a puddle of my own blood. Alone.

I arched my back and tried to buck him off. My flailing arms burned, already exhausted from long days of chores. Merrick easily pinned them with one hand. I gave in to the frustrated tears; there was no one to see my weakness but the asshole on top of me, and I didn't give a shit what he thought.

"This will be good." I couldn't tell if he was talking to me or to himself.

The knife swooped down in a graceful arc, warning me of pain to come. I couldn't remember from the last time if it was going to be sharp and clear, or more of a blazing ache. The blade sliced through flesh, but it wasn't mine.

A dark ribbon of blood appeared on Merrick's wrist. The first drop rolled hesitantly down his pale forearm, then more followed, gathering speed as they found their own paths.

"You are my first," he told me, sounding like he

thought I should be honored by his declaration.

"What are—" My confused words were cut off when he thrust his bloody wrist across my mouth.

Oh, my God. His putrid taste invaded my mouth, and I gagged. The flavor of death was quickly joined by vomit, but there was nowhere for it to go, because the vampire's disgusting bony wrist was still sealed against my lips. Choking on foulness and blinded by tears, I nearly passed out from lack of oxygen.

By then, I knew no one was coming to rescue me. If I wanted to live, the burden was squarely on my shoulders.

With my hands still held immobile, I used the only weapon I had. Opening my mouth wider, I bit down with every bit of strength I could funnel into my jaws. Flat human teeth obviously don't do nearly as much damage as fangs, but Merrick howled, letting me know he wasn't enjoying the impromptu amputation that I was attempting to perform on his hand.

"Ahh! *Oww—*"

His bones ground under my teeth, and when he tried to pull away, I locked my jaw like a pit bull.

"You *bitch!*" He toppled over and scrambled away, leaving a dark trail across my hardwood. The crimson smears made me smile; I had mastered the art of cleaning up bloodstains, and I was giddy that, for once, they weren't mine. Most of his wrist went with him, everything but the smaller bits of skin and sinew that were caught in my teeth.

I spat and wiped at my face with the bottom of my shirt. Gah, the taste refused to be purged from my mouth, and I spit some more. It was going to take more than toothpaste to rid myself of the taste of old garbage and decaying meat. Half a gallon of bleach wouldn't be enough.

"You stupid, psychotic, rabid *bloodsucker*!" I shrieked, as I crawled toward the closest wall and pulled myself up to standing. The shelf above me held the four writers' awards that I'd won over the last decade. My hand randomly grabbed one.

"This is *my* house." Avoiding the biggest spots of blood, I moved so that I was standing directly over the vampire's writhing figure. "And *where* the hell is my dog?" When he didn't answer immediately, I raised the etched glass over my head. The motion had become second nature after all the chopping of wood that I'd done lately.

I wished that I had something clever to say; something worthy of a woman with four writing awards and six best-sellers. The mewling vampire wasn't going anywhere; I should have stopped and composed something witty and audacious, something that a truly self-reliant woman would say. But I was worried about Dog, and not nearly sadistic enough to drag out the vampire's suffering.

Later, when I would tell Dog about this, I'd add a few cliché phrases. Purely for his entertainment, of course.

I brought the book-shaped cube of glass down on Merrick's forehead in a two-handed motion. It exploded into a million shards of glass that all sounded like little bells as they bounced across the hardwood. He screamed, the high-pitched sound full of pain and violent rage.

I stood there like an idiot, staring at the small dent in his forehead. Maybe I'd read too many books, but for some reason, I'd been expecting his head to implode, complete with a dramatic spray of blood and brain-bits.

Well, shit.

Of course, my dumb luck would never allow for such an easy conclusion to such a messy story. He was as fast and deadly as a rattler when he reached out with his good hand and hooked my foot. I pulled back to kick him in the face, losing my slipper in the process, but at least I was able to wrench myself free.

I didn't waste any time scrambling away from the enraged vampire in an awkward crab walk, until I bumped into the coffee table and used it to stand up. Glass crunched under my bare feet as I stumbled through the living room and pried at the deadbolts. It took me longer than usual to get them unlocked, because my shaking hands were slippery with blood, but once the door was open, I burst outside with my ripped sweatshirt flapping behind me.

"Dog!" I screamed his name as I flew down the stairs with my head twisting side to side, desperate to catch a glimpse of amber eyes in the dark.

I skirted the edge of the cabin and headed to the backyard, since I didn't think to bring the truck keys, and there was no way I was going to bang on Mrs. Swazle's front door with a deranged vampire on my heels.

"Dog!"

My feet automatically led me across the yard and into the trees. Branches tore at my loose hair, and more than once I left some behind, snagged on whatever branch was greedy enough to keep it. Behind me, a long angry howl shattered the air, and I skidded to a stop.

"*Dog?*" I whispered.

Dread twisted a path across my skin, leaving goose bumps in its wake. Dog never barked or yipped or woofed; when he was scared, he would growl, but this was no ordinary doggy sound. This was the call of a thoroughly pissed-off predator on the hunt.

Another howl split the silence, the tone vibrating through my skin and bones before reverberating back out into the darkness. It was too loud, too bold, too deadly to be Dog…But some part of me recognized it as familiar. So I stood barefoot on the path, shivering and scared, torn with indecision.

Ahead, the path branched off, and I would have to decide between going left toward the lake, or right toward the hawthorn tree. Either way was a dead end, surrounded by hundreds of kilometers of wild land.

I knew my bloody footprints were leaving a trail that Merrick could follow better than if I'd painted big neon arrows and a raised flashing sign that said, "SHE WENT THIS WAY!" I should have taken the gravel road; that would have eventually led me to the main highway.

Something called out, answering the howls with a guttural yell that was neither human nor sane. I sprinted back toward my yard, no longer caring about the trail of blood I was leaving in my wake. Maybe Merrick wouldn't see it. Yeah, and maybe an Uber would cruise by and offer me a ride home. Stranger things had happened in these woods.

Behind me, the clearing with the hawthorn tree buzzed, pulling at the edges of my awareness, bringing life to the pulse of magic inside me that I'd been trying so hard to stomp down. Even though I'd spent the last few weeks studiously ignoring that particular part of the woods, I could still pinpoint exactly where it was.

My breath came in ragged gasps, each exhale ending on a whimper that coincided with the lurching steps I took on my shredded feet.

The full moon slid out from behind a low-hanging bank of clouds just as I reached the end of the path. Merrick's pale skin had faded to a bloodless gray that made him stand out in stark contrast from the dark background. His coat was split down the center, leaving ragged edges of fabric hanging from his shoulders like limp feathers on a dying bird. A jagged slash bisected the skin in a vertical line from his right nipple down to his navel. Hints of white bone and darker, squishier things peeked out from between the edges of his skin.

He hissed and snarled like a rabid weasel, baring his fangs and then snapping them shut in a gruesome show of aggression. The tips of his fingers were sharp and pointy like claws, and I doubted he'd gotten a manicure in the last few minutes. Maybe it was a vampire thing? But Ozzy and Will hadn't had any claws. Marissa's nails had been perfectly filed and polished.

At first, I thought he was entangled in a loop of epileptic dance moves, but then I caught sight of the giant black shadow that darted around him. It matched his steps, staying just out of his reach, while keeping him trapped in the middle of the yard. It lunged back and forth, so graceful on four feet that it barely seemed to touch the ground. The only sound it made was a continuous low growl.

"*I am her sire!*" Merrick hissed, making a wide swipe with his hand. The shadow darted under his outstretched arm, teeth sinking deep into the tender part of the vampire's thigh, just above the knee. The crunch of muscle and bone tearing was drowned out by the hysterical shriek Merrick made, and I had to cover my ears.

The shadow continued to tug until Merrick toppled over. Its growl subsided into a low rumble that I recognized immediately; it was the sound of comfort and security, and it made me think of bad doggy-breath.

"Dog?" The word was barely loud enough to carry across the space between us, but two yellow eyes turned toward me, and there was a mountain of recognition and loyalty in those beautiful orbs.

"Dog!" My relief at finding him was quickly replaced with furious indignation that someone was trying to hurt my dog. *My* dog! Not happening, not on my watch.

I started forward, doing an awkward limping shuffle that would have made me a shoe-in the next time *The Walking Dead* was looking for zombie extras.

The swirling mass of shadows surrounding Dog folded in on themselves, condensing from something the size of a grizzly bear, into the shaggy black dog that I was used to seeing. He was still huge, his shoulders taller than my waist. I'd been unsuccessful in coaxing him onto my bathroom scale, but I'd bet he was about two hundred and twenty pounds.

He took a tentative step toward me with his tail wagging hard enough to uproot small trees.

Behind him, Merrick sat up, and I screamed a warning. "*No!*"

Dog turned back, just as the vampire reached out and sank his claws into Dog's flank and pulled him to the ground. I shouted again, but neither of them paid me any attention. Dog kicked with his back feet, tearing flesh open on Merrick's chest, while they both scrambled for traction on the carpet of dried leaves.

Knowing I had nothing but my bare hands and a heart full of vengeance as weapons, I detoured to the patio table and yanked my flint knife out of its hiding spot. With his back to me, Merrick held Dog down and tore at the flesh on his back with blood-stained fangs. If he managed to get Dog rolled over, the soft delicate skin on his belly would be exposed and vulnerable to the slashing claws.

"Hey, asshole! Over here!" I yelled, to get the vampire's attention away from my dog, but Merrick just clung to Dog's back like a giant lecherous barnacle.

I careened closer. Any efforts to sneak up on them would be wasted; girls my size just didn't sneak. It was a fact.

With both of my trembling hands wrapped around the hilt, I drove the knife into Merrick's back, hoping like hell my aim wasn't off. I'd seen more decapitation and throat slitting than I had ever wanted to, so I was counting on a shot to the heart to do the job.

Gravity took over, forcing all of my one hundred and sixty pounds into the downward motion. The blade slid halfway in before grinding against bone. I leaned harder, practically lying on top of the squealing bloodsucker until something gave way with a crack. The knife sank in like the suddenly motionless vampire was made of butter. One final breath wheezed out of his body, and then he was dead. Whatever magic was running through my veins recognized the sudden lack of his.

He'd said every vampire had a first death when

they were turned, so I wondered what I was supposed to call this? Second death? Final death? Plain old murder?

I shook off the bizarre tangle of thoughts that had been holding me immobile and crawled over to where Dog lay. With fingers that had gone numb from the cold, I tugged at my shredded sweatshirt and tried to use it to cover the gashes on his back. The makeshift bandages didn't seem sufficient against the furrows that crisscrossed his hide. When he whimpered, I gave up on playing nurse and flung my arms around his big neck.

"Oh, Dog…" Tears ran down my cheeks, but I didn't care. Dog had seen me cry before. "I'm so sorry he hurt you."

He sighed and closed his eyes.

"You're such a good dog. So strong and brave." I wrapped myself tighter around his furry body, offering what comfort and protection I could. Just as he'd done for me when I'd been stabbed. My fingers flowed through the tangled mess of his coat, already familiar with every sharp line of muscle and bone beneath his skin. He was still skinny, but not nearly as skeletal as before.

"Please be okay," I whispered into his fur. Why did he have to take on a vampire? I didn't know how I'd live with myself if anything happened to him.

"Dog?" He wasn't responsive, even when my sobs broke free from my chest, and the force of them shook his body beneath mine. He had to be okay. I needed him to be okay.

"Theo?"

Tension and dread curled in my gut when I recognized the familiar tingle of fae magic next to me.

Chapter Twenty-Three

I'm not sure how long I'd been lying on the cold ground in my sports bra and yoga pants with my bare arms clinging to Dog. The moon had disappeared behind a thick blanket of clouds, so I couldn't even use its journey across the stars as an estimate of the seconds slipping away. I'd been too scared to move him, too afraid that I'd upset the delicate pattern of inhaling and exhaling that proved he was still alive.

"Theo?" The dark prince knelt beside me with a concerned expression.

"He hurt Dog." I hadn't wanted to kill Merrick. He really shouldn't have tried to hurt my dog.

"You're injured." His eyes quickly assessed, taking in my ravaged shoulder before moving on to Dog. His eyebrows furrowed when he lifted my sweatshirt and saw the oozing wounds carved into Dog's rump.

I didn't protest when he removed his cloak and draped it around me. I'd already lost all the feeling in my feet or hands, and frostbite had set into the tips of my ears.

"Theo? I'm taking you to Eddesta." He tried to pull me away from Dog and panic tightened my chest.

"No! I'm not leaving him." I struggled in his arms until he set me on my feet and tugged the cloak tighter around my body.

"You need a healer." He kept his voice level, but I

could tell by the way he clenched his fists, that he wasn't going to waste time arguing with me when it would be easier to sling me over his shoulder and drag my butt to Fairie.

"Dog's hurt." My voice broke, and I braced for his bossy aristocratic tone to order me toward the gate.

"Very well." He sighed and gestured to the cabin. "We'll tend to your friend first."

I nodded as he bent and scooped up Dog, carrying him like a parent would carry a sleeping toddler. I followed in their wake with the makeshift blanket dragging across the old leaves and crunchy grass.

The back door was wide open, spilling weak light across the steps. Lief waited at the bottom so I could hold onto his elbow as I hobbled up the stairs. After depositing Dog on the living room floor, he steered me toward the bathroom.

"But Dog—"

"Shower first." His voice brokered no room for negotiation, so I allowed myself to be led into the bathroom. "You're hypothermic. If you pass out, I *will* take you back to Fairie." He reached past me and turned on the shower, cranking it as hot as it would go. "You warm up while I get a fire started."

He had too much faith in my water heater.

"*Theo!*"

I jumped and looked up in surprise. How long had I been sitting here staring at the wall? I thought he'd left. Or maybe he had, and I just hadn't heard him return. Steam filled the room and haloed Lief's dark hair and shirt, making him look like some sort of dark god. It was fitting, since Farranen called him the dark prince.

Pain pierced through the fog in my brain, and I

hunched my shoulders against the sudden onslaught of sensation. Just the thought of my guardian was like a spike of hot metal sliding into my gray matter.

Lief gripped my arms, keeping me from sliding off the edge of the tub.

"Easy, my dear, let's get you warmed up." He slid his arms around me, letting me burrow against his chest and prop my heavy head on his broad shoulder. I let him think the pain was from my injured shoulder; he didn't need to know it came from the sorrow that Farranen's betrayal had left growing in my heart.

Magic burned through my body, glowing and flexing everywhere Lief held me. I could feel him channeling it into me, adding to the power that I'd been trying so hard to ignore. His hands bit into my skin, and he let out a shaky exhale.

"Oh…*my.*" His voice was strained, and I would have laughed if I hadn't been so exhausted.

We stayed like that, clinging to each other long enough that I worried about my poor water heater. Moving seemed improbable, but Dog needed me to get my butt in gear.

"Why did you come back?" I couldn't stop myself from asking, even though I knew the answer might hurt. If this was some last-ditch effort to revisit the issue of my failed transition, I was going to plant my foot so far up his ass that he'd be able taste the dirt stuck under my toenails from my barefoot run through the woods. Just as soon as I had the energy to lift my head, of course.

"I never left."

I inhaled. Exhaled. Tried to find words. Nothing came to me.

****

A fire blazed in the fireplace, filling the cabin with heat and the smell of fresh-cut wood.

After ignoring my protests about needing a shower, Lief had stepped under the spray with me in his arms. That woke me up enough to slap at his hands until he quit trying to help me undress. Once we'd used every last drop of hot water, Lief glamoured our wet clothes into fluffy white bath towels. Fae glamour could be pretty darn handy.

Removing the glass shards from my feet had been a long, tedious process, with no small amount of explicit threats on my part, while Lief muttered something about the absurdity of someone with royal blood being reduced to a nursemaid. Seeing my depleted first-aid kit had only added to the grumbling, and he'd been forced to glamour the smaller bandages into bigger ones that could cover the bite marks on my shoulder.

By the time my feet were swaddled in gauze, the last bit of fight in me had drained away, and I didn't argue when Lief carried me out of the bathroom. The slight smattering of dark hairs on his chest rasped against my cheek, and my fingertips traced across a hard ridge of scars.

"You couldn't have glamoured a bigger towel for yourself?" I asked sleepily.

"I can take it off if you'd like." The smirk in his voice told me he was needling me on purpose, so I didn't bother responding. It would have taken energy I didn't have.

Every blanket I owned was piled on the floor in front of the fireplace to create a cozy nest. My couch and coffee table had been pushed back to the edge of the room, and my broken writer's award had been swept up.

"Thank you," I murmured against his neck, feeling awkward. I wasn't used to other people doing nice things for me, like scrubbing bloody footprints off my hardwood while I had an emotional breakdown in my bathroom.

"My pleasure," he replied, sounding just as awkward as I had. Apparently, he wasn't used to dealing with gratitude.

He knelt and gently deposited me on the floor. I immediately reached for the blanket covering Dog.

"Dog?" I tugged the blanket back, and I shrieked when I found a naked body instead of my shaggy friend. I scrambled backward, and Lief caught me in his arms.

"Who's that?" I demanded without taking my eyes from where the man slept.

"You've never seen him like this?" Lief laughed.

"Who is he?" I really, *really* didn't like strange naked men arriving unannounced.

"Theo, that's Dog." His humor was making me grouchy.

"No, Dog is a *dog*. That's a *man*." I jabbed my finger toward the stranger.

"No, Dog is a *shifter*. That's a *shifter*." Lief mimicked me, pointing toward the figure in question.

I looked back to see if he was joking, but there was nothing besides the usual arrogance on his face. He arched an eyebrow, daring me to argue with him.

"But…" My brain couldn't come up with anything even remotely logical. "That's *Dog*?" I asked in disbelief. "*My* dog?"

"You didn't know he's a shifter?" Leaning back on

his elbows, Lief chuckled.

I scowled and pulled up the towel that was slipping. "How was I supposed to know? He looked like a normal dog to me."

"He never looked like a dog; he looked like a wolf."

"A *wolf*?" I thought about his big golden eyes and black shaggy fur. "I've been living with a wolf?"

I wanted to be horrified that I had let a wild animal sleep in my bed, but when I thought about his sweet timid personality and sad eyes, I couldn't muster up any regret. He'd nearly died tonight trying to protect me, so I didn't care what he was. Human, wolf, shifter; labels didn't matter.

He was loyal and liked my cooking; I couldn't say that about many people I knew.

I crawled closer, until I could poke at the golden skin on his shoulder.

"Will he be okay?" My fingers trailed across his back and into his dark hair. It was soft and wavy, and it felt no different than his fur. Underneath, the skin was puckered and hard where layers of scars ringed his neck. I'd felt them before but hadn't been able to see the extent of the damage when they were hidden by his fur.

"Yes, his injuries are already healing. It'll be a while before he regains consciousness; keeping his wolf form for so long has exhausted him. He'll need sleep to recover."

"Oh. That's good." Now that I could see his face, I realized he was just a boy. Probably no more than fourteen or fifteen, judging by the soft edges of youth still lining his face.

Uncaring of the fae that lounged behind me, I snuggled up next to Dog and tentatively wrapped an arm around his middle. His skin felt strange against mine, but he still smelled like my dog, and my body responded to his presence by relaxing against him. He was safety and companionship; and exactly what I needed right now.

"Theo?"

"Hmm?"

Lief tucked a fluffy comforter around Dog and I, pulling the edges up to my chin before pulling my damp hair away from my neck and injured shoulder.

"Sleep well, my lady."

I didn't hear the back door open or shut. I should have thanked him and reminded him that he'd left his cloak on my bathroom floor. I wondered if he'd walk back to the gate in the ridiculously small towel, or if he'd glamour himself new clothes. And I really should have asked what he meant when he said he'd never left in the first place.

Did he mean he'd been lurking nearby for the past few weeks? Or was he implying that he hadn't yet emotionally distanced himself from me, like Farranen had done once my infertility had come to light?

I was too tired to figure anything out right now.

Sleep beckoned, and I went willingly.

****

I slid a pan of double-fudge chocolate-chunk brownies into the oven and set the kitchen timer for fourteen minutes. Any longer than that and they'd be too hard, any less and the center wouldn't completely cook.

"Hello, Theo."

I jumped at the sudden greeting and spun around to find Ozzy leaning against my kitchen counter with one hip cocked and his big arms crossed over his chest.

"Don't *do* that! You scared me to death!" I admonished, sounding slightly hysterical to my own ears.

"Sorry." He didn't sound a bit sorry.

"What do you want, Ozzy?"

"Don't call me that." His leather coat creaked when he inhaled.

I stared, refusing to be the first to speak. He'd been the one to show up uninvited; I assumed there must be a reason, and that, sooner or later, he'd get around to telling me.

"Why did you ask me if I'm part of a brood?"

I shrugged. "Just curious."

"I don't believe you."

"I don't really care what you believe."

He studied me, looking like a shark patrolling for any sign of weakness that he could exploit.

"See, here's the thing, Theo—your story just isn't adding up." His eyebrows rose challengingly. "You said that Will was acting on his own when he kidnapped you, that there was no one else involved."

I nodded hesitantly, even though he hadn't really asked a question.

"That's interesting, because he was a new vamp, no more than six years old. Vamps that young aren't usually strong enough to live outside the safety of a brood."

I stayed silent, knowing he was baiting me into admitting I'd lied.

"Help me out here, Theo; help me to understand

how you came to know what a brood was, without ever seeing one."

Oh, shit.

I tried to keep my face impassive, but he could probably hear my heartrate increasing as I struggled to come up with a plausible explanation.

"And another thing…" He tilted his head, looking mystified. "Why would you assume my brood was 'all dudes,' as you so eloquently put it?"

Oh shit, oh shit, oh shit.

He knew that I hadn't told him the whole truth about my abduction.

I quickly decided that the best defense, was a good offense. "Why did you kill the men in Marissa's brood?" I was even able to muster some indignant anger that was mostly genuine.

"Why did I kill…What the hell are you talking about?" He looked just as confused as I had been when he walked in.

"Marissa's brood. Someone raided their nest and killed all the men she had sired."

I stepped closer and yanked aside the shoulder of my shirt to reveal the ugly wound from Merrick's attack. My skin was a lovely shade of purple and green that nicely accentuated the perfectly shaped crescents of scabs. "One of the vamps got away, and for some strange reason, he thought *I* led you to his front door."

I took perverse satisfaction in seeing his shocked face.

"The Paranormal Intelligence Maintaining Peace Agency doesn't just randomly raid nests and murder innocent vampires!" He sounded horrified, as if I'd accused him of kicking puppies.

"Merrick said they identified themselves as PIMPs when they ransacked the place."

"Who's Merrick?"

"The vamp that stopped by to leave his dental imprints in my shoulder." I left out the part about him making me drink blood. I didn't want to give Ozzy any more perceived reasons to lock me up.

"I'd be happy to set the record straight. Where can I find him?" His dark look implied it wouldn't be a casual conversation over cookies and hot cocoa.

"He's dead." I waved my hand airily. "*Really* dead, not just first-death dead." Again, I kept it truthful. I saw no reason to bring Dog's involvement to Ozzy's attention.

The vampire pondered everything I'd told him with a suspicious look. When he let out a huff and ran his fingers through his hair, I knew I'd won.

"If there's nothing else…" I glanced meaningfully at the door.

Ozzy drummed his fingers on the counter before asking, "How did you know Vanessa's name?"

"She told me."

I saw an *Ah ha!* look cross his face and I thought, *Damn it!*

"How could she tell you? She was already dead." His triumph was obvious, but I couldn't figure out what he thought I'd given away.

"I talked to her," I insisted.

"Impossible. The coroner put her time of death roughly eight hours after she was abducted. You didn't get there until *four days* later."

My mind fumbled for an explanation, but all I could come up with was, "Maybe Will mentioned it?" I *knew* she'd still been alive when I'd woken up on the filthy mattress in Will's bedroom of horrors.

"So you had a chance to chat with your hubby? What else did you talk about?"

Shrewd vampire. I glanced at the wooden spoon I'd used to make the brownies and wondered if it was sharp enough to stab him in the heart.

"Where's your friend?" His eyes narrowed thoughtfully, and I wanted to smack myself for letting the conversation get out of control.

"I don't have many friends."

"Not even the guardian?"

Grief tightened my throat, and I had to swallow hard before I could speak. "Haven't seen him in weeks."

"Huh." His gray eyes were skeptical, and I struggled to hide my rioting emotions. "Probably for the best; those fae are deceptive bastards. Always dancing around the truth, twisting their words to suit their needs. You never know where you stand with them."

He was wrong about that; I knew *exactly* where I stood with my former guardian.

The kitchen timer went off with a loud *brrrrrring!* that made me jump, but I didn't move toward the oven. Ozzy seemed to realize that I wasn't going to say anymore. He sauntered toward the door.

"Wait!" I called.

He turned and smirked at me from over his shoulder. "Yes?"

"Will's gone and can't hurt me, and my magic is pretty much dead—so we're done, right?"

I tried not to fidget while he considered my

question. Yes, Will's stalkerish tendencies were no longer a concern, and my magic was pretty much dead—but not completely. I could still feel a tiny spark residing in the deepest part of my chest. It was slowly shrinking, but I wasn't sure it would ever totally go away. It felt like a part of me. And while I was okay with the tiny nugget of power, I wasn't sure if Ozzy would be.

"Yeah, Theo, we're good."

I held my breath until the door shut with a click.

Chapter Twenty-Four

"You really don't like vampires, do you?"

Dog slunk into the kitchen with his tail between his legs. It was uncanny the way he avoided being here every time Ozzy dropped by.

"Next time, give me a heads-up so we can both disappear, okay?" I tried to soften my words with a smile as I busied myself with prying slightly charred brownies out of the pan.

I'd had enough supernatural drama to last me a lifetime and was looking forward to returning to the normalcy of writing romance, baking cakes, and binge watching some TV with my wolf. It might not sound like everyone's version of normal—but it was quickly becoming mine and I was ready to embrace it.

Now that Will was dead, and Marissa's brood was gone, I doubted I'd be getting any more random vampires stopping by. Ozzy had seemed satisfied that my magic was too weak to be a problem, and the chance of me becoming a changeling was gone. At least I wouldn't have to keep looking over my shoulder for PIMP agents that wanted to drag me into custody.

I hadn't seen any sign of the one-eared skunk since Ozzy's warning about ghosts; and if I did see it, I definitely wasn't going to get close enough to touch it. If I *had* accidentally used some new grave-reaping superpower, I didn't want to know.

I hadn't seen any sign that Lief was still hanging around—which was probably for the best. I was grateful for his help the night Merrick had attacked Dog and I, but now that all the danger had passed and my magic was dying, I was happy to shut the door on that part of my life. Seeing him would just remind me of…Things I was working to forget. And speaking of things I was working to keep in the past, I had to assume my former guardian was continuing to guard the gate camouflaged with glamour. I hadn't seen him, but sometimes the lights were on in his cabin. Not that I was checking.

I dropped a plate of burnt baking on the floor and nudged it toward Dog. He jumped on it like a chubby kid on a chocolate bar.

Apparently, he did like brownies after all.

After spending two full days sleeping on my living room floor, Dog had stood up, poked at the bandages I'd taped on his lower back, then padded outside to pee on the bushes next to my truck. I know because I watched through the living room window. But only because I wanted to make sure he didn't fall down the stairs while he was getting used to walking on two feet, not because I was a perv who stared at naked adolescent boys.

Then, he'd disappeared into the woods to the west, which was good, because I didn't want Mrs. Swazle to have a heart attack if she saw a naked boy loping through her yard.

Once Dog's plate was empty, I added some cold meatballs that he happily swallowed whole.

"So…werewolf, huh?" I lowered myself onto the floor and studied his decidedly lupine features. Long legs, large paws, narrow chest, and long muzzle. All very wolfish, now that I was paying attention. His powerful jaw housed teeth sharp enough to tear a vampire's thigh in half.

He finished his meal and glanced at me uneasily while licking his muzzle.

"Come here." I patted the floor next to me, and he padded over, circling once before curling up against me with his head on my thigh. Sad yellow eyes watched me with wary adoration.

"I didn't get a chance to thank you for protecting me from Merrick."

Dog growled low in his throat at the mention of the vampire, making my thigh vibrate with the sound.

"Shhh, it's okay; he's gone now." I scratched behind his ears, letting him know that the danger had passed, that we were safe. "You were such a brave boy."

Now that I knew he wasn't actually a dog, I should stop treating him like one.

"So…You're a shifter, huh?" The word felt weird on my tongue. "What should I call you?"

He chuffed and gave me the equivalent of a doggy eye roll.

"Yeah, you're right. Nothing has to change."

Dog yawned, showing me his massively sharp teeth. How had I ever thought he was a normal dog? Those damn things were longer than my fingers and pointier than needles.

I continued to stroke his soft fur until my butt got sore from sitting on the hard floor. I shoved at his big head. "Get up." He growled in protest, and I shoved harder. "Come on, move it…I'm going to make some pork burgers for supper."

I knew that would do the trick.

"Next time we're in town, I'm going to buy you some clothes. You can't run around naked when you're on two feet."

That earned me another harrumph of disappointment.

"And one more thing." I crossed my arms and gave him my best stern look. "No more hanging out on the bathroom floor while I shower."

A word about the author…

Born and raised on the beautiful Canadian prairies, Everlyn prefers to spend her time outdoors with her family, kayaking, skating, fishing, and hunting. She loves reading and writing about vampires, witches, fae, and zombies that get to find their own version of happily ever after.

Ingram Content Group UK Ltd.
Milton Keynes UK
UKHW020624110423
419970UK00014B/293

9 781509 248087